The Vaporetto Driver

Published by Keldaviain Publishing

The rights of Kelvin Robertson to be identified as the author of this work have been asserted in accordance with the Copyright, Designs and Patents Act 1988.

This is a work of fiction. Names, characters, businesses, places, events and incidents are either the products of the author's imagination or used in a fictitious manner. Any resemblance to actual persons, living or dead, or actual events is purely coincidental.

A CIP catalogue record for this book is available from The British Library.

ISBN 978-0-9928599-30

Prologue

It was the summer of nineteen eighty-eight when Franco was just fourteen years old. He was a smart boy, good at numbers but he was not much good at reading, history, geography or any other of the disciplines taught in school because he was very rarely there. He had attended school only a dozen times in the past six months. The reason? He had joined the business. The business was always on the lookout for a sharp boy like Franco, one who could hustle, one who could persuade tourists to buy his roses. Though selling the roses was not his principal task, of course. His prime objective was to act as eyes and ears for the business.

He was a wild, carefree boy living with his brother and sister in the family home in the back streets of Mestre, close to the causeway leading to the island city of Venice. He had grown up there, knew many people, and through his circle of friends had found himself recruited by the mafia. At the tender age of fourteen, he had found his vocation in life. Together with his older brother, he moved through the side streets of Venice, ostensibly selling roses, but in reality they were checking out the numbers.

The numbers were important to the mafia, simple numbers yet ones that carried significance. The boys watched where people congregated, the restaurants they visited, and the shops where they spent their money. They watched everything, counted everything and reported to the men of the organisation. It was a simple occupation for the boys but an important one for a business that thrived on extortion. It was a beginning for Franco, for a fourteen year old, the first rung on the ladder of crime, one that would eventually propel him to a life where he could acquire great riches. For now though, he roamed the streets and canalsides of Venice selling his flowers. In future, he would progress to picking pockets and breaking into hotel rooms to steal from the tourists. That was just the beginning for a budding mafioso. If Il Capo took a liking to him, he could look forward to promotion, drug dealing and extortion and once the organisation accepted him he would make serious money, but today, he was simply the eyes and ears of the local mafia clan.

'Hey, Franco,' called a voice. It was Luigi, a youth of nineteen, a thug. 'The Pizzeria Roma, how many customers are in there?'

'Twenty-two, all dining.'

'How many men?'

'Nearly all men, that is apart from some tourists.'

'Anyone you recognise?'

'Six men at a table near the back; I think one is Umberto Da Silva, a big man with power, I know.'

'Good boy, now go away and don't come back here for a few days. Here, buy a gelato,' said the young thug, placing a few coins into Franco's hand, while slicking back his greasy black hair in a dominant gesture.

'Ciao,' said Franco, taking the money and slipping away into the shadows.

Something was brewing he knew, something big, and so, instead of disappearing from the scene, his curiosity got the better of him. Amongst the crowds of tourists, he was anonymous, invisible, and from a distance he clutched his flowers and observed.

Luigi had disappeared and for several minutes, there was no sign of him until Franco's eyes suddenly picked him out and widened in anticipation. Three other men, all very much the same in appearance, accompanied him: slicked-back greasy hair, each dressed in a fashionable, expensive suit, the uniform of aspiring mafia hit men. They entered the pizzeria, Franco moved closer, his breathing sporadic as the tension increased, then suddenly a commotion of shouting and screaming reached his ears. Something was happening inside the restaurant, it lasted only a few seconds and then he heard the sound of gunshots.

Franco could only imagine what was going on but then the men reappeared, self-satisfied grins on their faces. They were confident killers who had achieved what they had come to do and being so close to a mafia hit set Franco's heart racing. To see

3

killers perform their grim ritual both frightened and excited him and leaning back against a wall he wondered if one day he might attain enough status to join their exalted ranks.

The crowds of tourists seemed unaware of the terrible event that had just taken place until several survivors emerged from the restaurant, some weeping, others silent and ashen-faced. Then a second wave of turmoil erupted, sirens echoed from the canals as the police and ambulance service began arriving in fast launches. Franco watched with some fascination for the greater part of an hour, observing the drama, marvelling as men in police uniforms took charge. They held back the gathering crowd, made a safe route for the medics to dash into the restaurant to render help.

After a time everything calmed down, the only noise that of low voices in the crowd, and then the ritual of removing the bodies began. It was without doubt the most macabre episode of the whole drama, a part that excited Franco. The medical personnel appeared with stretchers carrying white-sheeted bodies and passed within a few metres of him. So close to death, so close to the still warm cadavers, his senses raced and he strained for a closer look, wondering which one was Umberto Da Silva.

Chapter 1

They were lucky, very lucky. I became aware something was wrong as I waited in line to board the ferry on my way home. I had just finished my first year at Edinburgh University and I was about to start the summer vacation, though it would not be a holiday because I still had to work. Helping my father with his small fishing boat was something I did every summer because we were not altogether a wealthy family and any extra income was welcome.

Originally, we were crofters and years earlier my grandparents, realising my father had little in the way of job prospects, sent him to live with relatives in Glasgow during the winters. It saved money for his keep, and in the city he found temporary work in the shipyards. He learned to become a carpenter and now he builds small boats and takes on any odd jobs he can find. Along with some inshore fishing and a smallholding, we survive well enough. Since an early age, my father had instilled in me the need for a proper education. His words still ring in my ears, 'No school at fifteen to go fishing – a profession for you my lad,' and it led to my friends considering me a swot. For many of them fishing was the only option, to work hard in the fresh airs blowing in from the North Atlantic and, when the sun shone, it seemed there was no better place on this earth. However, there was another face to the Western Isles: harsh, cutting winds could whip up big seas that would sweep the island for days on end putting a temporary stop to the fishing, which meant little or no money to feed the fishermen's families.

Let me introduce myself, my name is Malcolm McKenzie. I was nineteen only a few days before catching the ferry on that fateful day in June of ninety three and the memory still lingers. As we began boarding, I heard the whoosh whoosh overhead and looking up I caught sight of the giant yellow helicopter of the air-sea rescue service. Everyone around heard it, we all looked up into the sky and for a moment fell silent and then we began to speculate.

'Somethin's going on,' said a voice behind me and from further back in the queue I heard someone else say a fishing boat was in trouble.

'Where d'you hear that?'

'The Coastguard, he was leaning out of his office calling to someone who must be a member of the lifeboat crew, he said they had received a Mayday.'

A Mayday, something was happening all right. I climbed the gangplank and could see the other passengers dispersing round the ship and I thought the upper deck, away from the breeze, would be a good place to watch the fast disappearing Sea King. Then from the corner of my eye I caught sight of the lifeboat making its way towards the harbour mouth.

In my part of the world, the sea rules our lives; fishing is an important part of the economy of Stornoway where most families earn at least a part of their living from the sea. In days gone by the harbour would fill with all kinds of boats but during the past few years the numbers have dwindled, the fishing industry becoming a shadow of its former self.

Rory, my best friend from school, worked as a fisherman alongside his father and Angus, their only crew member, on their boat the *Lurach-Aon*. She is a forty-foot ring netter, a fine boat constructed from stout planking and fitted with a powerful winch for hauling the net. Hauling used to be backbreaking work but change was overtaking the industry. The fishermen of the Western Isles were finding that they had to embrace new ways as foreigners, the so-called 'Klondykers' from Eastern Europe and Russia, were destroying our traditional fishing grounds with their giant factory ships.

I looked up into the sky as the ferry's horn hooted and it began to move away from the quayside and I turned my mind to the emergency taking place. I wondered about Rory. As soon as he was fifteen, he left school to go fishing with his father and was probably out there on the blue expanse. I on the other hand had studied hard, spurred on by my parents to gain an education. They had seen a drop in living standards, seen poorer families struggle to survive and were determined that my sister and I would do well enough to find decent employment. 'Become a teacher,' my mother had said, 'there will always be jobs for teachers and the money is good.'

She was a canny lass my mother and her advice was still running through my head hours later as the ferry docked. I was home.

'You're looking thin Malcolm, what have you been living on at that university of yours, beer!' said Mother as I burst in through the kitchen door and she looked up from her baking.

My eyes gave the game away and she smiled and then, after a pause, 'don't be getting a girl into trouble when you are drunk, it will ruin your life before it's begun.'

'Mother!'

'Well I'm only telling you. They say the big cities are full of pregnant unmarried girls and I don't want you bringing one back here.'

'One?'

'Don't be cheeky. Come here and give me a hug, I haven't seen you for quite a while. Let's feed you properly and put some meat back on those bones of yours,' she said, wiping the flour from her hands, and then she fell silent. Her eyes took on a more serious look and she said, 'Have you heard a boat is in trouble?'

'I saw a maroon as we were Ullapool and an air-sea rescue helicopter flew over. Do they know who it is?'

'Not yet, but the lifeboat has launched and rumour has it that it is heading towards the south Minch.'

'Oh, and you think it might be one of ours?'

'I don't know. Come on, settle yourself back in, you have been relegated to the back bedroom.'

'The back bedroom!'

'Aye, yer sister has taken full advantage of your absence this term and I can't say that I blame her.'

I remember the shock of discovering that I was no longer top dog. My sister had finally grabbed the larger bedroom that once was mine and as I opened the door to her old room I was horrified to find that all my books, model aeroplanes and clothes had been piled up on what was once her bed. Oh well, I was philosophical about it, I would have done the same and at least she had waited until I left for the summer term before making her move.

I had completed the first year of university, I had made friends and there was talk of trekking through India. The Beatles had set a precedent. Many of my student friends had warmed to the idea of going travelling eventually and perhaps my sister was hoping I would disappear for a year or two. Tidying up the remnants of my earlier life, I piled the books in disorder on the shelf, placed my models on any surface I could find and then unpacked my haversack, returning to the kitchen with an armful of dirty washing.

'Put them in the basket, I will wash them later,' said Mother, stirring a pot of broth on the stove. 'Here, get some of this down you.'

12 hours earlier

The sun was still not over the horizon when the *Lurach-Aon* made her way slowly out of harbour and across a flat featureless sea. The storm of the past few days had abated, the crashing waves that prevented the little fishing boat from venturing forth were no more, just a memory, yet the three men on board knew the benign conditions might not last long.

'Take the wheel Rory while I have a look at the chart. The black clouds to the north are moving away and the forecast at six o'clock predicted no more than a force three today, maybe less. Time enough to fill a few boxes eh!'

'Aye Da, we'll need to catch some fish today if I am to pay for my new motorbike.'

Hamish MacLeod grunted. Catching fish was important to feed the family but wasting money on motorbikes, noisy and dangerous beasts in his opinion, was folly. What was wrong with a pushbike?

'And where will you be going on this motorbike of yours?'

'Anywhere it will take me, the Highlands and maybe Glasgow.'

'Glasgow? If you go there on a motorbike chances are you'll be walking home, a motorbike indeed.'

Rory's father was of the old school, walked everywhere, his only concession to modern transport an ancient black sit-up-and-beg bicycle. Nevertheless, he was a good fisherman, knew where the fish spawned, where they shoaled and developed. He had learned his trade from his father and his father before that, a fishing family stretching back over many years. Casting all thoughts of motorbikes from his mind Hamish turned to the small chart table to plan their day, the thump thump thump of the boat's engine an accompaniment to his deliberations.

A new day was beginning and the sky was turning orange as the boat cleared the headland. Rory relaxed his grip on the oak wheel and, with a faint smile on his lips, looked out through the window. They had reached the open sea and he caught sight of old man Macintosh's croft standing alone close by the shore. The old man was in his eighties, one of the last of the old crofters, and once he left this earth, Rory mused, the old ways would be gone forever.

'Do you want me to hold this course Da?'

'What are you on?'

'Ninety-five degrees.'

Hamish looked over his chart, his special chart, the one with black pencil markings. He knew the waters between the islands and the mainland like the back of his hand, where to find the best fishing grounds, and to make sure his secrets were safe from a casual eye he marked the chart in his own hieroglyphics.

'Aye, bring her round to one twenty degrees and steam for another hour and a half. That should bring us to the wreck where we caught all those fish a month ago. You cannot see any other boats can you? I do not want Campbell or that rogue McDougal seeing where we cast our nets. They are always trying to find out where we fish. I was in the Clachan bar on Saturday night when the pair of them thought they would fill me full of whisky and trick me into telling where to find the best catches. Well they did fill me full of whisky and I told them a cock and bull story. Saturday night was a good cheap do and they'll be heading north I think.'

Rory chuckled to himself; he had heard it all before. But Da's special knowledge, and them working hard together, meant they punched above their weight, most days bringing more boxes of fish ashore than the other boats – and more than one fisherman was eager to find out how they did it.

'Angus, will ye start our breakfast,' said Hamish through the half-open door to their only crewmember leaning against the wheelhouse smoking a finely rolled cigarette.

'Aye aye skipper,' said the wizened old man of no more than forty-five years of age, his looks testament to the hardship of a fisherman's life. 'Ah'll just finish this.'

Two minutes later, after flicking the still smoking cigarette end downwind, Angus came into the cramped wheelhouse and climbed the three stairs down to the galley.

'Will it be two eggs skipper?'

'Aye, it always is?'

'And three for you young Rory?'

Rory just grinned; it was a routine, a ritual, carried out whenever they put to sea and he enjoyed the gentle banter, the precursor to breakfast. There was nothing like a plate of bacon and eggs, a wedge of bread and butter and a steaming mug of coffee to set the day off. He was eighteen years old and he wanted nothing more than to be a fisherman like his father and grandfather. The old man had died when he was ten years old and he still missed him, still missed his far-fetched tales of the sea, of the catches they were never likely to see again. He always said that they never went hungry, 'not if your taste for herring didn't tire.' He remembered the soft, slow voice describing the days when herring was king, when hundreds of boats filled the harbour, when the herring girls lined the pier.

Then there was Grandma, one of those herring girls from the mainland, girls who followed the fleet. He remembered her hands: big hands, coloured red from gutting fish twelve hours a day. Every year from the age of fifteen, she had gone with the boats from harbour to harbour, following the herrings south, and when she was eighteen, she had met Granddad. He was smitten and the following season when she returned, he had watched out for her.

Slowly Rory turned the wheel and looked at his hands; they were big like his grandmother's hands. He remembered them, large for a woman and strong and she could never quite straighten her fingers, curled by years of hard manual work and bearing the scars of the gutting knives. The skin covering her fingers was thick and hard like armour plating, and

13

yet in her old age, those same hands softened and he remembered with fondness how she had stroked his forehead and sung the songs of the sea to him.

'Right, let me have a play with this new-fangled Decca,' said Hamish, breaking into Rory's thoughts. Reaching up he twiddled with a knob on the instrument, read off the numbers and after several minutes' scrutinising his chart, announced the course.

'There are still no boats Rory?'

Rory scanned the sea, 'Don't worry Da, there's no sign of McDougal.'

Rory sat back on his seat, one leg dangling over the edge, and he listened to the engine. He liked engines. He liked their sound, their power, all part of a man's world and he was nearly a man. To him there was no finer life than one spent steering a boat out on the open sea, hauling nets, the sun and the wind in his face. He looked towards the horizon and wondered about city dwellers, how they managed on a morning like this. They would never see the horizon going to work in their factories and their offices, sitting amongst the traffic and the pollution for hours on end. No, he had the better life; he had no need for riches because out here the riches of nature surrounded him.

A flock of sea birds appeared, flying low over the surface of the sea, turning to swoop over the solitary fishing boat before heading into the rising sun.

'Where did they come from Rory?'

'Straight behind us Da.'

'Good, there will be fish I'm sure of it.'

'Breakfast skipper,' Angus called from below and a plate of eggs and bacon appeared in the companionway.

'Thank you Angus, I see you have managed to keep the yolks intact this morning.'

Angus grunted, passed up bread and a mug of coffee. He had sailed with Hamish MacLeod for the past twenty years and had heard the same comment almost every day. Shrugging his shoulders, he gave Hamish a solemn look before returning below to prepare Rory's breakfast.

Rory grinned and watched his father tucking in, a peaceful scene that would not last long. Soon they would be shooting the net and, with his eyes on the horizon and an occasional glance at the compass, he steered the little boat knowing that once they had finished breakfast it would be down to work. When they reached the fishing ground, Hamish would take over the wheel and he would join Angus to set the net. For the aging Angus it was becoming a hard job, but with Rory by his side he would manage well enough.

Hamish finished eating his breakfast and took a long swig from his mug as he daydreamed, thinking of the future. Ten years before he had bought the boat and today he was within a whisker of paying off the loan. Time had moved on and he was thinking he should build a nest egg for his retirement. He still had a few years before that day arrived and, like most islanders, he was careful with his money. He would go and see the bank manager when they returned to harbour, see what investments were available, and then Rory interrupted his thoughts.

'Are we about there?' he asked, impatient to be casting the net.

'I think so son, let me have a look at this Decca thing again. Hmm . . . let me see.'

He leaned towards the instrument, read off the figures, transferred them onto a chart covered in red and green curves and after a few minutes declared, 'We're near enough, here let me take the wheel. Get your breakfast Rory and then you two get ready to shoot the net.'

Rory stepped aside to let his father take the wheel while he devoured his breakfast and after eating, he pulled on his waterproof jacket ready for the day's work..

'Looks like we're here Angus, are you ready to let go the net.'

'I was born ready,' said Angus one of his homemade cigarettes dangling from his lips.

'All right clever sod, we do not want any mishaps. If the net becomes tangled up we'll be all day clearing it and I will never get that motorbike.'

Angus looked at the boy with disdain for hadn't they worked together for three years, ever since Rory had left school, and hadn't they been amongst the most successful fishermen of Lewis, the largest of the Hebridean islands. Shaking his head he made his way towards the stern of the little boat and began paying the net out to make it easier to shoot into the water, but first they had to lower the dahn buoy attached to one end of the net line.

'Ready,' called Hamish from the wheelhouse and as Rory raised his hand to signal that they were, the boat was brought to a near standstill to allow them to slide the dahn buoy over the side and to begin paying out the line. Hamish watched and at Rory's signal engaged the gears, steamed slowly ahead, and the rope reel began to turn, paying out several hundreds of yards of line. Eventually it was time to shoot the net and as the two fishermen began dropping the light netting over the side Hamish steered the boat in a wide arc ready to return to the buoy.

'We should have a good run today on this calm sea Angus.'

'Aye lad, an' you'll be getting that motorbike sooner than you think eh?'

'Oh I hope so; I can't wait to take Molly for a ride on the back of it.'

'A word of advice lad, don't be lettin' her faither know or he'll be puttin' his foot down.'

Rory thought about that as he fed the last of the net over the side and then signalled to his father that it was time to return to the dahn buoy.

He had been seeing Molly for almost three months and only the week before she had taken him to meet her parents and he had found out then how fearsome her father could be when it came to his daughter. He knew he would need to be careful but the desire to take her for a ride was overwhelming and as the boat chugged back to the buoy he gazed out to sea thinking of the best way to secrete her away. He looked at Hamish, he was equally deep in thought, concentrating on his course. Then, with a force that took them all by surprise, the boat suddenly lurched sideways.

The movement was so unexpected and violent that it threw Angus bodily against the winch before he finally sprawled to the deck. Rory gasped in surprise, grabbed the rail and held on tight as the boat began to move rapidly in reverse. Instinctively he knew that they were in serious trouble and looking towards the wheelhouse saw his father struggling with the wheel. Hamish turned his head, fear written across his face, and that galvanised Rory into action. Struggling to gain a handhold, he forced his way along the sloping deck towards the wheelhouse.

'Something's caught us lad, I can't hold her, she's going over.'

Rory's heart was in his mouth, the boat *was* starting to tip over and at a dangerous angle. Water was beginning to flood the deck, he had never been so frightened and that fear drove him to grab the frame of the wheelhouse door and reach inside for an emergency flare hanging just inside the door. The forces acting on his body were almost overpowering, the angle of the deck, the rocking of the boat both working to dislodge him but miraculously he felt his hand touch a flare and closing his fingers round it he pulled it from its bracket.

He could feel the boat beginning to roll. Panic began to well up inside him but somehow he kept his nerve, bracing himself against the doorway, and with both hands free he managed to fire the flare. With a whoosh and a shower of red sparks, the rocket arced high into the air imprinting a smoky grey trail on a blue sky background. Rory did not see it; the boat had reached the point of no return and was slowly turning over. He heard his father shout, 'We're going under lad, save yourself. Where's Angus?'

'Aft, by the winch,' Rory called back.

'Bugger it, when she rolls jump,' said Hamish crawling out of the wheelhouse on his hands and knees.

Then the boom used to land the fish boxes began to swing wildly about and Angus, clinging to the side of the boat, took its full force across his chest, knocking him to the deck. Then it happened, in one last desperate act the boat rolled completely, throwing the three fishermen into the cold and shocking sea. Rory went under, struggling to catch his breath as he sank, finally managing to kick off his boots and swim to the surface. Gasping for breath his thoughts were for his father who, like most fishermen, was a non-swimmer.

Treading water, his arms ploughing back and forth, he searched the surface of the sea and to his great relief saw his father no more than twenty yards away clinging to a fish box. Then he looked for Angus but could see nothing, only a large circle of disturbed water and the boat sinking. For several seconds there was silence until the gurgling sound of air escaping the wooden tomb reached his ears. Whatever it was that had dragged the boat under had left little behind, just fish boxes and a few items that had managed to escape the sea's clutches. It was then the realisation that everything had gone sank in.

Looking furtively round for some buoyancy of his own he saw some half-submerged crates and struck out towards the nearest of them. As he took hold, he heard his father coughing and spluttering not far away and turned his head towards him.

'Relax Da, let your body go limp, spread your arms and legs, float damn you.'

With great effort, Hamish did as Rory told him, spreading his arms and legs whilst holding onto a precariously floating box. Then came a surprise. 'Ahoy,' called out Angus, paddling towards them with one hand and holding onto the dahn buoy with the other.

'Angus, thank God. You can swim!'

'Aye, but we're stuck in the middle of nowhere.'

'Hold on, with this buoy and the boxes we can maybe make some sort of raft.'

Rory kicked out to close the gap and taking hold of a trailing line secured a fish box to the buoy. Then he and Angus together dragged the beginnings of their raft towards Hamish.

The captain of the Uig ferry jerked his head to one side; a movement had caught his eye, a red glow arcing slowly across the sky.

'What was that?'

'Looks like a maroon sir,' said the helmsman.

'Bloody hell it is,' said the captain, grabbing a pair of binoculars. 'Helm, steer zero fifteen degrees; you, call the Coastguard and send out a Mayday,' he said glancing down at the chart.

Quickly he made some calculations and after reading out their position to the radio operator, lifted the binoculars to his eyes once again.

'I can't see anything but that maroon must have come from somewhere.'

The Uig ferry was the only vessel in the vicinity and if it had not been on schedule then the maroon would have gone unnoticed – the one piece of luck that saved them. Slowly the ship began to turn onto her new course. The captain scanned the horizon for the origin of the distress signal but could see nothing and after ten minutes ordered the ship to slow and to circle the area. For an hour, he scanned the water and in the background the ship's radio crackled as an ever-increasing search operation began to unfold.

'Helicopter sir,' said the first officer, peering at a different area of the sea.

'I see him; ask the Coastguard what he wants us to do.'

The radio sputtered and the order came to stand down, three lifeboats were already racing to the scene and the helicopter was best equipped to carry on the search.

In the sea, the young fit Rory heard the same noise and managed to turn his eyes skyward but he could see nothing.

'Hear that?' he said, but there was no reply.

The two older men were suffering from the onset of hypothermia and in real danger of losing their grip on the makeshift raft. Rory looked at them and then back at the sky, he could hear it, an engine, loud, seemingly overhead, and then he felt the downdraft and the calm waters suddenly began to dance.

I told you they were lucky, another half an hour and Hamish could have died, then Angus, but Rory's quick thinking had saved them. I had gone to the hospital as soon as I heard it was the *Lurach-Aon* but was unable to find out more than that the three crew members were being well looked after and it was believed all would return to good health. I tried again the following morning and discovered that the hospital had discharged Rory but the other two were still under observation.

'Well Rory it seems you had a lucky escape, what happened?' I said after catching up with him.

We were meeting in the small harbour side café and I had just carried our mugs of coffee to the Formica-topped table.

'Thanks Mal,' he said, spooning two sugars into his cup. 'It was a close thing they tell me. I had a word with John Thornton, the mechanic on the lifeboat, and he said we were lucky the ferry saw our flare otherwise no one would have found us and I would not be sitting here now.'

'What about the Coastguard, will you have to report to them?'

'Aye, when Da comes out of hospital, then they will have some sort of enquiry.'

'What did you hit, was it a whale?'

'Naw, something bigger than any whale we get round here. I think it was a submarine.'

'A submarine, one of ours d'you think?'

'I don't know but the speed at which we were dragged backwards meant it had to be a submarine.'

'The nearest base is the Gare Loch, surely they will know if there was a submarine out in the Minch.'

'If they do I bet they won't tell us. While I was laid up, I did a bit of thinking. We were well north of the submarine exercise area; we never go near it because the sea is too deep there for seine nets. I'm pretty sure it was a submarine but don't think it was one of ours.'

'Russian?'

'What else, maybe American. I don't know, perhaps we'll never know.'

'How's your father and Angus, are they both still in hospital?'

'Aye, we were all suffering from hypothermia when we were picked up.' Rory paused for a moment and looked out of the window. 'Bloody hell we were lucky.'

'I know, everyone says so and they say you're a hero.'

'A hero! I don't think so. I was near to panic at times, I'm no hero.'

'Well, hero or not I'm glad you're all still alive. I suppose the boat is lost. What will you do?'

'I haven't really thought about it, I just want Da home in one piece. I suppose it's insured but I don't know much about that and if it takes a while to get another boat I guess I'll have to find something else to do, maybe crew for someone else or perhaps I can find a rowing boat and lay a few pots.'

'You will find it hard to make a living from just a few pots.'

'What else is there?'

'How do you feel about working away?'

'What, leave the island? I've never thought about that.'

'We've had some lectures on the Scottish economy, towards the end of last term, and they are saying the oil industry in the North Sea is going to be even bigger than it is now. Why not look for work on the east coast, Aberdeen or Peterhead maybe. From what I can gather the American firms pay good money.'

'Och, I don't know.'

He fell silent and before he could speak again a voice called out from across the room.

'Yer bacon butties are ready lads.'

'Ah, breakfast; cheer up Rory a hot butty will make you feel better.'

I remember eating in silence, Rory had reached a kind of crossroads in his life, he had a head full of problems and was slowly working through them. Fishing had been his life, his family's life for the past eighty or ninety years, but now their boat was gone and there was no guarantee they could afford another. Compounding the problem were the changes afoot in the fishing industry. Since its heyday catches had dwindled, the advent of the common market had opened up the fishing grounds to Europeans who had only one intention, that of raping the sea for profit, and the locals were finding it harder and harder to make a decent living.

'Let's have a walk along the harbour,' said Rory, 'I haven't been there in over a week, not since the accident.'

We left the café, caught up on the local gossip as we walked, talked about who was courting who.

'I hear Linda is getting married, you know the pneumatic blonde everyone at school went with, everyone except us that is.'

'Everyone except you,' said Rory laughing, me to wonder if he was telling the truth or not.

'How's Molly, are you still seeing her?'
'She's fine, she came to see my mother when I was in hospital but I haven't seen her yet. We've arranged to meet for a drink tonight, why don't you come along?

Saturdays were usually busy and that particular Saturday evening was no exception. The fishing fleet had returned to harbour, the men were ready for some time off drinking and socialising. Nevertheless, it was not quite like the old days – the herring were not so abundant and the wages not so high, still, the bar in the Imperial was full when I arrived. I stood in the doorway, looking round until I caught sight of Rory. He was standing with a pint in his hand and he gave me a wave.

'Ah Malcolm, there you are. What will you have?'

'A pint of Deuchars, living in Edinburgh has given me a taste for it.'

'So you're a drinking man now are you?'

'Only when I'm in the students' union or when I go to Murrayfield, that's if I can get a ticket for the match.'

'Still playing rugby then?'

'Oh yes, I am in the university second team now and maybe next season I will make the first team squad.'

Rory handed me the glass and as I took my first mouthful, I noticed Molly peering round the door. She looked a little uncertain until her eyes met mine, and then she saw Rory and ventured into the bar.

'Malcolm, it's nice to see you. How's Edinburgh these days?'

'Fine, fun but hard work, I've just finished my first year exams and hope I have passed with enough marks to go back next year.'

'I'm sure you have, you were always top of the class. How's Alice by the way, I haven't seen your sister for weeks?'

'She's working hard on her A levels, well she was, she finished her last exam yesterday.'

'Is she going to university like you?'

'Aye, if her grades are good enough, she wants to become a vet and has a place at Glasgow. Depends on her grades though.'

'A couple of bright sparks aren't you?'

'You could say that but you have to work at it.'

'I wish I had paid more attention at school,' said Rory, handing Molly her drink and putting his arm around her.

'Your problem is that you have fishing and boats in your blood, you never seem to talk about anything else.'

'I like fishing; it's the only way of life I ever wanted to follow.'

'And look where it's got you, no boat and no job,' added Molly.

Rory's face changed, her barb catching him unawares, and he lowered his eyes.

'So Molly, what are you up to these days?' I said, trying to change the subject.

'I am the receptionist at the surgery,' she said with pride, as if it was the most important job in the world. 'I make sure the surgery runs smoothly and young Doctor Johnson can see as many of his patients as he needs to.'

'Needs to?'

'Yes, he works very hard and I don't want to see him overworked.'

It was obvious the subject had not changed enough and I wondered how long Rory's relationship with Molly might last. At school, she had always had a queue of adolescent boys waiting their turn.

'Are you still a Rangers' fan Rory?' I said awkwardly.

'Aye, it's a pity those left footers won the cup this year though. I thought we might have made the double.'

It was then, as we began discussing our respective sports, that Molly seemed to lose all interest, and when two of her friends turned up she went across to talk to them. I looked at Rory and could see hurt in his eyes; after all he had been through he did not need a floosy like Molly upsetting him.

'Cheer up, tell me about your dad, has he fully recovered?'

That seemed to work, he snapped out of his melancholy and looked at me with serious eyes.

'Physically he's fine but I think the experience has changed him, made him take stock. He keeps on about the decline of the fishing and how we have to go further afield to fish for anything worth catching and when we do catch fish we have to watch our quotas. Then, nine times out of ten, the bloody fishery protection vessel turns up.'

'Have you had problems with them?'

'Not too much, we've been boarded but each time we were within the law. Stupid bloody law, they do not seem to chase the foreign boats as they do us. I tell you if we fall foul of the fishery protection boys, it could finish us. We couldn't hope to pay some of the fines they hand out and I think that is what is playing on Dad's mind.'

'Will he buy another boat?'

'I don't really know but I suspect not. The insurance looks as if it could be a good amount and now the government have stopped paying us to decommission. He grumbles that if they allow the Spanish boats to fish these waters from next January he is better off staying ashore.' He paused for a few moments, took a drink from his glass and I could see that all was not well with him. 'We had a visit from the insurers and Dad thinks they will try to sue the Navy and that's why they offered us more than the boat was worth. Plus of course, we exaggerated our claim. If Dad decides not to buy another boat and keep on fishing, I don't know what I will do. I've already kissed the motorbike goodbye.'

'What about finding a job on one of the other boats?'

'Naw, they're all finding it hard and some have even started using foreign labour, East Europeans and Filipinos.'

'Filipinos! Bloody hell things have got bad,' I said with some surprise. 'Another pint?' I put my empty glass on the bar, hoping to lift the gloom that seemed to be descending again.

Rory took little persuading and as the night wore on we drank rather more than we should have, but our conversation at last moved from fishing and as friends arrived Rory began to relax. Then Molly returned wanting her glass refilling and I thought that at least she was spending some time with Rory. I didn't have a girlfriend, not if you didn't count Sandra, a girl at college, studying physics would you believe. But she was English and I wouldn't see her for another two months and by then she might have moved on.

'Mal, how are you?' said a voice from behind, causing me to turn round to see Pauline, a girl of more than ample proportions, smiling at me. Pauline was known as a man-eater and it seemed that I was the one she had her sights set on.

'Ah . . . Pauline,' I managed to splutter, looking round for Rory to save me but he and Molly had moved to the other side of the bar and were deep in conversation. I was on my own.

'Haven't seen you since, well when?'

'Aye.'

'Are you going to buy me a drink then?'

'Er . . . yes, what will you have?'

'I'll have a double vodka and orange if you're offering.'

I wasn't offering but her look persuaded me to dig my hand in my pocket. Pulling out the few coins I had left I saw through my drunken haze that she had no chance of a double vodka and orange.

'How about a half of lager,' I managed to say. She was not impressed and, to my relief, wrapped her arm around a passing man ready to try her luck elsewhere.

Thankful for my narrow escape I looked for Rory again but both he and Molly had disappeared so I decided that it was time to go home. It was getting late, I had practically no money left and I vaguely remember that I found it difficult focusing my eyes for although I had acquired a taste for the Deuchars, I was not a practised drinker.

I can remember the pub and, as with most drunks, I seemed to have an inbuilt homing device. I do not know why but I felt happy, very happy. On reflection, I had no real reason to be so happy yet I must have been because I began to sing. Now my singing voice is none too melodic and as usual I did not really know the words but in my state of inebriation I thought I was up with the best of them.

'*We're heading for Venus, and still we stand tall*,' I managed and then from a bench by the harbour side came the chorus, '*It's the final countdown, it's the final countdown, it's the final fuckin' countdown*.' Then I heard a sob.

Turning my head towards my accompanying singer, I saw that it was Rory.

'What are you doing here Rory, I thought you had gone off with Molly?'

'I did but she's not very game tonight in fact she doesn't want to know me anymore, we're finished.'

'Oh,' was all I could muster.

'She said I have no prospects and that the fishing is finished, reckons that's what doctor fuckin' what's his name says. I think she fancies him and I'm not good enough for her.'

I am not one for using expletives and when others use them it usually jars with me, but Rory was a fisherman and swearing seems to be a gift many of them are born with, so, again, all I could say was 'Oh.'

'Bastard bastard bastard!'

'Don't get so despondent Rory; there are always more fish in the sea.'

'No there aren't, if there were I wouldn't be in this state, fuckin' fish, fuckin' women,' he said and then he started chuckling.

'Now what's so funny?'

'Plenty more fish in the sea.'

The irony struck me and I too burst out laughing. Whether it was the alcohol or simply a release, I do not know but before long we were rolling about holding our sides, tears streaming down our faces until suddenly a stern voice cut us short.

'Now you lads, what's going on?'

'It was one half of the town's police force, and it must have been his bad luck to work the Saturday night shift.

'Nothing, we were just having a laugh.'

'Nothing wrong with that and you're both over eighteen but I must ask you to keep the noise down, it's nearly midnight you know. We can't be having a street party at this time of night, not here. Go on; get off home the pair of you.'

Slowly we got to our feet and made our way past the Constable, unaware of the grin spreading across his face. He must have had a boring shift and had decided to have some fun at our expense. At least the laughter and then the shock of seeing a police officer had sobered us both up, we had become sensible and before long found ourselves walking along the quayside past the remains of the once proud fishing fleet.

'It's such a shame that it has come to this, I can understand your father not wanting to return to fishing. I expect his insurance pay-out will go some way to supporting him and your mother for a while.'

'Aye, but what am I going to do?'

Rory's melancholy returned, weighing him down, and he stopped to sit on a nearby bench. Leaning back, he took a deep breath and stared out at the dancing lights reflected off the dark waters of the harbour.

'I'm feeling sorry for myself. It's no good, I know I have to sort myself out, have to find a job somewhere but all I know is fishing,' he finally said.

'And boat handling, you can do that. What about trying for a job on an oil platform support vessel, I would have thought that was right up your street? It's big business nowadays, the North Sea oil industry,' I said sitting beside him.

Slowly he turned his head towards me and his expression changed. 'Mal, you're right, I'll start looking first thing on Monday morning.'

Chapter 2

I found out later that Rory's father was serious about giving up fishing and Rory must have realised that because his promise to look for work in the oil industry became a pressing commitment. He began by looking in newspapers and magazines at the local library, finally making a visit to the job centre. Eventually his endeavours paid off and he attended an interview in Aberdeen. However, initially he was unlucky; the position was no longer open even before he reached the Granite City. But to his credit, he booked himself into a guesthouse for a few days and went knocking on any door he felt might present an opportunity and it worked. Two days after arriving in Aberdeen, he secured a position as a junior deck hand on a rig supply vessel. The company was looking for qualified merchant seamen but had a policy of considering fishermen with at least two years' experience and when Rory related his story they agreed to take him on. It would be almost two years before we would meet again.

The North Sea could be a cold and forbidding place in winter and Rory had only been aboard the *Norse*

Provider a month when the first of the winter storms hit. They were on their way back to Aberdeen from the giant Forties field after delivering a cargo of pipes when the weather front overtook them. The forecast was for severe gales: the waves were high enough to reach right up to the ship's bridge and for Rory it was a trial to just keep his dinner in place on the table.

'Will you look at that,' said one of the deck gang, glancing out of the window while trying to eat without his own plate sliding to the floor.

'I've not seen waves so big,' said Rory. 'We sometimes have seas like this at home but I've never been out in such conditions.'

'This is nothing lad, we get waves twice this big sometimes but I have to confess the skipper usually makes sure we are safely tied up in Aberdeen when a big one hits.'

'Good for him,' said Rory, 'I don't think I would be very happy out here in anything worse than this.'

He looked out of the window at the raging waters, the white crested waves stretching as far as he could see, and as the ship heaved under their pressure he had to admit that he felt at home. They had ridden angry seas in the *Lurach-Aon*, a much smaller boat, and he had delighted in steering her through the maelstrom but these seas were something else. Then his mind turned to the accident. The board of enquiry had still to sit, leading him to believe that nothing would come of it. If it were a submarine and he was sure now that it was, then there would be a cover up. The Navy would not admit to anything and if it was a Russian submarine then it was obvious there would be nothing but silence from the Russians. Sticking his fork into the last of his sausage, he mused that if the submarine had caught them in seas only a tenth as rough as these they would not have survived; he would not be alive to look out of the window. It was a sobering thought and it made a shiver run down his spine.

Rory survived that winter without mishap as the *Norse Provider* plied its trade across the North Sea where he enjoyed his time on her as much as anyone could. The money was far better than he could earn fishing and because his basic needs were met aboard ship he was soon relatively well off and as spring turned to summer he was able to afford a motorbike and home on leave his father asked, 'So you are happy in your new job?'

'Aye I am and it pays well.'

'I can see that. How long were you saving up for that motorbike when we were fishing son?'

'A year, maybe more.'

'And now you've managed it. Good for you but don't go killing yourself.'

'I won't, don't worry Da.'

The motorbike was a wonderful thing for Rory, his working pattern gave him three weeks' shore leave at any one time, long enough to explore the mainland. He would return home first to see his mother and then take his motorbike on the ferry to Ullapool from where he would ride to wherever his fancy took him riding hour after hour along deserted roads through the magnificent scenery of the Highlands. But it made for a lonely existence and eventually his wanderlust was satiated.

'So you're back to walking are you,' said Jimmy, a fellow deck hand as they stood waiting to cast off a heavy mooring warp.

'Aye, it's not a lot of fun on your own and there's nowhere to go on Lewis, only a few villages and nothing much to see except sheep. I've had a good time, been to places, but maybe I'll buy a car after this trip, I don't know.'

It's a waste of money, a car in this job. Why, it will just stand idle for weeks on end while we are out here. Better save your money, or spend it on something that's a bit more fun.'

'A bit more fun?'

'Of course, me and a couple of the lads are off to Thailand for a few days. You can have more than a bit of fun there.'

'Doing what?'

Jimmy was about to answer when the deck officer appeared, speaking into his radio, and then called out to them.

'Take your stations, wait for my signal to cast off and remember to keep clear of the lines.'

The orange-clad men of the deck crew took up their positions under the watchful eye of the officer and when he gave the command Rory and Jimmy began guiding the shoreline through the fairlead while another member of the deck crew controlled the winch. From the dock, the shore men let go the thick rope for the on-board crew to guide the heavy rope on deck and when they had almost finished a prolonged blast of the whistle announced the ship's departure. Slowly the giant propeller began to turn, thrashing the water, turning it from grey to white. The vessel began to move away from the dockside and once it was on its way, the order came to stand down. It was time for the work crew to go for breakfast and one by one the deck hands trooped through the door into the superstructure to make their way to the mess room.

'A young lad like you could have a great time with all those girls. They will do anything you know and you can have two at once, if you want. Why don't you come with us?' said Jimmy, still pressing Rory on Thailand as they hungrily devoured breakfast.

'I don't think so; I've heard stories about that place. I don't want to catch anything and some of the girls aren't even girls I believe.'

'Oh don't be such a prude, you'll have some fun.'

'No thank you,' said Rory, feeling decidedly uncomfortable. He was twenty years old, still a virgin and did not intend to lose it to a whore on the far side of the world. He had grown up in a quiet, gentle environment away from the vice and depravity that seemed to consume some of his shipmates and he had no desire to experience anything Jimmy was suggesting.

Finishing breakfast, he left the mess room and was about to go to his shared cabin when the deck officer caught up with him. He was slightly older than Rory, had qualified for his officer's ticket only recently and this was his first job. Although he was in charge and not really supposed to mix with the crew aboard ship, they had become friends, occasionally sharing a drink in a dockside pub before going on leave.

'Rory, just to let you know the old man has orders to take us to Leith after our next trip to the Forties. Seems there is a problem with the hull after that battering we took a few months ago. The surveyors have been having a look at her and they want a closer inspection. We've been taking on water and the engineers think that maybe the seal on the shaft is failing. We might get a few nights out in Edinburgh.'

'That's interesting David, I've never been to Edinburgh.'

'I did my training there, I know a few places to go. What do you say, we could manage a couple of nights out to sample the Edinburgh fare?'

'Fare?'

'You know, have a few beers and maybe we'll meet some girls. A bit classier than those whores in Thailand Jimmy and his pals will be chasing after.'

'From what I've heard they chase you.'

Less than a week later the *Norse Provider* headed south and along the Firth of Forth to Edinburgh. It was as pleasant a journey as Rory had made on the ship and the early morning caught him standing by the rail looking out over the calm sea of the Firth. Feeling the sun on his back, he watched a pair of tugboats working in harmony, guiding the ship into the Imperial dry dock. He and the rest of the deck crew knew what to do and under the supervision of the deck officer they passed the mooring warps to the shore men as slowly the ship came to a standstill.

'All secure aft captain,' David announced through his radio and after a crackled reply he ordered the men to go off watch. 'There is a list in the crew room lads. As we are in dry dock and there is not a lot for you to do the captain says because we should be here for around four days, there will be some shore leave. He wants at least two of you on watch for the duration and the list will tell you when you are working, other than that your time is your own.'

A cheer went up from the men as they slowly began to disperse and David came across to speak with Rory.

'Well Rory, we're here. It's a fine day for sightseeing and if you have never been to Edinburgh before, I suggest today would be a good time to start.'

'Aye it is David, ah think I would like a look round the castle at least.'

'That's unusual for a seaman; they usually find the nearest pub and stay there.'

'Och I don't want to be wasting my time in a pub, maybe on an evening but not all day.'

'A wise decision, I'll give you a few pointers. There are buses every few minutes to Princes Street and from there it is an easy walk to the castle. I have to work today but we can catch up tomorrow night for a drink and I can show you a couple of interesting places.'

Rory smiled, left for the crew room to discover from the rota what his time off was, and as he looked at the list, Jimmy caught up with him.

'Are you coming to the pub with us Rory?'

'No, I'm off for a look round, I've never been here before. It's our capital and I want to take this chance to see it.'

'You've a lot to learn young 'un, sightseeing is for softies. Come to the pub with me and the lads.'

'Later maybe, it's too nice a day to be sitting in a pub.'

Jimmy scowled and shook his head in feigned disgust, Rory to smile after him as he walked away. He was a good man, Jimmy, a good worker, but he played hard, drank more than his fair share, you could see it in his face, not a look Rory particularly admired.

Rory finally got off the bus on Princes Street at not quite mid-day to find it bustling with shoppers and tourists. He stood for a minute taking in the atmosphere, the surroundings, and looked up admiringly at a statue of a Scottish soldier on horseback. In the background, the skirl of a lone piper entertaining foreign visitors stirred his emotions and then, in the distance, he saw the castle, dark, imposing and sitting proudly on its impenetrable mound above the city. It seemed to proclaim the hundreds of years of Scottish history and Rory felt proud, standing for a few minutes to take in the view. He recognised the Scott Monument and began to walk towards it and to the bridge when he heard his name called out. At first, he did not react but the caller was persistent and as the voice grew louder, he stopped and turned round.

'Malcolm, what are you doing here?' he said in surprise.

'I live here don't forget, well I will for a while longer. More to the point Rory, what are you doing here? I wasn't sure it was you at first, hell we haven't seen each other in, what, nearly two years?'

'Aye it must be. I've been working on the supply ship for about two years.'

'Supply ship? I heard you were working in the oil industry. I told you that would be a good move.'

'You did and it was. I like the work and the money is very good but you know I miss the fishing with Da and Angus.'

'How are they both, I have never clapped eyes on either of them since the accident? Has your father fully recovered?'

'Yes he's well enough; he found a job working at one of the salmon farms and seems to like it. Ma thinks it is great not having to worry about him away fishing.'

'So, you still haven't told me what you are doing here in Edinburgh, I'd have thought you would be in Aberdeen.'

'We're in dry dock for repairs, four days they reckon, so I'm having a look round.'

'Listen, I have a lecture at two o'clock but if you like I'll come with you for a while, catch up on the gossip.'

'That would be great. I was wantin' to see the castle.'

'Come on, it's not far once we cross this bridge.'

Grinning hugely Rory fell in with Malcolm and tried to follow his rather energetic stride pattern.

'Do you remember the last time we had a drink, the Imperial, when we both got drunk and I found you sitting on that bench?'

'Aye, happy days I don't think.'

'Molly's engaged to that doctor you know.'

'It was on the cards, she never stopped talking about him.'

'So, are there any more fish in the sea?'

'What, girls you mean?'

'Yes, girls.'

'I've not really had the chance to meet any girls, only the ones back home and most of them are courting.'

'We'll change that. You can come with me to a student party, I will find out where one is happening or maybe we can go to one of the pubs we use. There are always lots of girls about.'

'Phew, sounds interesting but if they start talking about degrees and stuff I will probably feel lost.'

'With your looks Rory you will never be lost. They will be up for a Viking lookalike I'm sure.'

It was a good day for Rory as together we explored the Royal Mile and Edinburgh Castle. He learned a lot about his heritage, about battles long forgotten, people long dead and in the process, I somehow forgot my afternoon lecture.

'There is a good pub round here, do you fancy a pint?'

'Ah do, I haven't eaten since breakfast on the ship so a pint and a pie would be a good idea. Tell you what, how about I treat you to an Indian for showing me round.'

'An Indian! I wouldn't have thought you were into Indians.'

'Sometimes, only sometimes. I've had a night or two out with the crew in Aberdeen and they introduced me to Indian food.'

'So you like Indian food?'

'Yeah, but not the real hot stuff, they used to have competitions to see who could eat the hottest curry but I only did that twice.'

'Twice?'

'Too much to drink the first time, so I forgot how bad it can be the second.'

'Ha ha, you're not the only one, we've all done that and I must confess I can't handle a vindaloo. Come on, we'll have a look in the Brass Monkey first. It's a bit of a walk but not too far and I know a decent enough Indian restaurant nearby.'

'Where do you live Mal?'

I told him 'Just a few doors from the Brass Monkey.'

'That sounds useful.'

The Brass Monkey was heaving as we arrived, full of students and we had to force a way through the noisy throng.

'What will it be Malcolm, you still on the Deuchars?'

'Aye, a pint of if you please.'

Rory ordered the drinks and handed me his glass just as the throng round the bar was becoming a little too oppressive. I saw Rory's discomfort and nodded my head sideways, encouraging him to follow me to a less congested area.

'I've never seen so many people in a pub. Is it always like this?'

'Not always, but it usually is. Come on there's some space by the door over there.'

Following closely behind, Rory looked on in wonder at the gaggle of students thronging the pub, the sound of clinking glasses and their banter filling the air. I thought that perhaps Rory was used to the self-contained existence on board ship and after his lonely travels, was finding a first impression of student life a little overwhelming. I guessed that to him their dress seemed strange; their unkempt appearance mildly shocking but at least there was an abundance of girls. I could see that almost all of them were attractive to him in one way or another and he was finding it hard not to gawp.

'How do you like it in here, noisy isn't it?'

'Bloody well is, you can hardly hear yourself think. Hello Mick, did you get your bike back?' I said as my flatmate appeared pushing through the crowd.

'Naw, I reckon it's gone. I bet it was those smack heads who were loitering round here last night. The police say I will be lucky to see it again. Not to worry though, the cops told me that there is a sale of recovered stolen property next week and there are at least ten bicycles. The sergeant said I should be able to buy one even on students' money.'

45

'That's helpful isn't it?'

'Yes, though I guess it's back to walking for a while. Who's this?'

'A friend from home, he's working on a rig support vessel and he is in Leith for a few days. Rory this is Mick, a good friend and flatmate of mine, and Mick this is Rory.'

'How d'you do,' said Mick reaching out to shake Rory's hand. 'So you're from Stornoway are you? Quite a place I understand, not like my home town.'

'Where are you from?'

'Essex, near Southend.'

'It's a long way for you to come to study.'

'It is but I do like it here, a bit more soul than down south. Everywhere is beginning to look the same round London and I don't like it.'

'What are you studying?'

'I'm doing a PhD in organic chemistry.'

'Oh,' said Rory, beginning to feel out of his depth. 'Er, what's that?'

'Never mind organic chemistry Rory, if you get him talking he does not stop and there is nothing more boring than organic chemistry,' I said.

Mick pouted, annoyed to have been stopped in his tracks and he lifted his glass, draining half of it in one go before saying, 'Sandra, Barbara, how are you?' to two girls who had just appeared carrying pint glasses. Half ignoring Mick, one of them began talking to me and once she realised Rory was with me, demanded an introduction.

'This is Sandra; I told you about her didn't I?'

Rory looked puzzled, unable to remember and not much interested, stunned as he was by Barbara's clear blue eyes. He was not good with girls, not a smooth talker and in this company, he had little idea of where to begin.

'Who is he Malcolm?' Barbara asked as she broke off her conversation with Mick. 'We haven't had such a good-looking stud round here for ages. Have you got a girlfriend?' she said holding Rory's gaze.

'Er . . . no, not at the moment?'

I think Barbara's forthright manner took Rory by surprise but recovering his poise, he swallowed the last of his pint, and then emerging from the crowd came Emily to stand squarely in front of Rory.

'Hello, I'm Emily. What's your name? I see you are with Malcolm, are you on the same course?'

'No, I'm not a student I'm afraid, I'm a friend of Malcolm's from back home.'

'And where is home?'

'Stornoway, Lewis.'

'Oh yes, Malcolm has told me a little about his home and I would love to go there, different from the city, peaceful I imagine.'

'A bit more peaceful than here.'

'I bet,' she said, draining her glass. 'Malcolm, don't be so rude,' she said poking me in the ribs, 'my glass needs filling.'

'Are you all right Rory, I see you have met my flatmate?'

'Flatmate, her!'

'What do you mean her? My name's Emily if you don't mind.'

'Sorry, er, Emily.'

'Take no notice Rory she's just winding you up. Here give me your glass and I'll get another couple of pints,' I said.

Rory handed me his glass and so did Emily with a look that dared me to refuse her and when I returned from the bar they were deep in conversation.

'What are you doing in Edinburgh if you're not a student; you're not a travelling salesman are you?'

'No I'm not a travelling salesman, I work in the offshore industry, on a supply vessel. What are you studying, organic chemistry?'

'No, that's boring. Look at Mick, that's what organic chemistry does to you.'

I glanced at Mick talking animatedly to a girl with the look of boredom spread across her face and could not help laughing. Emily too saw the funny side of what she had said and began to giggle.

'Nice to see you are both getting along. Here take this,' I said, handing over the drinks.

'So what are you studying?'

'English literature, I hope to be a writer one day.'

'A writer, that's interesting.'

'Where are you staying, is your ship here?'

'Not quite my ship, but yes, it's in Leith dry dock.'

'So that's where you sleep?' she said, looking thoughtful for a fleeting moment. 'Leith's quite a way from here; we have a mattress in the flat you can use that for tonight if you want. We are all off to a party later. Why don't you come along? He can come can't he Malcolm.'

I just nodded.

'I would love to but I have to be back by mid-day tomorrow for my watch.'

'No prob. Hey Malcolm, Rory is coming to the party with us and he can sleep in the flat.'

As I recall, as the evening wore on Rory became more relaxed, drinking and mixing with the students. He was happy enough chatting with myself, Sandra and Emily and then Barbara reappeared.

'Are you coming to the party Sandra?'

'Are we going Malcolm?'

'Hey, of course, I wouldn't miss it for the world,' I said.

'You, sailor boy, are you coming?' said Barbara.

'Am I invited too?' asked Emily indignantly.

'Of course you are.'

'Where are we going?' Rory asked.

'Student party down the road, six of our friends have a house between them, and it's a great place for a party,' I said.

'Do I need to take a bottle or anything?'

'You can if you like but we'll probably only be drinking coffee.'

'Coffee! Doesn't sound like much of a party?'

'Come on Rory,' said Emily, grabbing hold of his hand, and with little in the way of resistance he let her lead him from the pub and into the chilled evening air.

'Have you smoked much, sailor boy?' said Barbara catching us up.

'No I don't smoke, do you?'

Barbara smiled a wicked smile and began walking faster towards an open door.

'Hi guys, come on in, up there,' said a smiling friendly face attached to an arm pointing up some stairs.

Rory and Emily were the last to arrive, passing the smiling face to follow the clatter of shoes on the bare wooden stairs to the first floor. It contained a spacious room with little more than a threadbare square of Persian carpet, an old three-piece suite and several people chatting.

'Come over here Rory,' said Emily. 'Do you want a coffee?'

'Aye, a coffee would be fine.'

'I see you have made friends with Emily, don't get too stoned will you; we have to get you back to your ship in the morning,' I told him.

'Stoned?'

Emily reappeared handing him a mug of coffee 'I didn't put any sugar in it, you don't need sugar,' she said.

'Won't I, why?'

'Blood sugar levels, Mick told me if you smoke *Bob Hope* your blood sugar levels go up and you risk getting diabetes. He should know he's an expert on dope.'

Rory looked at the coffee and then at Emily who was grinning from ear to ear. 'I don't expect you will develop diabetes after just one smoke.'

Rory expression changed as he noticed the smell, a strange sickly smell, and he watched as the partygoers began sitting down on the carpet and forming a circle.

'Come on Rory, sit here with me,' said Emily, taking hold of his hand. By now, it was dawning on him what was about to happen, they were taking drugs. I knew that he had never taken drugs and would have little idea of how to when Emily squealed with delight.

'Ooh it's my turn.'

A cylindrical smoking white object had appeared, passed to her by her neighbour, and taking hold of it, she placed it carefully between her lips. Rory watched in fascination as with eyes half shut she slowly inhaled and then, after a short pause, blew smoke into the air.

'Phew, that's good,' she said, passing the glowing spliff to Rory. 'Just inhale a little to begin with, that's it, nice and steady.'

Rory inhaled and by the look on his face, half expecting to have a coughing fit. But it did not happen, instead, a strange warm glow seemed to come over him and I guessed he was feeling the sensation of dizziness and numbness associated with smoking marijuana. Then someone gently removed the spliff from his fingers.

'It's Moroccan, good isn't it? Mick got it from somewhere,' said Emily, her eyes dark and dreamy.

Rory didn't answer; instead he just looked into those eyes.

'I can see its having an effect Rory. Drink your coffee, it will be round again soon and you can have another go,' I said

Rory lifted the mug to his lips and then he looked around at the circle of people. Most were sitting cross-legged, silent and simply staring, their minds elsewhere, and then the spliff returned. It was shorter and the end was soggy, no deterrence to Emily who inhaled deeply, then it was Rory's turn once more. I watched as he drew the smoke into his lungs and then we heard a banging noise.

He told me later that in the depths of his mind, he had begun to believe he was back on the fishing boat, on a flat blue sea with the summer sun beating down and the sound was that of the engine.

It was not an engine and certainly not the engine of the *Lurach-Aon* he could hear. It was Mick, the supplier, clattering up the wooden stairs.

'Hello everyone, I see you have started without me.'

'And finished,' said a voice. 'That's the last of it.'

'Have no fear people, look,' he said, opening the palm of his hand to reveal a small greased-paper package.

Now I cannot tell you much more about that evening for I was just as stoned as the rest of them. Between smoking the marijuana and returning to the flat my memory failed but I can guess most of what happened. Rory, unused to smoking the *Bob Hope,* would no doubt have become legless for a time and from what I heard later, he did. Then there was Mick, arriving late, and I remember thinking that he looked a little secretive. I was not too far gone at that stage and when he declined the spliff, I became suspicious.

When Mick refuses a spliff it can only mean one thing, he has already taken something stronger or weirder. Mick was a clever chemist and even in those days, we suspected him of concocting his own designer drugs and years later, when his case went to court, we had proof.

Rory related the rest of the evening to me the following day, told me as far as he could remember, that he found it hard to stand up when it was time to leave the party.

'I don't know how she did it but Emily managed to help me,' he said. I managed to stagger up to your flat, banging my head in the process and with Emily's help I managed to sit the armchair.

'That was a strange experience,' he said.

'First time wasn't it?'

'Yes, I had no idea how thirsty it makes you.'

'Amongst other things. How are you feeling now?'

'A bit strange but I'm okay,' said Rory, rubbing his face in his hands.

'How did you get on with Emily?'

'Oh, well I woke up in her bed,' he said rather sheepishly. 'I don't know how I managed that but I got out of the bed without waking her, and sneaked out of the bedroom. Then I saw your friend Mick lying on the settee. He was lying flat on his back with his arms straight out as if someone had crucified him. His hair was disorderly, his face had streaks of dried blood all over it and his knuckles were skinned red raw. For a minute, I really did think he was dead. Then he opened his eyes and looked straight at me.

What happened to you I said, have you been attacked?' He just blinked and wiped his tongue across his lips and tried to speak.

'What is it?'

'Water.'

'He was in no fit state to help himself so I looked for the kitchen and a tap. The first door I opened wasn't the kitchen I was your bedroom and there you were with Sandra and Barbara, all three of you fast asleep. 'Bloody hell what have I got myself into,' I thought, anyway I found the kitchen and a glass amongst all those dirty pots. I was in need of a drink as well and then I took the glass of water to the living room and saw Emily looking at Mick.

'What have you been up to this time Mick?' she said.

'What did he say?' I asked.

'Told her he had synthesised some sort of acid in the lab and thought he would give it a try.'

'Was it lysergic acid?'

'Yeah, I think that's it. What is it?'

'LSD, an hallucinatory drug, it makes the world a wonderful place, for a while anyway. The Beatles used it, remember?'

'Oh yes, anyway he was beginning to liven up and Emily queried him about his injuries.'

'What injuries?'

'Oh he just had cuts and bruises. He said it was a very small dose, said he put a couple of drops onto a sugar cube and when we were in the pub, popped it in his mouth. then he said he was listening to some music and thought how beautiful it was and for some reason it inspired him to go for a walk.'

'A walk, where?'

'Across the city.'

'What do you mean, across the city!'

'Nowhere in particular,' he said, 'just a walk across Edinburgh – in a straight line.'

'And how far did he get?'

'Into the next street, said he spent a couple of hours trying to get over a high wall. Each time he got near to the top he fell off but was pleased that he managed it in the end.'

'It was no real surprise to find out what antics Mick had performed while under the influence of his home made LSD but I worried that one of these days he might really hurt himself, get run over by a car or something. In the event he survived long enough to gain his PhD and other than a newspaper report of his case I have not seen him since

Chapter 3

The man's natural reaction was to retreat from the powerful fingers gripping his throat, his head pushing hard against the wall in the secluded alleyway. He had half expected that one day to have to face clan members but three of them had surprised him, cornered him, and he knew that there was no escape.

'Where is the money you piece of shit,' growled Franco, his grip tightening.

The man could hardly breathe as he frantically clawed at Franco's hand. Franco released his grip momentarily only to swing the clenched fist of his free hand into his victim's stomach leaving his the man incapable of coherent speech.

It was not as if he was an enemy, a rival mafioso or even a criminal in the wider sense, he too was mafia and of the same family as Franco but Luigi Bellincioni had sinned. Selling twenty barrels of the family's virgin olive oil to French gangsters from Marseille, he had pocketed the proceeds. He had done the same thing before bearing the scar on his cheek, but he had not learned.

'One more time Bellincioni, what have you done with the money, where is it?

The man mouthed several words as his blood dripped from his lips and Franco leaned closer to catch his whispered words.

'I didn't catch that,' he said hitting him again.

'It is in the church.'

'Church, which church?'

'*Santa Maria.*'

'*Santa Maria*, where?'

Any resistance Luigi Bellincioni might have summoned up disappeared, leaving him incapable of coherent speech and able only to mumble his words.

'The...the presbytery...a leather satchel... behind the curtain.'

'We shall check.'

Franco released his grip and clicked his fingers summoning one of the two Mafiosos watching.

'Carlo, you heard that, the presbytery in the church of *Santa Maria*. Go and have a look, we will follow with this worthless toad. Go into the church, find the money and we will meet you there.'

The man nodded, crossed the canal bridge to set off at a brisk pace towards the church while Franco and the other man frog marched the unfortunate Luigi over the bridge between them. It was late, the poor street lighting concealed them from the few pedestrians in this part of the city, they could as easily be seen to be been helping a drunken friend as beating the man unconscious. They traversed several narrow streets turned into a narrow ally and crossed a second stone bridge before entering the paved

57

square in front of the church. It was deserted and silent save for the faint noise of a television coming from an open window high above them and keeping to the shadows, they waited for the church door to open.

'Have you looked inside it?' Franco hissed as Carlo emerged carrying the satchel.

'Yes, it's full of Lire and French francs.'

'Good, let's go.'

They had accomplished their task, retrieved Luigi Bellincioni of his ill-gotten gains and now all that remained was to dispose of him but that was not Franco's job, he was simply carrying out the order to find the money and not yet an executioner. He nodded towards his accomplice and together they dragged Luigi from the square to the canal side where he began to shake uncontrollably. Franco looked at Fabiano and the satchel, reaching out his hand. It was the end game for Luigi, as the satchel changed hands Franco's eyes gave the order and with one swift movement the executioner's stiletto knife plunged deep into Luigi Bellincioni's ribs.

Luigi had expected death; the oath of allegiance made in his own blood came with a price. Even so, his eyes still widened in shock as the blade found its mark and coughing once, with blood beginning to trickle from his lips, he slumped to the ground. The three gangsters said nothing, standing silently and down at the corpse with macabre fascination. Franco was the first to react, using his foot to roll the body into the canal and with a sound no more than a plop, Luigi Bellincioni became history.

Half an hour later, the three Mafiosos delivered the satchel to one of *Il Capo's* lieutenants, receiving in return a buff envelope containing the rewards for a job well done. The three killers parted company with the briefest of goodbyes and Franco, living outside the city of Venice, made his way towards the railway station. His scooter was waiting for him and after quickly releasing its security chain; he kicked the starter and twenty minutes later arrived at the tree-lined avenue and home.

'Franco you are late you should have been here an hour ago,' scolded his mother. Francesca was annoyed with her son and not for the first time. 'Where have you been, what have you been doing to be out so late? Wash your hands and take the pasta to the table for me.'

She lifted the large pot from the stove and drained the water, stood it on the cooker top and waited for Franco to take it into the dining room. Franco did as his mother told him for, although he was a minor gangster, his mother still held sway when it came to the affairs of home. Picking up the steaming bowl, he used his back to nudge open the door and carry the steaming bowl of pasta to the dining table. Already seated were his sister and brother, his father, a small balding man stood apart holding a glass of wine.

'Ah Franco you have decided to grace us with your company at last,' he said.

Franco's brother Claudio sitting opposite his sister looked up. He was a good-looking young man with differeing characteristics to his brother; he did not possess the same arrogance or desire to compete as

Franco. Sitting next to him was their sister, Nadia, the youngest of the Foscari's three children and the apple of her parents' eyes. She was a typical dark eyed Mediterranean beauty and with intelligence to match.

'Nadia, good to see you,' said Franco placing the bowl of pasta on the table and leaning over to kiss her on each cheek. 'You have your degree I hear. Clever girl, you must get it from me,'

Nadia's eyes flashed at her brother. All her life he had teased her, tried to dominate her but she would have none of it. As children, he always tried to take charge, to dominate her and even Claudio, a year older. Franco was one on his own, she knew that, and she knew as well that he mixed with bad and dangerous people.

'Franco, you can't even spell your own name properly, don't tell me I get it from you.'

Franco frowned, felt his blood begin to heat up but his mother had entered the room and her look prevented an escalation of the situation.

'Now children don't be fighting, it's a time for celebration not conflict. All that childish argumentative stuff is in the past, you are grown-ups now, don't be fighting.'

'Sorry Mamma,' said Nadia.

'Hm, sorry,' said Franco with some difficulty.

'Now sit down while your father dishes out the pasta,' she said placing the bowl of sauce on the table.

'What have you made Mamma? I have missed your cooking. In the hall of residence, we had a canteen that served the most horrible food.'

'It's salmon and prawn in my own mascarpone sauce.'

'Mmm, I cannot wait, me first papa?'

Mario laughed at his daughter. She was making fun of Franco for as a little girl she would use the same expression to make sure she got her fair share at the dinner table.

'I think Nadia that Mamma is first and then you. Pass this plate to your mother and then give me yours. What about you Claudio, are you hungry?'

He was and so was Franco and after he filling everyone's glass, the family settled down to dinner.

'I hear the police are cracking down on the water taxis Claudio. Have you heard anything?'

'No papa, I do not think there is a problem, too many of the city's officials have a stake in leaving things as they are. The last time they tried to impose their rules nobody took any notice and after a few months we heard no more. I think the taxi licences are lucrative business for some of the city officials and they don't want anybody looking too closely at how they run thing.'

'Quite so,' said Mario. 'And you Franco, how is your job in the market, you are still working as a porter for the Morettis?'

'Now and again, I have other jobs.'

'What other jobs?' asked Nadia.

'Other jobs. What about you, do you have a job now you are a qualified person. Tell me what job will you be doing?'

Everyone looked at Nadia, inquisitive to know the answer for she was the first person in the family to

61

gain a real qualification, one on paper and that meant that she could expect a well-paid job, for a woman.

Nadia stopped chewing for a second or two before swallowing and taking a drink from her glass.

'I am not going to work for a year.'

'What!' exclaimed Franco? How can you not work, we all work, Papa as an accountant and your mother has the shop. Claudio and I work so you should too.'

'Now leave her alone Franco, said his father. Your sister will work eventually but she has something she wants to do first.'

'Like what.'

'I am going to travel the world.'

'The world, what world?'

'Don't be silly Franco, she deserves a reward for what she has achieved and she wants to travel for a while before getting herself a proper job,' added Francesca.

'Where will you go, India? If you do we might never see you again,' grumbled Franco imagining the kind of gangsters that might well roam India.

'We are not going to India, though I wouldn't mind, no the plan is to go to Australia and then America, find temporary jobs and learn better English. If I can speak English well, then that will help me get a decent job. Don't you see brother that with a degree and the ability to speak English, the world will be my oyster.'

'Oyster?'

'It's an English expression; I can go anywhere and do anything I please.'

For once, Franco was silent. His mother and father were looking at him, his sister was their favourite and he stood little chance of winning any argument with then on Nadia's side. As the talk of travelling to Australia and America dominated the conversation around the table, he began to feel out of his depth. His world had always been the back streets and the canal sides of Venice and formal education was for other people. He learned on the job, hustling, cajoling and threatening people to make a living, a very good living. Today his reward amounted to a week's work as a porter in the market – no wonder he only turned up to work when it suited him.

'You said we, who are the others?'

'Just Lucia Rossi, a friend from university. We shared a room and she studied geography so to travel will help her more than me.'

'What do you say father, are you going to pay for all this?'

'Nadia is a grown woman and she has a mind of her own. She will be gone for maybe a year, no more and as far as financing her trip she has saved some money and they both propose to work their passage. Now what is wrong with that? You could do the same if you were so minded Franco.'

Franco retreated and said nothing; his world was changing his siblings were no longer relying on him for favours, protection. Claudio had a decent job with his water taxi and now Nadia was leaving home. Subtle changes were taking place; his power over them was evaporating and watching his face, noting something in his eyes his mother said.

'Franco you are all growing up, it is time for each of you to take control of your own destiny. You are successful at work no, you have money and you have friends. Let Nadia find her own way.'

Franco looked at his family one by one, finished his Chianti and got up from the table.

'Very well, if that is how things are... I am going out; I will see you in the morning.'

He kissed his mother on the cheeks and then he went to Nadia to do the same.

'*Ciao*,' he said as his family watched him leave.

Nadia tumbled out of bed later than usual, another reward for passing her finals, and went downstairs in her dressing gown. The house was deserted, her parents and Claudio had left for work and as far as she could tell, Franco had not returned home the previous night. She went into the living room and picked up the telephone, dialled in a number and waited. She could hear clicking on the line as the connection was made and then the tell-tale tone as it rang at the other end.

'*Ciao*, this is Lucia.'

'Lucia, Nadia here.'

'Ah Nadia I was hoping you would ring. Any news?'

'Yes, I have spoken with papa and he says yes I can go. What about you?'

'Si, my father was reluctant at first but my mother persuaded him. Yes I can go.'

'Whoopee,' shouted Nadia down the line, Lucia responded in a likewise manner and for several minutes the girls let their delight run riot. They had planned their gap year trip with precision, obtained the necessary visas and paper work, had acquired Italian passports. The only item left on their list was their parent's permissions and now they had them.

'We need our flight tickets Nadia. Why don't we meet up and go to the travel shop, book the tickets and celebrate with a coffee somewhere?'

Franco was not happy to know his sister was leaving home on an adventure. He never had adventures, never travelled far but he had a dream, one day he would own a red Ferrari sports car just like the one parked outside *Il Capo's* house. Today was his first visit to the secluded villa, he was not yet an important player in the organization, but he would be one day of that he was sure.

'You are?' asked the dark suited man near the door.

'Franco Foscari,' he said looking into the man's eyes and realising his limitations.

It was not often Franco looked into someone's eyes and felt forced to back off but this man was a true mafioso, a killer.

'Stay there kid, I will see if you are expected.'

Kid! Who was he calling kid? The man was no more than three or four years older and the thought triggered a rise in Franco's temperature rising. The short fuse that catapulted him into trouble on more than one occasion was beginning to burn but for once, he had enough self-control to hold back. Luckily for him the minute or so he waited for his nemesis to return was enough for his rising anger to subside.

'It looks as if you are to see Angelo Di Fiore. A word of advice *kid*,' again he emphasised the word *kid*. 'Don't think you can square up to Angelo like you were going to do with me. He is an important man, be respectful.'

The words had their intended impact, restraining Franco's impetuous nature, a warning to heed.

'Follow me.'

The man led Franco into the house, knocked on a door and after hearing a voice, pushed the door open. With his outstretched palm, he indicated that Franco should enter and stepping forward Franco found himself confronted by a middle-aged man sitting at a desk. Smartly dressed in a dark grey suit with swept back grey hair to match the man looked up.

'Ah... Franco Foscari, come in, take a seat.'

Franco sat opposite wondering why the family had summoned him, had the murder of Luigi Bellincioni caused trouble, were the police investigating perhaps.

We have been watching you and we think you have potential. As from tomorrow, you will learn to take over the tax collection in the Rialto district. We had a tax collector but he met with an accident recently, Luigi Bellincioni. Ever heard of him?'

'No I can't say I have.'

Angelo Di Fiore pursed his lips and said nothing, simply thinking that this young man had the credentials to do the job.

The flight to Australia seemed to go on forever but eventually the blue of the Indian Ocean gave way to the parched scrub of Western Australia and soon the aircraft was making its final approach. Both Nadia and Lucia were weary from the journey but for the next few hours, adrenalin would keep them going.

'Isn't it warm, just like home in the summer,' said Lucia as the taxi whisked them from the airport to the heart of Fremantle where they had followed the advice of a friend from college and booked a room from where to begin their exploration.

'Do you think we should only speak English?'

'Yes of course, that is why we have come here to learn to speak better English. First though is a shower and some clean clothes and then we will explore a little.'

'Let's have a few days off first and then we can start looking for a job. We have work permits so we should be able to find something.'

'And then we need a place to stay, maybe the rooming house where we are staying for the first week will be okay. Look Nadia, I think we are here.'

The taxi pulled up outside a white washed wooden structure with a small well-tended garden between it and the road. Stepping from the taxi the girls picked up their cases and wandered into the small reception area manned by a healthy looking youth in a bright yellow shirt and blue shorts

'Good morning we have a room booked in the name of Foscari.'

'Ah g'day, Foscari you say, just a minute. He rummaged around on the desk in front of him, finally producing a card. 'Yeah, two females, I can see that. Just a mo an' I'll get the key.' Pulling open a desk drawer, he rummaged around, producing several keys with tags attached. 'Let's see, room twelve. Yeah here it is, follow me people.'

The youth led Nadia and Lucia along a short corridor, through an outside door and across a second garden area to a low building with several doors.

'Here we are room twelve.'

He unlocked the door and led the two women inside, showed them round and then he handed the key to Lucia.

'Get settled in and then come to reception and we can do the paperwork okay.'

'Thank you, is there somewhere nearby where we can have dinner.'

'Couple of good diners, the Mad Hatter is fair dinkum.' I'll show you where it is when you come to reception.'

The door closed behind him and Nadia and Lucia, gave each other a puzzled look.

'Far Dunk them, what does that mean Nadia.

'I don't know, it seems that we have a lot to learn.'

For two days, Nadia and Lucia relaxed, recovered from their journey and began to explore their new surroundings. The climate was familiar, warm and sunny and with their Italian tans, shorts and light tops they drew admiring looks. They wandered the precincts, explored the harbour side and after a morning window-shopping they came across a small coffee shop and decided to spend time watching the world go by.

'I like Australia Nadia. What about you?'

'We have only been here two days but, yes, from what I have seen so far I like it. The room is a bit dingy though and I have heard stories about spiders and snakes,' she said shuddering inwardly.

'We are in the city; I think the creepy crawlies are more in the countryside, nothing to worry about.'

Nadia admired Lucia's confidence; even so, she would keep an eye open for anything that might want to take a bite out of her. Pushing her fears to the back of her mind, she sat back in her chair and adjusted her sunglasses to watch the passers-by. As she did so, two men of about the same age and carrying large glasses of beer sat at the next table. From a brief sideways glance, she could see that they were healthy sunburned specimens of Australian males, more relaxed than the boys she knew back home and much less fashion conscious. They wore long shorts and scruffy denim shirts; one was blonde, his curly locks spilling over his forehead and the other, darker and Italian looking.

The blonde one looked them over and caught Nadia's glance, encouraging him to speak.

'G'day girls, we haven't seen you two before. Have you come for the surfing?'

Nadia tried to ignore him but Lucia was more amenable and pushing her sunglasses to the end of her nose, she peered at the two men.

'No we don't surf, do you?'

'Of course, everyone in Australia surfs, it's our national pastime. Hey that's a European accent isn't it. You French?'

Lucia giggled.

'No we are Italian.'

'No kidding, Tony here is Italian aren't you Tony.'

'Naw, no really, my granddad was a prisoner of war over here and never went home. Once they found out how good a pasta chef he was they wouldn't let him go anyway.'

'So where in Italy are you from?' asked the blonde one.

'Mestre.'

He looked at Lucia.

'Mestre, never heard of it. Where is that?'

'You have heard of Venice?'

The man nodded his head.

'Well Mestre is near Venice, at the opposite end of the causeway. Mestre is not like Venice though; we have industry and a port with big ships, not the tourists you get on the islands.'

'I have always wanted to visit Italy and especially Venice. My Granddad used to tell us about his childhood in Italy. I don't think it was easy from what he told me. He came from Naples,' said the dark one.

'Are you from round here?' Nadia found herself asking.

'Naw, we are here for the surfing, a week's holiday from work. We come from Newman up in the Pilbara.'

Both Nadia and Lucia had no idea what he was talking about, the expressions on their faces a manifestation of their bewilderment.

'Let me explain, we are miners. The Pilbara is one of the richest regions in the world for iron ore and we work at the Yandi mine about ninety miles from Newman.'

'It sounds like hard work,' said Lucia.

'It is but it pays well. We work at the mine for fourteen days continuously and then we get seven days off. That's why we are here, to get away from the heat and the dust and live a little.'

'Yeah, to surf in the heat and the water and drink a few beers.'

The two miners laughed at the joke explaining that at least they could cool down in the sea and a cold beer always helps.

'I'm Jake and this is Tony. What are your names?'

'Lucia and this is Nadia.'

'Pleased to meet you. 'Have you ever surfed?'

'No.'

'What about you?'

'It's not something that appeals to me. I prefer water skiing, a sport that seems safer. Anyway I have heard that sharks can be a problem in Australia,' said Nadia

'No need to worry, we get the odd shark but if you stick to the rules, keep inside the net, stay near the lookout posts you will be safe enough. All sightings of sharks are reported to the water police and there is a helicopter patrolling the coast to keep surfers as safe as they can,' said Jake.

'Yes I have heard about the nets and the lifeguards but maybe we will just stick to walking for the time being.'

'The surfing isn't so great round here by the way, the water is shallow and they don't get the big waves. We are on our way to Rottnest Island where the surfing is better. Why don't you take the ferry and spend some time watching the surfers over there and maybe you will catch the bug.'

'Catch the bug, what bug?' said Lucia wondering what else Australia was hiding from her.

'Ha ha, not an infection, it is just a turn of phrase. Catching the bug simply means that you have a strong interest in doing something. If you watch the surfers out on Rottnest, you might feel like joining in. If you do decide to go there you will have to ride bicycles everywhere as cars are not allowed on the island.'

Jake lifted his glass and downed the last of his beer.

'Ready mate?'

'I am. Sorry girls but we must go now we have to collect our boards and catch the ferry. It has been very nice meeting you,' said Tony pushing his empty glass away.

Nadia and Lucia watched the two Australians leave and then they turned to each other.

'Nice boys, I hope all Australians are like that. What about this ferry, do you want to go and see the island?

Lucia looked thoughtful for a second or two.

'As long as I don't get bitten by a bug. Yes, tomorrow we will go there, tomorrow for the whole day and ride bicycles.'

Nadia and Lucia rose early, walked to the pier and joined the queue, of surfers and tourists waiting to catch the ferry. As the line of people shuffled on board, they found a space against the rail and waited there to watch as the ship cast off. The dock receded and they turned their attention seaward to search the horizon for their first glimpse of the low-lying island lying twenty kilometres offshore and after twenty minutes Nadia excitedly gesticulating towards the horizon.

'Look Lucia, I can see it, look there,' she said pointing to a flat dark shape on the horizon.

The island had suddenly come into view, rising above the horizon and for the next fifteen minutes, they watched it grow. It did not appear particularly impressive, a rocky coastline covered in low, grassy sand dunes and as the Ferry sailed nearer, they became aware of wide expanses of white sand and aqua marine waves turning white as they crashed ashore.

'I can see why those two like surfing so much. We should try it sometime,' said Lucia eyeing several surfers riding the waves.

Nadia remained silent, watching, intrigued for it did look inviting but she would need a little more convincing as to how safe it really was. Finally, she said, 'maybe in a week or two after we have found our feet. Today though we will hire bicycles, explore and watch the surfers.'

As the southern summer approached, temperatures were rising, people they met advised them to protect themselves from the strong sun and as they neared the landing stage, both girls applied plenty of sunscreen and donned their floppy hats. They followed the line of people from the ferry and joined a shorter queue of tourists of similar mind who were intent on hiring bicycles.

The riding was easy to begin with but their expectations of a very flat landscape soon evaporated. The many undulations along the way made for some strenuous pedalling and after two hours, they reached the far end of the island, stopping to take in the view.

'Look there Nadia, the surfers,' said Lucia laying her bicycle against a grassy bank. Let's sit a while and watch them.'

Nadia wiped her forearm across her sweat-covered brow and did the same. Sitting on the bank and unscrewing the top of a bottle of water. She took a long slow drink and lay back for a moment, recovering from her exertions and then she sat up to watch the surfers gliding towards the beach on the breaking rollers. It was a magnificent sight, the sea with its shades of green, aquamarine and blue, the sun bleached sand and the blue sky above. It seemed a paradise.

'What are you thinking?'

'I'm thinking that Australia is all I expected it to be, it's wonderful,' she said looking out to sea and then along the beach. Suddenly she let out a scream and jumped to her feet, shaking with fear. '*Ratto, Ratto, là.*'

'Rat, where,' said Lucia, an equally alarmed look upon her face.

'There.'

Nadia pointed to a small sand dune and in the shade of overhanging grass, two black eyes peered out from a furry brown face at them.

'Oh, *ratto*,' echoed Lucia and together the girls picked up their bicycles and rode away as fast as they could.

'I think I have had enough exploring for today Lucia, let's ride back and have a drink, a proper drink.'

Nadia took little persuading and together they rode at a steady pace until they finally caught sight of the buildings along the waterfront.

'The first to find a bar doesn't have to pay for the drinks,' said Nadia laughing and peddling hard, pulling away from Lucia and causing her to rise immediately to the challenge.

Nadia was a fit young woman but Lucia was better, a member of the swimming team at university she had kept up a reduced training schedule and as her friend began to distance herself, she stood up on the pedals and pushed as hard as she could. After two hundred meters her superior fitness showed and she drew level with Nadia.

'Nice try Nadia but it won't work,' she said laughing and slowing to Nadia's pace.

Nadia grinned, her face red with exertion unable to do no more than could capitulate, breathlessly calling out that she would pay.

'This will do,' said Nadia as they pulled up outside the first bar. She dismounted and pushed the bicycle's front wheel into the parking frame. 'We need to talk about our future you know, we will soon need jobs, my money has gone down far more than I expected. If we are to stay where we are we will have to find money to pay the rent pay.'

The conversation went no further, Nadia let out a scream and took a pace back. '*Ratto*.'

Lucia saw it immediately the same black eyes and furry brown body of the rat they had seen on the sand dunes. She grabbed Nadia's hand and together they rushed into the bar past customers sitting in the open air and once inside the bar they felt safe and able to relax. The lone barman was busy cleaning glasses and on hearing them clatter over the threshold looked up.

'G'day ladies, what'll you have?'

Nadia looked at Lucia and then at the barman, 'you have rat, big rats. We saw one out there,' said Nadia pointing towards the open door.

'Rats? Naw you are mistaken, they are not rats. Don't you know about the Quokka, the furry little animals that live on the island? They are the only mammal we have here.'

'No, I never hear of them. They look like big rats.'

'If you take a good look at them they are cute little guys but don't get too close as they can turn a bit nasty. Don't worry about our Quokkas they are harmless if you don't provoke them. Now what can I get you?'

'Two Cokes.'

'Comin' right up, take a seat and I'll bring them over.'

The two girls did not move, instead they each sat on a bar stool only feet from the barman who had already turned his back and was busying himself preparing the drinks.

'Oh, you've decided to stay here have you?'

He was a good ten years older than Nadia and Lucia, probably in his mid-thirties and with dark shrewd eyes that weighed them up as he slid the drinks across the counter top.

'You two back packing?'

'No, not backpacking but we are hoping to stay in Australia for several months.'

'I thought so; I get quite a few youngsters in here like you. You're going to ask me if I know of any jobs I guess.'

Nadia looked at Lucia and then at the barman.

'Si, we are from Italy and we are here to learn better English but we will have to find a job.'

'I thought so, you don't have a confident look about you and I've seen it before. Where are you staying?'

Nadia told him and he pursed his lips.

'Well you are in the best part of Fremantle for the holiday trade; here it's just the beach bums, the surfers and the day trippers who come across on the ferry. There are a couple of Italian restaurants in town, they might be your best bet, or maybe the Imperial hotel, they take on workers for short periods. We are approaching the busy season so there should be something. Pretty girls like you two should have no trouble getting a job, probably one like mine, behind a bar or waiting on. Tell you what, take a walk along South Terrace near the old Markets and the Colonial era prison, there are any number of bars and restaurants, shops too. There must be someone looking to hire. That will be five dollars,' he said, his smile receding.

Nadia opened her purse and handed him a five-dollar note, quickly estimating her remaining money and realised that she had spent rather more than she should have.

'Come Nadia, let us go outside and watch the sea,' said Lucia catching Nadia's mood.

She led the way, finding an empty table away from most of the other customers and sat down.

'I see you are becoming worried Nadia. We know we have to find jobs but we are nowhere near desperate yet.'

'Yet, that's what worries me, if we relax, dawdle and let time slip by we will be in trouble.'

'*Che*, you worry too much. We will find jobs soon and then we ca...' Her voice tailed off as she looked past Nadia towards a small gate, the entrance from the dusty track that served as a road.

'What is it?' said Nadia turning round, immediately spotting two men she recognised, Jake and Tony, entering the grounds and too busy in conversation to have noticed them.

'Our friends from yesterday?'

'*Si*, the miners or are they really surfers. I understand that surfing is a way of life out here. I bet work is just an inconvenience to them, surfing is what it is all about.'

Simultaneously they lifted their glasses and took a drink, their eyes on the two men, watching them for a few seconds until, as if by some telepathic signal, they glanced across the open space. Nadia and Lucia immediately averted their eyes, concentrated on their drinks, not a word passing between them. However, it was too late to hide, no red-blooded surfer was going to pass up the chance of meeting a pretty girl and very soon the two surfers were standing over them.

'G'day, we meet again,' said Jake. 'Mind if we join you for a drink?'

'No,' said Lucia a sparkle coming into her eyes.

'Great, do you want another drink?'

'*Si grazie.*'

'What is it, coke?'

'Bacardi and coke,' said Lucia bringing a cheeky smile to Nadia's lips.

It was not the first time Lucia or Nadia, for that matter, had upped the stakes when a man had offered to buy a drink, and why not.

Jake grinned, pulled up a chair and Tony left for the bar.

'So you made it to Rottnest Island after all. Have you had a good day?'

'Yes we have been riding bicycles round the island and we saw the surfers in every bay.'

Lucia described a part of their ride across the island and was about to broach the subject of the little furry animals when Tony returned carrying the

Bacardis and two large glasses of straw-coloured beer in his large hands.

'Cheers,' he said lifting his glass to his lips.

'They have been out riding Tony, had a good look round the island and watched the surfers.'

'Did you see us, we were in Strickland Bay. The surf was okay 'till it walled out and I slipped. My board fish hooked me in the ass! I still can't walk straight,' said Tony rubbing his thigh.

Both Nadia and Lucia looked at him with wide eyes. What was he talking about; they had no idea and were beginning to wonder if they would ever be able to speak decent English.'

Jake noticed their look and began laughing.

'You Sheilas don't know what he's talking about do you.'

'No,' said Nadia, 'and what is a Sheila?'

Again, Jake laughed and Tony grinned from ear to ear.

'We call girls Sheilas that's all and Tony was just using a bit of surfing slang. He said that the waves were collapsing and one knocked him off his board. On the way down the board turned over and the fin caught him in his crack.'

'Crack?'

'You don't need to know that. Say are you catching the ferry back?'

'Yes we are,' said Nadia.

'So are we, the last one goes at six so we have an hour or more, time for another drink,' he said downing the rest of his beer in one gulp. 'Another drink girls?'

The journey back to Fremantle was uneventful except for the fact that Jake never stopped talking. He was humorous to a point, but by the time they stepped off the Ferry, he was beginning to repeat himself and Nadia guessed that perhaps he had drunk too much. On Rottnest Island, he had bought several more rounds of drinks. Lucia and Nadia declined his offer having experienced the boys in college, lotharios who thought they were god's gift to women.

'Where d'you live, do you want to stop off at a bar for some more drinks?' said Jake beginning to slur his words.

'No thank we have had a busy day and tomorrow we must look for work.'

'Aw come on just one, you'll enjoy it.'

'No thank you.'

'Leave 'em be Jake, they don't want anymore and we don't want to spoil their day.'

Jake looked a little crestfallen, his attempt to ingratiate himself with the two Italian girls a failure and reluctantly he grunting agreement.

'It has been a pleasure meeting you, I hope we meet again, we are here for another few days. We usually eat and have a drink in the bar called Nashville, just down from the old jailhouse. It's mainly burgers and beer but that is all we need. If you feel like a drink, one night perhaps you can join us.'

'Thank you,' said Lucia, 'Thank you both, we had a wonderful day because of your advice. *Ciao*, good night.'

'Chow,' said Jake.

A smile came to Tony's lips and he could not help poking fun at his friend.

'You'll soon be speaking Italian at this rate mate.'

For a second or two there was silence, a puzzled look on Jake's face as he took in Tony's words and not to be outdone he said.

'Eyetalian, easy when you can speak kangaroo like an Abbo mate.'

'Come on Jake, we can grab a couple more beers on the way home and tomorrow it's back to surfing. Good night ladies, nice to have met you.'

'Yeah, couple of smart Sheilas, hope we can meet up again,' said Jake. 'How's about a goodnight kiss?' he added.

The girls did not reply, embarrassed by Jake's suggestion.

'Maybe some other time,' said Lucia firmly before she touched Nadia's forearm and turned to walk away, leaving Jake to stare after them.

'He was a little overpowering don't you think?'

'A little Nadia but we can handle him. What did you think about the other one, Tony?'

'Good looking and he was more polite, his Italian background no.'

'Maybe, or perhaps he is naturally quieter than his friend.'

'You liked him didn't you?'

'A little, but we do not want boys spoiling our time here. What would our mother's say if three or more of us returned home next year?'

Chapter 4

I was sorry I did not see Rory before he left
Edinburgh but I was rather indisposed. After the girls
dressed and left I got up and went into the living
room to look for him. I knew Emily had a lecture that
morning and was not surprised to find her gone but I
thought Rory might have still been around. Even
Mick had recovered enough to leave the flat and I
was alone. I was into my final term and with exams
just over the horizon I needed to get down to serious
work so it was then I decided no more parties and no
more marijuana and that was how it was until one
day weeks later, there was a banging on the front
door.

'Rory, what are you doing here?'

'I have some time off, I told you I would come
back to Edinburgh if I could.'

'I don't remember you saying that, anyway good to
see you, come in and I'll make us a coffee, I'm ready
for a break.'

Together we went into the kitchen and I filled the
kettle and started to wash two cups.

'How have things been since the last time I was
here?'

'Different, exams you know. If we want a degree, we have to knuckle down to work. I have not had a proper drink for ages.'

'So you'll be ready for one?'

'I guess so, but not a binge; I really must put some work in.'

I handed Rory his cup and we went into the living room. He sat on the settee and I in the big armchair, one leg dangling over the arm. 'So, how is the North Sea these days?' I could not think of anything else to say, guessing that the purpose of his visit was to see Emily and I knew Emily.

'Fine, we have been taking drilling mud out to the Forties field for the past two weeks. It's hard work unloading and a bit boring but it pays well.'

'Do you still miss the fishing Rory?'

He went quiet for a moment. 'Aye ah do. I miss the boat, our boat; she was part of the family. But she's gone and Da is happy enough working at the fish farm so here I am making a living in the oil industry.' He became quiet again and looked out of the window. 'You know I miss the mornings the most, when Da let me steer the boat out to the fishing grounds, the power of the engine, the open sea.'

'I'm sorry; it's a sign of the times I'm afraid. What with overfishing and the foreigners, things are not as they used to be. I know a bit about the problem, it is unfortunate that one of our proudest industries is in such decline. Can you remember the fleet when we were boys, when the harbour was full and those that couldn't get in had to anchor outside?'

'Of course I do. Even then I thought I would become a fisherman.' Then he asked, 'How's Emily, I was hoping to see her again.'

'She's fine, she's working in the library, says it's a better working environment surrounded by all those books.'

'So maybe she will come for a drink with us?'

'Rory, don't get your hopes up too much. We had a good time when you were here before but it was a drink and drug laden night. Funny things happen; she is young and attractive and has had a string of boyfriends. You're not the first, you know, I don't want you to get hurt.'

'Oh . . .' was all he could say and his eyes avoided mine.

'Cheer up, there are plenty more fish in the sea.' There was another pause before we both burst out laughing at the memory of the last time I said that. 'We're not going to sing the final countdown again are we?'

'I hope not I've had too many final countdowns.'

'Cheer up, I could be wrong about her but I have seen similar situations before. I don't know what it is about her, she uses men like toys, plays with them until she gets bored and then she dumps them, but they all seem to come back for more. I have an idea, it's nearly five o'clock, how's about a drink in the Monkey and then a curry. Maybe a bit of relaxation will help me with my studying. Come on, I'll tidy up my work ready for tomorrow and see how much money I have.'

'Don't worry about money, I'll treat you.'

The Brass Monkey was less than half full when we walked in because most students had wised-up, were taking their work seriously and their money had just about run out.

'Usual Mal?'

'Yes please,' I said, looking round to see who was there and to my horror I spotted Emily clinging to one of the university rugby team. 'Shit,' I said under my breath, unfortunately loud enough for Rory to hear.

'What's wrong?'

'Let's sit over there,' I said, steering him away from a collision. 'Emily is in the other room with one of the rugby team. I know him and he's not a particularly pleasant fellow. It's those steroids; a few of the lads take them to bulk up, it can change their personalities, make them aggressive.'

Rory leaned forward to try to see Emily. 'So what are you saying?'

'Let's find another pub, I don't want you upset and I don't want Alistair pumping up. Bloody women.'

'Pumping up?'

'Macho man, clever sod who thinks he can push anyone he likes around.'

'He won't push me.'

'Shit,' I said again.

In my head. I could see trouble brewing and then it all began to unravel.

'Malcolm,' said a voice from near the bar.

'Alistair.'

He had come to refill his glass and he had spotted me.

'How are you, you have dropped out of training I see?'

'Not much point, I will probably not be here next season and anyway I need to study.'

'I'm with a flatmate of yours. Emily, come and sit in here,' he called into the other bar.

My heart sank as Emily appeared and Alistair passed her drink to her. I could not tell whether she had seen Rory or not because Alistair was blocking her line of sight and then, as she reached the table, she did recognise him, yet made no acknowledgment.

'Who's this?' asked Alistair.

'Rory, a friend from home, you know him Emily.'

'Do I? Oh yes he was here a month or two ago. Hello.'

Rory's face was stern, impassive, and he was probably wearing the right expression to combat Emily's indifference but underneath I could see that he was upset. He didn't speak, simply nodded and Emily turned away to slip her arm into Alistair's.

'So what do you do?' asked Alistair, sitting down opposite him.

'I work on a rig supply vessel.'

'Officer?'

'No, just a deck hand.'

'A deck hand! That doesn't sound much of a job.'

'No I don't suppose it is but sometimes you have to take what you can.'

'What do you reckon, Emily baby?'

'That's what not having a college education does for you, no prospects.'

I could see that Rory was becoming incensed, angry at Emily's comment, that she could be so dismissive of him. He was angry too with Alistair for looking down on him and that seemed to spur him on to retaliate.

'It didn't seem to bother you when I fucked you,' he suddenly said turning back to Emily, his eyes piercing hers.

'What did you say?' said Alistair, coming to life.

'I fucked her last time I was here. I wasn't the first by a long shot, seems she fucks anything that moves when she's had a drink. Do you move big boy?'

I could not believe what I was hearing and as Alistair began to go red in the face my heart levitated into my mouth. I was sure his pumped-up frame was about to burst and I braced myself.

'Outside you, let's see who can move. I don't take kindly to anyone calling my girl.'

'Your girl, yours and who else's?'

It was then the fireworks went off, Alistair could contain himself no longer and lunged across the table towards Rory. I feared for my friend because Alistair was tough and fit from rugby training; what I had not allowed for was his conditioning and training as a forward. Without warning, he thrust himself at Rory as if engaging with the opposition front row, his broad shoulders and thick neck heading towards Rory's midriff like a tank. However Rory was ready for him, leaping to his feet to sidestep the onrushing bull and to bring his fist down hard on Alistair's exposed neck. If it were not so serious it could have appeared comical as with no more than a soft groan, Alistair collapsed onto the table, a big man, too heavy for a light wooden table.

It gave way with a crash, splintered wood and broken glass was flying everywhere, and Alistair crashed helplessly onto the floor. His eyes rolled for a second or two before closing and Rory stood back to admire his handiwork. Emily could do no more than stare at Rory with an open-mouthed admiration and I do believe my own eyes were wide in panic.

'Fuckin' hell Rory, you've started something now. Come on let's get out of here,' I said, dragging him by the arm out into the street and together we ran for a hundred yards before stopping to look back only to see Emily standing alone, glass in hand, watching our escape.

'I think the best thing we can do is to disappear Rory, there's no telling what Alistair might do now. How did you manage to flatten him so easily?'

'Chinese cook.'

'What Chinese fuckin' cook? Look, you've got me swearing,' I said, upset and shaking at the thought of the w university rugby team coming after us.

'The Chinese cook on the ship. He is an expert at something or other. I bring him lobsters from home sometimes and he shows me a few moves in case I run into trouble.'

'And you have run into fu . . . trouble, we both have.'

'He won't hurt you – will he?'

'Perhaps not, I train with the team and play for the seconds now and then but I do not expect to be here much after my finals. I just need to keep my head down until the end of term and then I will be leaving Edinburgh. That is if I get a degree, because the way I feel right now I can't see me holding my pen steadily enough in the exams to write down the answers.'

'I'm hungry, I thought we were going for an Indian?' he said.

'A fu . . . Indian! Oh heck, if that's what you want who am I to stop you. After that performance I couldn't anyway.'

Rory just grinned and I was beginning to calm down.

'Alistair lodges in Morningside I think, it's miles away over there,' I said pointing. 'If we head for Saint Mary's Street we should be safe enough.'

This time, without a backwards glance, we set off at a brisk pace to put as much distance between us and the Brass Monkey as we could. There were two Indian restaurants nearby and after a toss of the coin, we plumbed for the Himalaya. We ordered two beers and when the meal arrived we ate in silence until Rory said, 'I hope everything will be all right for you Mal, I had to do something.'

'Well you did wind him up rather.'

'He was belittling me and that cow you share a flat with ignored me, then said I had no prospects. I could not let that go. I might not have had a university education like you but I am not worthless. I can't see him standing a twelve-hour watch in a force nine or even managing one day fishing on the *Lurach-Aon*.'

He seemed unfazed by the events of the past hour, more annoyed at Emily I thought, and I watched as he tore off a piece of naan bread and dipped it in the sauce. My appetite, unsurprisingly, was not what it was only a few minutes earlier and then I noticed a faraway look in his eyes.

'Penny for your thoughts.'

'I miss that boat, I hadn't realised just how much I have missed the fishing until I started mixing with your poofy friends.'

'They're not poofy, just young and sometimes stupid I guess. Listen, are you intent on staying a deck hand, are there any prospects in your job?'

'No prospects unless I get some qualifications.'

'Have you thought of that?'

'Nope.'

'Maybe you should, you could sign on as a mature student.'

'A mature student and get lumbered with that lot for three years. No thanks, I'll manage as I am, I like the sea and I like driving boats. Maybe I'll save up and get my own fishing boat, something small to start with.'

'It's an idea but don't forget fishing isn't what it was. Where are you staying tonight by the way?'

'Your place, I'll sleep on the mattress. You don't mind, you still have the mattress don't you?'

I nearly choked, after our narrow escape from Alistair I was concerned that he might be in the flat with Emily and the fireworks would start all over again.

'What if Alistair has gone back there with Emily?'

'What if he has? You can go in first and signal from the window. If he's there I'll have to either wait till he's gone or find somewhere else or – he spoke with a twinkle in his eyes – I could come in with you and really sort him out.'

'No . . . don't even joke about that,' I said, reluctantly agreeing to let him stay the night.

So much for my new regime and so much for cutting back on the booze and settling for an early night. I let myself into the flat just after midnight after we had called in to what seemed every pub on the way back home.

'Oh, hello,' I managed to say, finding Emily alone and reading in the communal living room.

'Hi, where's your friend?'

'Where's Alistair?'

She looked at me in silence and then, as a grin slowly spread across her face, she told me I did not need to worry as he had gone home. She said he was unaffected by his experience and as she had agreed to see him again was not holding a grudge against me. 'That's rugby players for you I suppose,' she said.

'Aye, well I'm glad he's not looking for me I must say,' I replied, walking to the window and waving.

Rory, standing in the shadows, waved back and a minute later, he walked into the room.

'Where's the mattress?'

Emily's jaw sagged visibly and, without speaking, she closed her book and went to her room.

'What's wrong with her?'

I did not feel like giving him an answer, I was just happy enough that we had landed back in one piece.

'The mattress, it's there, standing against the wall behind the settee,' I said, pointing.

'Thanks,' he said, pulling it out and letting it fall to the floor.

'Are you going to be okay on that?'

'No problem.'

'I'll give you one of my blankets and I will see you in the morning then,' I said, staggering towards my own room to wrestle the top blanket from my bed. With some relief, I gave it to him and bid him good night and then the following morning I woke up surprised to see he had somehow acquired a second blanket for his mattress.

Years later, I found out why. Emily had paid him a visit during the night and they had managed a brief and clandestine relationship, known as a one-night stand in some circles.

'Want some breakfast?'

'That would be great, what have you got?'

'Cornflakes.'

'I think I need something a bit more substantial than cornflakes after last night.'

'It is all we have I'm afraid. We're all a bit skint, we are getting to the end of term and the money's running out.'

'Come on, let's find a café and have a proper breakfast. No fuckin' cornflakes, eggs and bacon and a slice of black pudding for me.'

I had to admit it was tempting and agreeing I left the flat with Rory in search of the nearest café where we managed only to sit in silence for the first ten minutes, the previous evening's adventure and my hangover filling my head. Rory on the other hand seemed unaffected and was deep in thought. Finally, I asked him if he was thinking about the *Lurach-Aon*.

'What? No my mind was on something else.'

'What?'

'Oh nothing. What are you doing this summer Malcolm?' he asked, changing the subject.

'What do you mean?'

'Are you going home, will you get a job? If you pass your exams you can get a good job can't you?'

'Bit soon to make those sorts of plans. I don't know what I will do this summer but if I pass my exams I'm thinking of doing a teacher training course.'

'You want to be a teacher?'

'I think so; it pays well and is secure employment.'

His eyes dropped but before I could say more our breakfasts arrived and for a further ten minutes nothing disturbed the silence except the odd scrape of cutlery on our plates.

'Well I feel better for that,' he said, mopping up the remnants with a last slice of bread.

'So you're intent on buying a fishing boat?'

'Yes, if I can find one I can afford.'

'It will be hard to make a living, most of the older fishermen are retiring and the younger ones don't want to know because the rewards are not worth the effort.'

'Some of them manage well enough.'

'Aye, one or two maybe. How much do you think you will need, why don't we have a look at some figures now my head is clearing?'

He visibly cheered up and for the next quarter of an hour our conversation centred on Rory's ambition to own a fishing boat. He was adamant he could afford one, said he had saved almost two thousand pounds and with a bank loan was sure he could at least go after lobsters and shellfish. I listened and with the aid of a napkin we worked through the figures, discussed bank charges and repayments and when we finished, his eyes were bright with enthusiasm.

'Don't get too excited Rory, if you have to go to the bank for a loan I guess they might be reluctant to give you one.'

'I'll worry about that when the time comes. Here let me pay the bill, I need to be off to catch the train. The sooner I get home the sooner I can look for a boat.'

'How long will you be there?'

'I have another two weeks off, why?'

'I have my finals over the next few weeks then I'll be heading home. If you get yourself a boat you can take me fishing.'

He pursed his lips and nodded his head, confident his plans would come to fruition, and with that, we parted company.

I did not catch up with Rory as planned. My finals went well enough, I managed a second-class honours degree and applied for a place on a teacher-training course at Sterling and I had an offer of a summer job on a building site in Inverness. I did not know it at the time but Rory did not buy a fishing boat and it would be quite a while before I saw him again.

'How long will you be away?' asked my mother when I told her I had found temporary work in Inverness.

'Angus McLeish, one of my friends from university, has got me a job with his father's firm. It's for the whole summer, working almost every day, weather permitting. The money is good and I need all I can get so guess I can't get back here until early September.'

'I was hoping to see a bit more of you this summer Malcolm. It's a pity your father doesn't have enough work to take you on.'

'That's the trouble, not enough work. We had a lecture on the movement of labour in Scotland and it did not make pleasant reading. Apart from the oil industry everything else seems in decline, shipbuilding, engineering, we need to find new industries.'

'Did you know Callum Macintosh has sold up?'

'That old rogue, no I didn't. Who has he sold out to?'

I half expected her to say Rory had bought Macintosh's boat but it wasn't him, it was someone from the mainland.

'Another one gone, we'll have no fishing fleet left if this carries on.'

I felt sad, I had watched the boats come and go ever since I was a boy. Many of my friends came from fishing families, almost all had left the industry and many of them had even left the Isle of Lewis in search of work. It made me wonder what I would do once I qualified as a teacher, would I too have to leave.

'Have you seen anything of Rory, Mam?'

'He was home a few weeks ago. I was talking to his mother and she said he was still working on the supply ship out of Aberdeen.'

'I guess I won't see him then, not unless he is home by the weekend. I am on the early ferry on Sunday. You don't know whether or not he's bought himself a boat do you?'

She did not and I did leave on the ferry for Ullapool on Sunday to spend the summer labouring on the building site. As for Rory, it would be some time before our paths crossed once more.

The crane swung the last of the steel pipes onto the ship and below a young deck officer watched its progress He lifted his short wave radio, spoke into it and slowly the long metal tube descended towards the waiting men.

'Take the line Rory,' he said.

Rory reached out to take hold of a line hanging from the end of the pipe and carefully guided the half-ton tube into its resting place in a wooden frame fastened to the deck.

'That's the last one,' said David, the deck officer, signalling to another of the deck hands and ordering the release of the wire sling. 'Secure the load and I will inform the captain we are ready for sea.'

The men set about their work and an hour later the ship slowly began to move away from the quayside, twin propellers churning a wide wake as the ship made its way towards the open sea.

'I hear you had quite a time of it in Edinburgh Rory,' said David, after dismissing the rest of the deck crew.

'Aye, a bit of an eye-opener I have to say.'

'What do you think of Edinburgh?'

'Good, those students are an idle bunch though. All they seemed to do was drink and party.'

'That's student life, but there is a serious side to it, if you ain't qualified in something then the good jobs pass you by. Have you thought about going back to school, you're bright enough and a hard worker. You could do more with your life.'

'I'm saving up for a fishing boat of my own, paper qualifications are no good to a fisherman. You need to know the sea, the fishing grounds and the weather. What good are paper qualifications for that?'

'I must admit I admire you for that Rory. By the way did you know I'm getting married next year?'

'That's a bit of a shock; I didn't even know you were courting.'

'She's from back home in Dundee; she's never been up here.'

'So there will be a bit of a stag night will there?'

'More than that, I'm off to Las Vegas with a few mates. Do you want to come? It's a way off yet, give you time to save up.'

'Las Vegas! That *will* cost won't it?'

'It would do except I've had a word with someone I know at head office who organises accommodation for crews working abroad. Thought I would see if he could get us cheap flights and a hotel. What do you say?'

'I don't know what to say, when is it?'

'Next September, we're getting married at the beginning of October. Plenty of time for you to save up, come on, you'll enjoy it and you know Alan don't you.'

'Alan, he is going is he?'

'Yes, and a friend from home called Mike.'

Rory paused for a few moments and, strangely, Emily's face came into his mind and he remembered how he felt mixing with Malcolm and his friends. It was all very different from Stornoway and the solitude of the sea. Then it struck him that perhaps a bit more adventure was what he needed in his life and without thinking he said 'I'm in.'

Chapter 5

To the passengers sitting aboard the Boeing the vibrations of the undercarriage swinging out in preparation for landing was almost imperceptible. To some though, it signalled the aeroplanes arrival at its destination and sitting in a window seat Rory gazed down at the landscape below.

'Will you look at that,' he said to Alan, sitting next to him.

Alan leaned across and together they shared their first view of the city of Las Vegas – desert, long straight roads and finally, as the aircraft descended low over the city, they could see the vast casino resorts under construction. They had arrived at Sin City.

Clearing immigration was for most a boring but necessary pursuit but for Rory it was exciting, the first time he had visited a foreign country and he could not help looking everywhere at once. He had grown up watching Hollywood productions and to see the security staff wearing broad brimmed hats and carrying side arms fascinated him.

'Let's hope they don't want to use one of those on us,' joked Alan as they collected their bags and walked out into the hot sunshine.

Leading the way David hailed a taxi and after they had all piled into the car it took them along Las Vegas Boulevard. For Rory it was awe inspiring, New York New York, Luxor, MGM Grand, huge buildings taking shape as Las Vegas transformed itself. Big business had come to town. The resort casinos under construction would accommodate thousands in the lap of luxury but, for Rory and his friends, lesser accommodation awaited – a cheap motel not far removed from Fremont Street and the old Las Vegas. The shipping company's travel manager had recommended it, told David that they could not get any closer to the action so cheaply.

The taxi drove north, the huge building sites behind and abruptly the scenery changed. Intersections and architecture of a previous age replaced the ultra-modern and eventually they arrived at their destination. A small motel, a scruffy wooden establishment with a weather-worn sign outside and as the taxi came to a halt Mike pointed to a neon sign on a building opposite.

'Hey look over there,' he said. 'It looks as if we are in good company.'

'You don't believe that do you?' said David. 'I doubt very much that Elvis really did sleep there.'

'He might have done. Where are we staying, not here I hope?'

The laughter was subdued as it dawned upon the four friends that it was their final destination.

'It's here all right, the Lone Apache,' said David paying the taxi driver. 'It's cheap; it's somewhere to lay our heads. What more do you want?'

The other three feigned disappointment, casting their blank and tired eyes over the building. Two floors of identical rooms arranged around three sides of a concrete parking lot. It was not their idea of Las Vegas but it would have to do.

'Tidy enough,' said David, trying to put on a brave face. 'Well at least we're here and it is cheap,' he repeated.

He picked up his suitcase and led his friends through the security gate towards a small office in need of decoration. Opening the flimsy door, he walked in beneath a large, slow turning fan hanging from the ceiling. Beneath its arc, an oversized black woman of indeterminable age sat behind a desk.

'Yeah?' she said.

'Hello, we have rooms booked.'

'Name?'

'Holman, David Holman. The booking might be in the name of my company.'

The fat woman said nothing, simply picked up a clipboard with several pages attached and flicked through them.

'No Holman here, what's the company name?'

David told her.

'Aw yeah, four people two rooms,' she said, looking up to count her visitors. 'Yeah, you're booked in for five nights, right?' she said.

'Er . . . yes,' said David, a little unsure of how to handle her.

'Here,' she said, opening one of the desk drawers and pulling out some keys, 'rooms eighteen and twenty, first floor, far end. We lock the gates of a night but there's a night man to let you in.'

'Don't we have a key?'

'No fear sonny, have you seen the characters that hang round here after dark? No sir, the security guard will let you through the gate. Password today is Dragonfly. We change it every day, so make sure you pass by this office of a mornin' for me to tell you. I'll need your passports for a few hours; you can collect them after the police have finished with them. Here are your room keys. There are a couple of coke and ice machines on each floor if you want a drink. Alcohol's allowed but if'n there's any trouble we call the cops okay?'

David nodded and after handing over their passports, they trooped out of the office and up the stairs to the first floor.

'You sharing with me Alan?' asked Rory.

'I might as well, what number is it?'

Rory looked at the key David had passed to him and then he looked along the balcony.

'That one, number twenty,' he said, walking towards it and inserting the key in the door.

Pushing it open, he looked apprehensively at the simple yet comfortable-looking room containing two very large single beds and in one corner there was a sit-up-and-beg armchair. On the sole chest of drawers sat a television.

'Not quite what I expected for Las Vegas,' said Alan, following Rory into the room.

'What *did* you expect; we didn't pay a lot did we?'

'Naw, suppose your right. Mind if I have the bed near the door?'

Rory did not and for the following quarter of an hour they settled in, unpacking and filling drawers. After an inspection of the bathroom, Rory went to lie on his bed and, staring up at the ceiling, took stock of his first hour in Sin City. It was hot, he was tired from the flight and he wanted a few minutes to relax.

'She's a bundle of fun Rory, the woman on reception.'

'Fun, ha, a bundle maybe but not much fun. What's the password, I've forgotten already?'

'Dragonfly, I had better write it down, I don't fancy spending the night out on the street especially if some of those characters she mentioned really are about.'

'I didn't quite expect that either, I thought we'd be in a proper hotel, one of those you see on television. I suppose the action is somewhere in those big casinos we passed.'

'Action, that sounds good,' said Alan, shaking off his fatigue. 'Let's go and see the others, head for a drink somewhere. Look there, some maps on the table and is that a safe?'

'You don't think anyone will break in here do you?'

'Dunno, it's a strange place and they are strong on security so I guess someone might try but so long as the night watchman does his job we should be okay.'

'I'm going to have a shower, if I don't I'll be falling asleep,' said Rory.

'Hurry up, I'll do the same.'

Fifteen minutes later, refreshed and dressed in clean clothes they were ready to explore. David and Mike in the room next door were in a similar frame of mind and soon the four of them were ready to head downtown but first they had to call in the grubby little office. David took Rory's key, walked in followed by the others to find the woman concentrating on her computer screen.

'Settled in?' she asked, without looking up.

'Yes, just wanted to know the best way to the casinos. Fremont Street isn't it?' asked David.

'Yep, turn right and just keep goin' honey, or git yourself a cab.'

Standing near the doorway Rory watched the woman and could not help smiling. Absorbed in her computer, her eyebrows rose in pleasure every few seconds, the repetitive clicking noise coming from the machine a clue as to how she was doing.

'Hundred bucks,' she said to herself and then, 'leave your keys on the table, if I'm not here the night man will give them to you.'

'Well that's a good start,' said Rory as they left the office. 'They even play the machines when they should be working.'

'I guess that's why it's called Sin City,' said Mike, raising his arm as a cab approached and minutes later they found themselves on the famous strip.

'We should be driving a Mustang like James Bond,' said Alan leading. 'Did you see how he drove the car along this street? Look, there is the Golden Nugget. I remember it from the film.'

'We'll win one,' laughed David. 'Come on Rory, we don't want to lose you.'

Rory grinned; he had fallen behind, absorbed by the glitzy lighting and booming country music. The street was crowded, the Golden Nugget casino beckoned and reaching the entrance, they paused for a few moments, taking in the sights and sounds of Las Vegas before walking inside. Rory could do nothing more than stand and gawp, his senses overawed by the flashing lights and alien sounds of row upon row of gaming machines. He almost believed that perhaps he was on another planet.

'I could do with a beer,' said Alan, 'it was hot out there.'

'Where's the bar?'

'I have no idea,' he said looking round.

Rory was having the same thoughts, spotting a dark-haired girl carrying a tray of drinks. She caught his eye and walked towards him.

'Scuse me miss, where is the bar?' he asked.

'You a no need the bar if you play the machines. I come with your drinks. Play these machines and I come back.'

Rory nodded a kind of understanding. 'She says we should play the machines and she will bring the drinks.'

'Good idea,' said David, searching his pockets for some coins and for several minutes the others watched as he clumsily played a machine until the girl returned with her empty tray.

'You want drinks?'

'Yes, four beers please and do you know where we can get change?' asked David.

She smiled and pointed to the machine he was facing. 'There, look you can put notes in or a credit card, no need for coins. You put a note in and choose your bet then the machine does the rest. Four beers, I bring a them to you.'

'How much is it?' asked Rory.

'Is a free when you play the machines so make sure you do or I am in trouble,' she said, a practised smile filling her face.

'Look, you feed a note in here,' said Mike with some authority, demonstrating and within seconds began to lose his money. 'See, easy isn't it.'

They watched him put another bill into his machine, copied him and sat back, hypnotised by the spinning reels.

'Have you won anything yet Rory?'

Rory looked at him with a hangdog look.

'Oh well, I'm sure you will.'

'Have you won?'

Alan was about to speak when his machine's tone changed and it began to rhythmically drop coins into the win tray.

'Five dollars, looks like I've got my money back.'

'We're not going to go home rich men then are we, not at this rate anyway?'

'You never know,' said David, sitting two machines away and inserting a five-dollar bill.

Rory grinned at such certainty, felt in his pocket for some money and for the next few minutes concentrated on playing the machine in front of him.

'Blimey, that was ten dollars, gone in a flash,' he said. 'What about you Alan?'

Alan looked crestfallen. 'I've just lost twice that amount.'

'Never mind, she's back with the drinks,' said David, taking a glass from the waitress.

'For you,' said the girl handing a glass to Rory. He reached out and could not help but look into her eyes, dark, attractive eyes. Then she turned away and the moment was gone.

'Nice looking girl,' said Alan. 'Foreign I think by her accent.'

Rory hardly heard him, the girl's lasting image clouding his mind.

'Ever played cards or roulette Rory?' asked David, breaking into his thoughts.

'No, I don't know the first thing about cards other than a game of snap.'

David laughed. 'Snap! I think the games here are a little different to snap. Look, I can see card tables in the other room, let's go and have a look.'

Finishing their drinks the four friends wandered across the lush carpet towards a room filled with the sound of plastic chips clicking like a million crickets.

'Are you playing?' asked Mike.

'Are you?' asked David.'

'I might, let's watch for a while, see how they do it over here.'

For twenty minutes, they wandered around the room, stopping occasionally to watch a game in progress, marvelling as piles of chips constantly changed hands.

'The dealer seems to win a lot,' Rory mused.

'Yes but if you get lucky you can win serious money,' said Alan, nodding towards a large man dressed in a white suit and wearing a cowboy hat one size too big. 'Just look at the pile of chips he has and there, look, he is scooping up even more.'

For several more games, they watched the white suit, cool, confident and with a look of indifference as he placed his bets. Rory was puzzled, the man seemed to know where the ball would stop, winning on three occasions out of four.

'Will you look at that,' said Alan. 'We could do with a bit of luck like that.'

Rory nodded and watched again as the man placed a large bet, more than half of the chips in front of him. The wheel began to spin, all eyes on the small white ball as it click click clicked its way across the roulette wheel. Finally, the wheel slowed and the ball tripped over its last few hurdles before settling on the winning number. The man in the white suit lost and yet his expression did not change.

'I think that's more the reality,' said Rory. 'It's the house that wins every time.'

'Don't be such a spoil sport, we're here to have some fun and if it costs a few dollars then what the heck.'

Rory did not answer; it was futile to engage in an argument over the rights or wrongs of gambling. He remembered his days fishing with his father, when they hauled nothing more than a few mackerel, forcing them to eke out the little money they had. Frugality was in his nature, gambling was not.

He noticed David glance at Mike, say something he could not hear but it must have been an invitation to play cards for both moved away to sit in vacant chairs at a nearby card table. Rory followed, watched as each placed several twenty-dollar bills on the table and the croupier slid modest piles of blue and red chips towards them.

'Looks like they are in with the big boys Rory.'

'Aye, this should be interesting. Do you play cards Alan?'

'A little.'

'Tell me what's going on. They are playing pontoon right.'

'Yes but it's not called pontoon.'

'What is it called?'

'Blackjack, but it's basically the same game.'

Rory nodded, knowing enough to follow and for the next half hour he watched the ebb and flow of the game. David seemed particularly good, or maybe he was just lucky. Rory didn't know, but still he did feel a sense of excitement when his friend scooped up a heap of chips to stack them neatly on the table in front of him.

'How much did he win?'

'Not sure, they are mostly one-dollar chips, maybe fifty dollars. Mike isn't doing so well though, his chips have nearly all gone.'

For a few minutes longer, the two men played on until the croupier's rake took Mike's last chip.

'How much did you win?' Rory quizzed David.

'Not a lot, maybe doubled my money. Come on happy Jack,' he said, noticing Mike's expression, 'let's have a look round and then find somewhere for a drink.'

They strolled past the clanking, flashing gaming machines, past the roulette and craps tables, finally arriving at the Keno Lounge.

'What's this?' asked Alan.

'Keno, it's a bit like the national lottery I suppose,' said Mike. 'You've played that haven't you?'

'I've had a go a couple of times but never managed to win anything.'

'Let's have a look in,' said David, 'I could murder another beer.'

The room was spacious though not on the scale of the main gaming rooms – an oasis of quiet with comfortable seats and on one wall a large screen filled with numbers announcing the game's progress.

'Looks like she is serving drinks,' said Mike, pointing to a cocktail waitress just entering the lounge. 'Can we get drinks here?' he asked as she passed.

'Sure, what'll you have?'

'Four beers?'

'Sure,' she said again.

'That was easy enough. Now how do we play this game?' said David as she left.

'You want tickets?' asked another girl, appearing as if from nowhere.

'Yes please,' said Mike taking the lead. 'I have to win back some money.'

The girl, unimpressed, lowered her tray onto the table. 'How many?'

'How much are the tickets?'

'A dollar, more if you want. You can bet as much as you wish but the minimum is a dollar a go. Here,' she said, 'I'll leave you some tickets and crayons.'

'How many numbers can we choose,' asked Rory, looking a little puzzled.

'You guys don't know how to play Keno do you?'

'Not really.'

'I will explain then. Look, you fill in the tickets like this, give me the money and I will go to the desk for the writer to make a copy and bring it back to you. Watch the screen and if you think you have won just call me and I will check your ticket.'

For several more minutes, the girl talked them through the game, showed them how to fill in the tickets and for good measure wished them luck before them to their own devices.

'Seems easy enough,' said Alan, scratching his head.

For once, they were quiet as they tried to figure out how to play the game and then the girl reappeared to see how they were managing.

'I think we've got the basic hang of it. Here, can you take these?'

'Sure, let me have a look,' she said, running her expert eyes over the tickets and informing them of how much to pay and for an hour they sat talking, drinking and playing the game. They watched the

113

screen, noted the numbers as they came up until finally Mike let out a whoop of joy.

'Four numbers, I've got four numbers, that's a winner I'm sure, hey,' he said, waving to the Keno runner. 'I've got a winning ticket, I think, can you check it?'

'Sure,' said the girl walking over to him.

'How much do you think you've won?' asked David.

'I've no idea but if it's like the lottery it might be a big win,' he said enthusiastically.

A minute later, the girl returned from her visit to the writer's desk and offered Mike the contents of her tray, a few one-dollar bills, enough to change the expression on his face from one of delight to one of disappointment.

'Eight dollars, is that all,' he said, looking a little glum. 'Sorry miss was there something else?'

'We make our money from tips buddy. If'n you don't want to tip me that's okay,' she said, giving him a deadpan look.

Mike looked back at her and then at the money in his hand and for a second or two seemed to be in limbo until finally he grinned and placed a dollar bill on her tray.

'A dollar for the ticket, a dollar for a tip leaves me with six dollars. Not much is it?'

'We haven't won anything, at least you have six dollars,' said Alan.

'Come on lads, time to go I think, I'm ready for my bed,' said David rising from his chair. 'One last drink, where we came in, and maybe we will win something on the slots.'

The others nodded agreement and slowly the weary tourists made their way back through the casino, past the rows of gaming machines until they reached the main gambling hall.

'Lucky machine this,' said David, feeding a ten-dollar bill into the one he had played earlier.

Rory smiled and shook his head. He had only been in Las Vegas for a few hours and already he could see from the glitz and glamour of the place that there was only one winner. Then he noticed the waitress who had brought them drinks earlier. She was cruising slowly between rows of machines looking for custom and Rory raised his hand to attract her attention.

'Beer lads, last one for the road?'

'Good idea Rory,' said Mike.

'I don't need to ask you two do I?' he said to Alan and the back of David's head as the girl approached.

'You want drinks?'

'Yes please, four beers.'

'Hokay,' she said turning to walk away and as she did so Rory could not help but look her up and down.

She was no more than five feet four he guessed, about his own age but what really took his attention were the shapely legs protruding from the short skirt.

'Fancy her do you?' said Alan, equally mesmerised.

Rory just smiled and a little embarrassed turned to watch David and Mike playing their machines.

'Ho ho,' chortled Mike, sitting back in his chair as the machine began a thumping rhythm and coins began cascading into the tray. 'Twenty-five dollars, about time I got something back.'

Grinning broadly, he scooped the coins from the small tray and stuffed half of them into his trouser pocket just as the waitress returned with the drinks.

'Four beers,' she said, placing the glasses on the shelf next to the machines.

'Thanks,' said Rory, putting a dollar tip on her tray.

'Thank you,' she said with a smile and for a brief second they caught each other's eye. Rory felt a strange sensation in his chest and for a few moments was unable to do more than simply look at her before finally managing to speak.

'You're not American are you?'

'No I am from Italy.'

'Oh Italy.'

'Yes, *Venezia*.'

'Where's that?'

'In the north, Venice to you Americans.'

'I'm not American I'm Scottish.'

'Scotland, I know a little of Scotland, hills, green and . . .' she laughed, 'skirts, the men wear skirts.'

'No we don't, they are kilts,' he said relaxing, laughing with her. 'Anyway what's an Italian lady doing here in Las Vegas?'

'I am touring round the world with my friend Lucia. We are working here for six weeks before we go to New York and then we go home after almost a year away.'

'That's a long time away from home.'

'Yes. I must go now, we are not supposed to talk with the gamblers, it stops them losing money. *Ciao*.'

'Er chow,' said Rory, watching her drift off between the rows of machines.

'Are you going to give me that beer or not?' said Alan to Rory, holding a glass of beer in each hand and gawping after the girl. 'You like her don't you?'

Before Rory could answer, Mike wanted to know the time.

'Midnight,' said David, glancing at his watch.

'Midnight here or midnight at home?'

'Here.'

'Bloody hell, we have been on the go almost twenty-four hours,' said Rory, suddenly feeling fatigued.

'Let's go back to the digs,' said David.

Their long day was finally catching up with them and as they made their way towards the casino entrance, Rory scanned the room for a last glimpse of the Italian girl.

Chapter 6

With a subdued grunt, Rory half-opened one eye and listened, unsure for a moment of just where he was. Then he remembered, opened both eyes and turned to look at Alan in the next bed. It did not make for a pretty sight, the bed's occupant lying half-naked on top crumpled bedclothes. Breathing deeply he ran his tongue round his desert dry mouth, felt the dull pain of a hangover. He should have known better, known he would feel rough after the long hours of travelling and the alcohol. A cold shower and a toothbrush were the first steps to recovery and forcing himself from the bed he went to the bathroom to stand under a stream of cold water until his senses began to return.

A voice called out.

'Rory is that you in the shower?'

'Aye, who did you think it might be?'

'How's your head?'

'Fine, how's yours?'

'Don't ask.'

Rory understood, finished showering, dressed and told Alan he was going to see what David and Mike were doing and then said, 'Get yourself in there; a cold shower will bring you round. It did me.'

A few minutes later he returned to find Alan had made it into the shower and called to him.

'They are just getting up. It's a good job I banged on their door otherwise they would be in bed all day and time is precious.'

'Is there a plan?' Alan asked, emerging from the bathroom.

'Not really, just a case of finding somewhere for breakfast.'

It was almost mid-day when the four of them finally made it into the hot desert sunshine and eager to see Las Vegas and for them it meant Fremont Street.

'Penny for your thoughts Rory,' said Alan.

'I was thinking about that over there, it must be costing a bomb.'

'I'm sure it is, it's a heck of a height isn't it? said David, pointing a finger towards the tower rising above the strip.

'What's it called?' asked Mike.

'Stratosphere,' replied David.

'How did you know that?' said a bemused Alan.

'Because that sign over there says so. What's the expression, in the land of the blind the one-eyed man is king?'

Laughter broke out and Alan looked sheepishly across the road at the billboard with the legend 'Stratosphere Opening Spring 1996'.

'Fancy not seeing that, obvious isn't it?'

'I'm just a bit tired I guess, what's the plan Dave?'

'I don't know, probably Fremont.'

'Yeah I reckon that's the best, have a look in the Golden Nugget again, see if we can win anything this time,' said Alan.

'David did all right last night,' said Rory.

'He did but what about the rest of us, did you see Mike's face when the runner brought him his eight dollars? It wasn't much of a return was it? I don't think you have to look at it that way though, just have some fun.'

'How about something to eat, over there look, a real American diner, let's go and get a hamburger and a coffee,' said David.

The diner was busy, the line of people waiting for seats stretching right to the doorway but they did not have to wait long. American efficiency had them sitting amongst some Japanese and German tourists with plates piled high in next to no time.

'Busy place David,' said Rory, turning to look out of the window.

'How about taking in a show one night?' said Alan.

'How's about a strip show,' said Mike.

'Now that sounds like a good idea, after all, it is supposed to be Dave's stag party.'

'Sounds good to me,' said David. 'Where will we find a strip club?'

'I imagine they are all over the place,' Mike said. 'Let's ask someone.'

'Ask who? These Japanese people won't know and the two old ladies by the window won't know either,' said Alan.

'Somebody will.'

Cheetahs Gentlemen's Club was what they were looking for said the doorman at the Golden Nugget. They had asked as soon as they reached the casino and discovered that Cheetahs was the place to go but that the fun did not start until after midnight.

'Sounds good to me,' said Mike grinning. 'We might win a few dollars in here before we go and then, who knows.'

'Who knows what?' said David.

'Who knows what you might get up to; it will be your last chance.'

David's face blushed, eliciting laughter and a few ribald comments and to escape his embarrassment he began feeding a machine.

'You're not wasting money on them again are you?' said Alan.

'Who says I'm wasting money, it's an investment,' said David.

'Investment, ha!'

'You never know, I might win big and then what will you say?'

'I will say well done, how about you getting the drinks in.'

'That's a good idea,' said Mike. How's about a beer?'

Rory's ears pricked, he remembered the Italian girl and looked round the room for her. He did not see her, but he did see another cocktail waitress moving slowly between some machines. Waving his arm, he caught her attention; she acknowledged and made her way towards him.

'Drinks? If you want drinks you have to be playing the machines.'

'They are.'

'Then *they* can order drinks.'

'We're with them.'

'Sorry buster, house rules. Put a dollar in one of the machines and I can bring you a drink.'

Rory and Alan looked at each other, grinned and felt in their pockets for some money.'

'There, how's that?' asked Rory, sitting back on the stool.

'Fine, what can I get you gentlemen?'

'Four beers please.'

'Coming right up,' said the girl, her face deadpan.

'Nice girl,' said Alan.

'I suppose she gets fed up of tourists.'

'Maybe, anyway never mind her; it looks as if Mike has won something.'

A few machines along the row Mike was looking lovingly at his slot machine as the clunk clunk sound announced a pay-out.

'Twenty dollars,' he said.

'That will cheer him up,' said Alan, putting another 5 dollar bill into his machine.

'Four beers,' said the returning cocktail waitress.

'Excuse me miss, is the Italian girl working tonight?'

'Italian girl, we have several Italian girls working the casino. You want one for the night or just a quickie?'

'Quickie.'

'It's a hooker you're looking for right?'

'Er . . . no, actually she was serving drinks like you last night in this room.'

'Hey buster, we're not hookers in here, we try and earn an honest living. If you want a hooker there are plenty of them cruising the casinos. You need to have a quiet word with a pit boss if that's what you want.'

'You've got it wrong,' said Rory, beginning to feel decidedly uncomfortable. I just had a short conversation with her last night and thought I might see her again.'

The girl looked at him, weighing him up. 'She is on her break; she'll be back in half an hour.'

'Thanks.'

'You're welcome, have a nice day.'

'Did I hear hookers?' asked Mike, reaching for his drink.

'You've got ears like a shit house rat. How could you hear above this racket?'

'It's one of those words that make his ears prick up, isn't it Mike?'

'Prick up; I like the sound of that. When are we off to this strip club?'

'The doorman said it doesn't really kick off until midnight so there is no point in going there any earlier,' said David. 'Are you playing the machine Rory, the reels haven't moved since the waitress told you to put some money in?'

'Oh, just thinking, watching the world go by,' he lied as his eyes scanned the room for the Italian girl.

She saw him first; well she recognised the group as good tippers and slowly she made her way into their line of vision. Rory had turned his attention to

123

the machine and he was busy watching the rotating symbols when he heard David say, 'Four beers please.'

He looked up, saw her and smiled; she did not reciprocate and yet her eyes seemed to convey something. She did not dwell, to fetch the drinks, and when she returned he could not take his eyes off her.

'Hello again,' he said, taking a glass and putting a dollar bill on her tray.

'Hello.'

The conversation ground to a halt, Rory became tongue-tied and then she was gone again, him with a feeling of deflation.

'Fancy the roulette David?' asked Mike, eager to try anything he considered might make him rich.

'You're a proper gambler Mike; you'll have nothing left at this rate.'

'It's about winning Alan, if I can win enough to keep going I know the big one is just around the corner.'

Alan did not answer, he could not argue with Mike's logic, the logic of a gambler.

'I wouldn't mind a flutter, let's have a wander through there,' said David, beginning to head towards the next gaming room.

It was the largest area of gaming machines, roulette and card tables in the casino and there, at the roulette table, David and Mike's luck seemed to change. Steadily winning small amounts enabled them to remain at the tables for almost an hour and when they finally came away, Rory could not help quizzing David.

'How much did you lose Dave?'

'That's a leading question Rory but as you ask, about fifty dollars. I still have plenty left; it would not do to run out before we even get started. How did you get on Mike?'

'I'm up twenty odd I think, not enough to break the bank but it's a great feeling to win.'

'Fifty dollars is a lot.'

'Relax Rory; we're here for the experience and some fun. Don't forget I'm getting married when we get back and then my days of fun will be over.'

'Don't talk daft. Did you get your house sorted out? You told me you were waiting for the mortgage when we were on the ship.'

'Yes it's sorted out now. I signed the papers last week as soon as I went on leave and by the time we get back the solicitor should have exchanged contracts.'

'Shouldn't you be saving instead of spending?'

'Rory, shut up, you're making me feel guilty, this is supposed to be my stag do not an inquisition into my long term finances.'

'Just teasing. You won't be going with a hooker will you?'

David flicked the back of his hand none too gently across Rory's chest and looked him sternly in the eye before breaking out into a broad grin.

'What's the name of that strip club?' he said.

They explored the casino for two hours more, playing machines that took their fancy, drinking, listening to a pop band blasting out the latest hits and by eleven o'clock they were eager to get to the strip club.

'Let's make for the door; we'll be heading to the club in an hour. We can have a last free drink and maybe play the machines,' said David, leading the way.

The room was busy with both locals and tourists playing the machines and for a time the four friends joined them. Rory put a dollar bill into his machine but had little interest in playing, looking instead round the room for the Italian girl. He saw her walking slowly between rows of machines and was about to draw her attention when a man appeared and seemed to confronted her. By her expression, she appeared alarmed, on the defensive, and immediately he decided to see if she needed any help.

The man appeared South American, dark skinned, a drooping moustache almost as if he had just come out of a spaghetti western. His eyes were dark, menacing and he seemed intent on dominating the girl and did not notice Rory's approach. The girl was defensive, not interested in the man and when she saw Rory her eyes seemed to plead for help.

'Excuse me miss the drinks you brought us just now, there is something wrong with them. They taste awful, can you please come and take them away and bring us some more.'

'Oh . . . yes sir, I'm sorry, right away I come and change them.'

It was enough to break the spell, enough for her to escape the clutches of the dreadful-looking Mexican whose attention now turned to Rory.

'Who you?'

'I'm sorry; I'm like you, just looking for some better service in this establishment.'

'You, where are you going?' he said to the girl.

She didn't answer, instead she looked at Rory for direction and he turned to lead her across the room, away from a tirade of Spanish expletives.

'What was all that about?'

'He thinks I am a hooker and wanted me to go with him.'

'Can't he see you're a cocktail waitress?'

'The girls try anything for business in this town. Prostitution is illegal in Las Vegas but that doesn't stop some of them. You must have seen them.'

'No, can't say I have. You okay?'

'Yes, this sort of thing, it happens, but usually the casino's security men are around so nothing gets out of hand.' She looked up and waved briefly to a large black man who had appeared by the doorway.

'It's okay, George is keeping an eye on me now.'

'George?'

'Over there, he's part of security. If there's trouble it doesn't last long.'

'What's your name?'

'Nadia, and you,' she said, smiling.

'Rory.'

'You are English?'

'Hell no, I'm a Scot,' said Rory indignantly.

'Oh yes I remember, nice country, and green I think.'

'If you say so.'

They looked at each other for a few seconds before Nadia announced that she must go, for even though he had rescued her, she still had her work to do.

'We would like four beers if you can manage it?'

'Okay.'

She glanced around the room and confident the Mexican had gone, headed for the bar.

'What was all that about?' asked Mike.

'Mexican, I think, was bothering her so I just asked her to change our drinks because they tasted off.'

'We haven't got any drinks,' said Alan.

Rory looked up at the ceiling and then at Alan.

'No, quite right, we don't have any drinks but we soon will have. Look, she's coming back now.'

The waitress arrived with her tray full and handed out the drinks, lastly placing Rory's on the gaming machine shelf in front of him.

Their eyes met and she said, 'Listen, you helped me and for that, I tell you secret. Do you see the machine over there at the end of the row, that one with a spaceship?'

Rory looked round.

'Is a special machine, no pay big win for nearly a year and the service man tell me he thinks it is ready to pay out big. Try it, you might be lucky for helping me.'

And then she was gone, gliding silently across the carpet and a bemused Rory with no choice but to watch her go until, recovering, he looked at his friends.

'Listen to this, she told me there is a machine over there that has not paid out a big win in nearly a year and she believes it's due to cough up. Shall I have a go?'

'Good idea, which one is it?' asked Mike.

'Not so fast clever Dick, let Rory try it first,' said David, aware that Mike was capable of selling his own grandmother to gain advantage.

Alan laughed and nodded to Rory, 'Go on then.'

Rory felt in his pocket, pulled out a twenty-dollar bill and with a mixture of bravado and apprehension fed it into the machine. The large buttons in front of him began to flash and with little idea of what to do, he pressed the red one.

The reels span for a short time, eventually coming to a halt with a clunk clunk clunk, then nothing, only a myriad of lights flashing and inviting him to try again. He pressed the button, the lights flashed and he was at a loss until Mike said, 'You've got three nudges. Try the middle reel.'

Rory pressed the green flashing button with the down arrow and the reel inched round and still it was not a winning combination. But at least he had a better idea of how to play. Pressing the buttons again, he set the wheels in motion and after five more minutes of trying managed to lose his twenty dollars.

'Not a very good tip was it Rory, does she do horse racing as well,' laughed David.

Rory grinned but felt little pleasure.

'My turn,' said Mike, pushing Rory to one side. 'Watch the expert.'

Mike proved no better than Rory at playing the machine, coming away ten dollars poorer and with his lips pursed in disappointment.

'Bloody machine, it's just like all the rest. I don't think it has any intention of paying out. Maybe she earns commission talking people like us into shoving their money into it.'

Rory just looked at him, said nothing and felt in his pocket for a dollar coin.

'One last go.'

'One last go, that should be a slogan for Las Vegas, one last go,' laughed Mike.

Rory put the coin into the machine, said *abracadabra* as if he had some mystical power and closed his eyes just as he pressed the button.

For a second or two there was silence save for the quiet whirring of the reels and then the inevitable clunk clunk clunk as they came to rest. Still silence and Rory opened disappointed eyes but then the machine began to convulse. Every light flashed at once and then the wonderful thump thump thump as it began to pay out, the clatter of coins cascading into the metal trough announcing a big win. Rory was euphoric and his face beamed with delight.

'Bloody hell,' said Alan, grabbing a plastic container to hold close to the tray as coins began to fall from it.

Then, as suddenly as it had started, the thumping noise stopped, it was all over, the end of the pay-out. Rory still had a huge grin on his face and could do nothing but stand watching in amazement as Alan and Mike got to their knees to collect those coins spilling over and onto the floor.

'Well done buddy,' said David, standing up and slapping Rory on the back. 'Looks like a small fortune but we can't carry all these coins around with us.'

At that moment, a man dressed in a smart suit and holding an earpiece close to his head approached them.

'Guys, I am the floor manager here and I see you have won. Congratulations, now if you will follow me to the cashier's desk you can exchange the dollar coins for notes, much easier to carry.'

'Er, thanks,' said Rory, coming to his senses.

It wasn't the jackpot, not thousands of dollars, just five hundred, but still a substantial sum and enough to make Rory feel as if he were a rich man.

'Well it looks like your waitress friend came up trumps after all,' said David.

Rory only half heard him as he stuffed the dollar bills into his pocket, his mind on both his good fortune and the cocktail waitress.

'Oh . . . yes, she did, I must find her and give her a tip. Come on, I guess you all want to be moving on. What time is it?'

'We certainly do,' said an eager-looking Mike, glancing at his watch. 'It's coming up midnight.'

'We can get a limo to take us there, easier than walking and anyway I don't know where it is,' added David.

'We can have one last go on the bandits Rory and you can get us some drinks, come on.'

They thanked the floor manager, made their way back to the gaming machines and almost immediately Rory saw the waitress and walked over to her.

'You won I see. Don't tell anyone I said to try that machine or I will get the sack.'

'No, I won't do that. Can you bring us four more beers please?'

'Okay, I come back in a few minutes.'

Rory turned to his friends and saw them clustered around the machine with the spaceship, hoping no doubt to emulate his success.

'It won't pay out again, you're wasting your money boys.'

'You don't know that,' said Mike.

'No I don't suppose I do. Good luck.'

Mike gave him a defiant look and put a ten-dollar bill into the machine, pressed the button and sat back.

'See I told you it won't pay out again. Never mind that, she is back with our drinks.'

'Thanks, here, a few dollars tip for helping me,' said Rory, placing the money on her tray and taking his glass.

She looked up at him and smiled.

'Listen,' he said, his stomach beginning to churn, thinking to himself that it was now or never. 'Can I take you for a drink sometime?'

She lowered her eyes for a moment before looking up and nodding. 'I finish my shift soon, you can buy me a drink then, but I will not be alone.'

'Oh,' he said wondering, disappointed.

'My friend Lucia will come with me. We always stick together, she works the same hours I do.'

'That's okay; bring her along, where shall I meet you?'

'Here, wait here and we will come. I see you in half an hour right?'

'Yes, brilliant.'

She smiled, turned to walk away and Rory watched her go. Something was happening, his heart was beating like never before, his chest felt tight and he was happier than he could remember.

'You're getting along well with your waitress friend I see.'

'Ahem, yes and I have a date with her so I'm afraid I will not be coming to the strip club.'

'Bloody hell, you're a fast worker Rory. I didn't know you had it in you. Did you hear that boys, Rory here has a date with the cocktail waitress?'

'And I'm feeling a little guilty not coming with you but to soften the blow here's a hundred dollars for some drinks,' he said, peeling several twenty-dollar bills from his winnings and giving them to David.

'That's mighty generous of you, thanks.'

'Well, time to go if we're going,' said an eager Mike.

'You okay here on your own Rory?' asked Alan.

'Yeah, she said she would be back in less than half an hour. Go on, bugger off and don't do anything I wouldn't,' he said, immediately regretting his words as each of them gave him a knowing look.

He did not have long to wait, Nadia appeared from a side door with her friend, her working clothes replaced by sober black slacks and a red blouse. He looked at her, delighting at her minimalist make-up, her black hair pulled back in a short ponytail and her air of cheerfulness.

'Hello,' he said a little shyly.

'Hello, this is my friend I told you about. Lucia this is Rory.'

Lucia was almost Nadia's double, dark haired, with bright brown eyes and the same light tan.

'Hello Lucia, I'm Rory.'

'*Ciao.*'

'Well girls where would you like to go? The drinks are on me after my good fortune.'

The two women gave each other a knowing look and Nadia giggled, 'Lucia knows about your winnings and about the machine paying out. Do not tell anybody I mentioned that you should play it.'

'Of course not, you said you would get the sack and I wouldn't want that to happen would I? Where shall we go, I expect you know all the best places.'

'There is a bar just off Fremont Street where we sometimes go after work. We don't earn a lot so we've found the cheapest places to go.'

'Don't worry about that, it's my treat, we can go somewhere a bit more up market if you like.'

'What about Fitzgerald's?' said Lucia. 'From the balcony you can see the light show. Perhaps your friend hasn't seen it.'

'Light show, you mean in the roof over the street?'

'Yes it is nice to watch.'

134

'We had a look at it when we first arrived but I hadn't really bothered tonight.'

'Fitzgerald's is as good as anywhere, we can watch the lights and the bands in the street will play another hour.'

'Sounds good to me, lead on,' said Rory with a sweep of his hand.

Ten minutes later the three of them were sitting in the warm evening air and and looking at the light show when Rory turned to Nadia.

'Where are you from?'

'Italy, *Venezia*, I told you that before.'

'Oh of course you are Italian. What's *Venezia?*'

'Venice to you English.'

'And I told you I'm not English.'

Nadia's eyes flashed playfully and she smiled, 'I know you told me, *Scozia*. I like to go to Scotland.'

'You'll like it I'm sure but you had better take a thick jumper and an umbrella. It rains all the time in Scotland, it's not at all like here but at least Scotland is green.'

'Which part of Scotland do you come from, Edinburgh?'

'No, I hail from the Western Isles, well away from the big city. Another drink, can I get you another drink?'

'Just one more red wine please,' said Nadia.

'And me,' said Lucia.

'You don't drink a lot do you?'

'Not like you British or Australians. The Australians drank a lot Lucia, didn't they?'

135

'Oh, you met some Australians here?'

'No we lived there for almost eight months before coming here.'

'You got about then? Was Australia good?'

'Fair dinkum.'

'I see you have picked up some Australian,' said Rory, a grin spreading across his face.

'We are travelling the world to improve our English before we look for a job.'

'Well you have impressed me. Where are you going to look for a job, Las Vegas?'

'No, Italy, we finish here in two weeks and then we go to stay with my uncle in New York before we go home.'

'Wow, you've had a good look round then.'

'*Si*, it has been a good experience, no Lucia?'

'*Si, molto bene.*'

'And you Rory, where have you been in the world?'

'Not very far I'm afraid, Edinburgh and here is about as far as I've managed.'

'Oh you should see the world while you are young.'

'Not much chance of that on my wages.'

The girls laughed and for a time talked of their adventures in Australia. Rory reciprocated, describing his time on the North Sea, and then he hesitated before telling them briefly about his time fishing before finally falling silent.

'What is the matter, you are quiet?' said Nadia.

'Oh . . . just thinking back to the accident.'

The girls looked at him with enquiring eyes and then at each other.

'What accident?'

'The *Lurach-Aon*, my father's fishing boat, we were sunk by a submarine we believe.'

'A submarine, you are lucky to be alive I think,' said Nadia, her eyes softening.

'Yes I know, but I *am* still alive and I am here in Las Vegas with two pretty girls. I guess I am very lucky.'

Nadia lowered her eyes, her mood seemed to change and Rory worried that he had said the wrong thing.

'I am tired,' said Lucia reading her friend's mood. 'I have been on my feet all day and tomorrow I have to do it again.'

'What about you Nadia, are you working tomorrow?'

'Yes but I have Thursday off. When do you go home with your friends?'

'Friday, perhaps you can show me Las Vegas on your day off. Erm . . . if you want to.'

'Maybe,' she said, uncertainty showing in her eyes. 'Lucia is right we must go now, it is two o'clock and the bar is closing. We will take a cab from the casino; they pay for a cab every night for the workers.'

Standing up she glanced at Lucia and something unspoken passed between them, then the three of them left the bar to walk back towards the Golden Nugget.

'I will go and find the concierge and ask him to send for our cab.'

'I wait here for you Lucia,' said Nadia, turning to Rory. 'Thank you for a nice time.'

137

'No problem, it was really good to meet you. Er, can I see you again, on your day off perhaps, it will be my last chance.'

She smiled her wonderful smile. 'I would like that.'

Rory had no time to say more before Lucia returned with news of their cab and all he could do was look at Nadia. Then, as if on instinct, she reached up to him and planted a soft kiss on his lips. 'I meet you here at mid-day on Thursday.'

The quiet hum of the air conditioning and heavy snoring was enough to wake Rory. Opening his eyes, he yawned, stretched his arms above his head and thought for a full minute about Nadia before turning to look at Alan. He had returned to their room a little after two o'clock, fallen into a deep sleep and now, with just a single sheet pulled up to his chin, he looked his roommate over and could not help grinning. Alan was fast asleep, covered from head to toe with a white sheet and, apart from the snoring, had the appearance of a corpse lying in a morgue. Holding back from laughing aloud Rory slipped quietly from the bed, went to take a shower and as the water cascaded over his body Nadia's image filling his mind. It had been fun and tomorrow he would see her again he thought as he dried himself and began dressing. He gathered the remnants of the previous evening's good fortune, stuffing the dollar bills into his pocket and crept silently out of the room. He walked down the staircase knowing that the others would sleep for a few hours yet and, for a while, he would be on his own. He decided he would take a walk to Fremont Street, find a diner and treat himself to an American breakfast, pancakes and all. He still had over three hundred dollars left from his winnings, money he was not going to waste on gambling.

'Morning,' he said as he passed the office.

'Hiya honey, how're ya doin.'

'Good thanks. Do you have the password for today?'

'Sure do honey, 'Stratosphere, big word ain't it?'

Rory smiled, amused by her enunciation as he committed the word to memory.

'They're building the Stratosphere just down the road so if'n ya forget just have a look at the tower risin' up, that should remind you. I see your friends had a good time last night, must have, because they were just coming back here as I arrived for work at six o'clock.'

'Yes I could see they had a late night. Can you do me a favour miss, they are still in bed and I'm going for a walk so can you let them know that I will be back here for one o'clock.'

'Sure, have a nice day.'

'Thank you.'

Rory left her to her computer game and set off at a brisk pace. Why were there so many wedding parlours he wondered and then he saw yet another sign proclaiming 'Elvis slept here'. Elvis, he liked the idea of seeing Elvis but the King was dead, almost twenty years before, so there was very little chance of hearing the real thing. Perhaps Nadia knew of an

139

Elvis impersonator who would do the King justice and he would get the chance to hear some real rock and roll.

He reached a Fremont Street already busy with tourists and looked up at the ceiling of the mall. It was too early for the light show, the bands and street entertainers would not appear until the evening. That left him with time to amble along, gaze into shop windows filled with everything western he could imagine. There were cowboy hats, boots, replica guns and the finest Indian headdresses he would ever see. Pausing to look in the window of one shop, he tried to envisage what it was like to live in the Wild West. Then the sound of a woman crying drew his attention, a black woman, the same size as the one in the office. She must have just come from the side door of the casino and he could see that she was distraught.

'Mister, can you lend me a dollar for the phone?' she called out to him.

Rory looked at her with some puzzlement.

'Ah have lost all ma money an' I can't git home,' she said, beginning to wail once more. 'Ah need to phone ma man to come an' git me, just a dollar for the phone mister,' and as an afterthought – 'Please.'

This larger than life character amused Rory and he did sympathise with her for losing her money.

'Here,' he said, offering her a dollar bill and adding a little sarcastically, 'Don't go and spend it all at once.'

'Gee thanks mister, say are you English?'

'No I'm not, I'm Scottish, and I'm from Scotland.'

'Scotland, what's that?'

'Never mind,' he said, beginning to walk away and then, to his amazement, she burst into song, Gospel music, and she was good. It made him feel good too, made him feel as if he was some sort of latter-day Samaritan and he stopped to watch her go until his attention focused on a more pressing need. Food, he had not eaten properly since mid-afternoon the previous day and he was ready for one of those big American breakfasts.

A sign advertising all day breakfasts caught his eye. Denny's, just fifty yards away, was offering everything you could ever want on a breakfast plate for five dollars ninety-nine. Pushing open the door, he joined the queue, and noticed that although the food was plentiful it was unappetising. However, he was hungry and he was sure it was probably no worse than the breakfasts Hamish served up. Grabbing a tray, he shuffled along with the rest of the diners towards a black woman dishing out plates and recoiled at the sight of the one she gave him.

'Excuse me, this plate isn't clean.'

'It's as good as you goin' to get em. Next.'

That was it, eat off a still greasy plate or starve – no contest. Shrugging his shoulders, he moved along the line towards another black woman who was serving the food. She smiled at him, seemed less hostile and he smiled back. He was not going to upset this woman; she was the one piling his plate with scrambled eggs, streaky bacon and flapjacks.

141

Though the food did not appear to be of a high standard it was surprisingly good and after eating, he sat for a while to watch the world go by. He could not help thinking of Nadia and Lucia, two girls who had toured the world and it caused him to reflect on how narrow his own life was. He had felt content enough until the accident, had no ambition other than to be a fisherman, but that had been taken away from him.

Feeling a little glum, he left the diner, walked the length of Fremont Street and made his way back to the motel room to find Alan just about to go into the shower.

'Where have you been?'

'I went for a walk to Fremont Street to have a real American breakfast. No wonder Americans are so big.'

'Was it good?'

'Yes, apart from the bacon. I have never seen such measly slices. Anyway, what happened to you three last night?'

'Oh blimey, what a time we had. You missed some sights. How did your date go?'

'Good, she brought a friend along and we had a couple of drinks in a bar overlooking the street.'

'A friend? That will have cramped your style boy.'

'I don't need my style cramping thank you very much.'

Alan looked at Rory and wondered. 'You like her don't you?'

'Aye,' said Rory rather shyly.

'You hardly know her and in a couple of days we'll be gone and you'll never see her again.'

142

'Aye,' he said again, hoping that would not be the case. 'I'm seeing her tomorrow at twelve.'

'Dumping us for a woman again are you?'

Rory looked away with some embarrassment. What was it about Nadia that was affecting him so?

'We're off for a beer in half an hour. You will be coming won't you?'

'Yes of course, where are the others?'

'Around, they told me you were coming back about now and I guess they will be waiting by the coke machine.'

They were.

'Well look who's here, the wanderer returns,' said Mike, greeting Rory as he came down the stairs. 'Hey you missed a good night, wall to wall girls and most of 'em with hardly a stitch on.'

'I hope you were not up to any mischief.'

'Naw, but I could easily have been, we had to hold Mike back or he would have gone off like a shot with one of those girls.'

'Too true,' said Mike.

'So what stopped you?'

'Money, I ran out of money and the one I fancied wanted fifty dollars for an hour.'

'What happened to the money I gave you?'

'Didn't last long,' said Alan, 'I've never seen such expensive drinks, your hundred only stretched to one round.'

'Sounds to me like you were had.'

'I guess so; we're not quite the high rollers they expected. We had two drinks and spent four hours

143

watching the girls' pole dancing. It was worth it just for that.'

'He didn't tell you he spent another hundred sticking twenty-dollar bills into the girls' bras and knickers did he.'

'Oh aye, what's this then?'

Mike looked a little sheepish. 'Well if you tip them they climb all over you.'

David started laughing and slapped him on his back. 'Come on Mister Gigolo, we're going out.'

Chapter 7

With slicked-back dark hair and an expensive choice in clothes, Franco had grown into a good-looking young man, flash, confident, and he liked the girls, but he had a mean streak.

'Hey Franco.'

'*Ciao* Rocco, how are you?'

'I'm good. Il Capo wants to see you.'

Franco felt himself stiffen – Il Capo, if the boss wanted to see him it could mean trouble. Had he found out about the money he had been skimming from the restaurants? He was handling a lot of it these days, protection money mostly, from the restaurants near the Rialto Bridge, his patch. He had been careful; nevertheless, he was taking a big risk. If Il Capo suspected he was robbing the clan it could mean losing a finger or even worse. He remembered Luigi Bellincioni and felt his stomach turn and then he shrugged his shoulders to look pleased to know that Il Capo had summoned him. He was young, he was resilient and his swaggering confidence always got him through and it would again he was sure.

'Where?'

'Follow me, he is on the canal.'

The two men walked in silence towards a private mooring on the Grand Canal where a beautifully rigged motor boat rocked gently in the wake of a passing craft. In the cockpit stood two men wearing dark suits were smoking and talking quietly. They were Il Capo's personal bodyguard.

'In there,' said one of them motioning Franco to come aboard the boat.

'Franco, take a seat,' said the portly, kindly-looking man ensconced inside the small cabin. 'Smoke?'

'No thank you, I don't smoke.'

'A wise man, you will live longer if you don't smoke eh?'

Il Capo's face remained kindly as his dark eyes penetrated Franco's soul, searching for any sign of disloyalty, and Franco felt his throat run dry.

'I could do with a drink though boss.'

'You want wine?'

'No sir, just water, it's a hot day and I'll live longer if I drink water.'

Il Capo's eyes softened, his face creased into a half smile.

'We live dangerously Franco; I think our way of life is worse for our health than a few cigarettes or alcohol. You remember Umberto, Il Capo of the Luciani clan?'

'Yes, I was only a boy but I remember.'

'You put the finger on him Franco, you were my spy and you did good. Umberto was meeting with some discontents who thought they might take over our, my, patch.' The boss paused, took a cigarette

from an expensive-looking cigarette case and lit it
with an equally expensive lighter. Drawing the smoke
into his lungs, he blew it back out again straight into
Franco's face. 'You have been cheating me Franco,
no?'

'No.'

'What about the money you skimmed and are still
skimming?'

'Expenses boss, expenses. I have a network of
boys to pay, just as you did with me. They tell me
who, when and where so that I can maximise the
take. Do I not bring in the most of any of your
collectors, boss?'

Il Capo smiled a crocodile smile. 'It is true you
bring in the most money but I don't like to think you
are cheating me. We all know what happens to those
who cheat the Family, eh?'

'Yes boss, how about that drink?' Franco's throat
felt like sandpaper. He was worried.

'Luigi, get the boy a drink of water,' he called to
one of his men. 'Okay, we both know where we stand.
You have been loyal enough all these years and a bit
of enterprise is no bad thing but I warn you – be
careful.'

'Yes boss,' said Franco, taking the glass from the
bodyguard, swallowing the water just a little too
quickly and eliciting a thoughtful look from Il Capo.

He was sure he'd got away with it, but it was a
close run thing.

'Now to more pressing business, I am promoting
you so you can earn more and steal less. We are
planning a heist that requires brains as well as brawn

and I want you involved. Your job will be to look after some tools.'

'Tools?'

'Yes Franco, tools, and you will be a part of the team. We will only have a short time to pull off the job and I want my best lieutenants running things.'

'What is it boss, the job?'

Il Capo gave Franco a look that said 'you do not ask a question like that'.

'In time, all in good time, I will send for you when we need you. In the meantime, I suggest you learn the oath of allegiance; you are to be welcomed into the Family. *Arrivederci* Franco.'

The villa was large, hidden from the road in expansive grounds and as Franco turned his scooter into the drive, he could not help but notice the expensive-looking cars parked in the driveway. Dismounting, he gazed enviously at them – big German cars, BMWs and Mercedes, parked side by side, and a beautiful yellow Lamborghini. They certainly impressed him but what he really wanted was a Ferrari, a red one that would turn the girls' heads.

Parking his Vespa, he looked towards the house and waved at two, suited men smoking, slouched against the wall. They came to life, stood up straight, as he approached and Franco noticed each of them involuntarily touch a bulge in their jackets.

'*Ciao* Silvano, Luciano.'

The two men nodded as one, Luciano, the bigger of the two, opened the front door to the house and stood aside to let him enter. Inside, another gangster sat guarding a closed door and, on seeing Franco, stood to tap lightly on it. Seconds later the door opened a little, he spoke to someone inside and then it opened more fully.

'Go in,' he said to Franco.

As he entered the room, the young mafioso saw several men sitting around a large polished table. Il Capo was at the head with his lieutenants along each side. Franco recognised two of them, but the clandestine nature of the mafia trade meant the others were unfamiliar. It was the mafia code of secrecy that kept them together and out of the reach of the law.

Il Capo gestured, ordered him to stand near him.

'Franco, I want you to join this meeting because we are ready to welcome you into the Family as a man of honour. Put your hand on this bible,' he said, rising to his feet.

Franco did as he was told, proud that at last the moment he had dreamed of had arrived. Then Il Capo produced a flick knife, its blade flashing wickedly as he opened it.

'Show me the palm of your left hand.'

Franco held out his hand, flat, with his fingers spread and without flinching allowed Il Capo to cut the palm, drawing blood as he marked it with a cross.

'Repeat the oath of allegiance.'

Franco, emotions high, spoke in a clear controlled voice knowing that with this ceremony the mafia clan were accepting him as one of their own, as a man of honour. Then Il Capo kissed him on both cheeks to endorse the brief induction.

'Good, welcome to the brotherhood. You have taken the Family's oath of allegiance and you know the penalty for treachery. Il Capo drew his index finger across his throat in the manner of a knife, the meaning all too clear.

Several kilometres away, the main office block of the Padua regional police headquarters sported an impressive main entrance. However, there was also another, less conspicuous, entrance, one tucked away from prying eyes, an entrance useful for those not wishing to draw attention. Through this door a scruffy-looking man in his early thirties passed, avoiding the lift, taking the steps two at a time to the third floor where he walked briskly along the corridor and into an office.

To the police officer sitting at her desk his entrance came as no surprise; she had witnessed the comings and goings of this man and others like him many times. Reaching out, she pressed a button to alert Colonel Barbonetti and seconds later a second door opened across the room and a uniformed police officer appeared.

'*Ciao* Roberto, do you want a coffee?'

'Yes, that would be nice captain.'

'Come into my office and you can tell me what you know.'

The man named Roberto followed the captain of police into his spacious office and watched in silence as he filled his coffee machine.

'Take a seat, the coffee will not be long. Now what have you found out about the Manor, what are they planning?'

'I don't know exactly but Il Capo is calling in his thugs. I saw our young friend Franco Foscari aboard his boat yesterday and then others I did not recognise.'

'What about Foscari, we've been watching him for some time and thinking of pulling him in once we have enough evidence to charge him? He is young and chances are he does not have the connections some of the old birds have. Unless he can afford a good lawyer he'll be the next one we can lock up.'

Roberto pursed his lips, shrugged his shoulders. 'He is small fish, Foscari, but small fish are eaten by the big fish and if we can use him as bait . . .'

'First we need to know what they are planning. Have you any idea?'

'No but rumours are beginning to surface. I think this is a big one, a bank, casino, something like that. What do you want me to do?'

'Keep undercover and let me know the minute you have something. We will use the drop off in the railway station if you cannot get here to report, there are always the crowds to give you cover. The director has given me permission to mount a serious operation once we know what the mafia boys are planning – more men and a magistrate that will not signal our intentions once we get the warrants.'

Roberto nodded his head slowly, thoughtfully, convinced that the local clan were planning something. His job was to discover their intentions, work alone under cover, a dangerous occupation but it was a career choice he had made when they had killed his brother, Giovanni. The mafia had murdered a good police officer with an exemplary record and he had discovered that corrupt officials were involved. That discovery had shocked him to the core, the pain running deep and undermining his faith in the service so much so that he had resigned from the Milan police. He had wandered aimlessly for a time, reflecting, until one day a change had come over him. A realisation of where his vocation lay had grown within, prompting him to contact a magistrate untouched by mafia tentacles. The official agreed to a meeting and it was at that meeting Roberto elucidated his desire to put mafia gang members and the corrupt officials who protect them behind bars. The magistrate was receptive and after a phone call to a contact, Roberto began a new career as an undercover officer working out of the Padua headquarters building.

The second time Franco found himself summoned to the house he walked past the BMWs and the Lamborghini hardly giving them a glance. For the time being, the Ferrari could wait, Il Capo had given him responsibilities, he was moving up the ladder and his mind was set on his task. The last of the inner circle to arrive, he entered the main room and as the door closed behind him he looked at each of the men sitting round the table. Five of them, all dressed in dark business suits – Il Capo, three of the men who had witnessed his admission into the clan, and a fifth individual. He understood now just how secret the organisation was for the fifth man was Mario Foscari, his own father. He had known for some time that his father was connected to the family but until this moment had not realised how close he was to the leadership.

'Good, we are all here, now down to business. I can tell you who do not already know that we are going to hit the *Banca d'Italia*. We have it on good authority that on occasion the bank holds almost a million United States dollars. They open the vault twice a day, before the start of business and at the close. There is more, a security company collects the week's takings every Friday after the bank closes. We have someone on the inside and that person will let us know when the vault is holding a significant sum. We also have someone working for the security firm and he will arrange for a delay in the collection of the takings long enough for us to clean out the vault. We have conducted a survey of the bank and are at an advanced stage of planning so now it is time for action. The Sicilians will supply us with guns and explosives and we are in the process of acquiring Carabinieri uniforms. Franco, your job is to find a safe place for all these things, a place the police will never think of looking.'

Franco nodded, took a sideways glance at his father and turned back to listen as Il Capo, and then two of the lieutenants, described the basic plan. Then it was the turn of Mario to speak. Mario was the organisation's accountant, he did not control the purse strings but he did advise on which ones to pull and when. He spoke quietly, outlining the costs of the equipment, transport and bribes to be paid and from which income streams the money would come. He was the one with a contact at the bank who could tell them how much they might expect to steal.

'At close of business last Friday the vault held eight hundred and forty-two thousand dollars. This is a large sum of money and when you consider there will be a high proportion of low denomination notes it will also be bulky. You will need to be aware that to move such an amount of money requires transport and an escape route unless we want to be caught red-handed.'

The men looked at each other and then at Il Capo, who added, 'We will hit the bank hard at closing time and, as Mario says, we need an escape route that will get us and the money out.'

He rose from his seat to face an artist's easel placed near to him and grasping the corner of the cloth draped over it, pulled it aside. The men around the table all leaned forward to see he had revealed a plan of central Venice with the Grand Canal as its centrepiece. He pointed out several features, described how he envisaged the operation might unfold, timings, who should be involved directly in the raid. 'Luigi here will gather together some of his best men, two as technicians and two dressed as Carabinieri to take care of the staff and set the explosives. Franco, as well as concealing the guns and explosives you will take care of the getaway. Questions anybody?'

The men round the table remained silent for several seconds until the one called Luigi spoke.

'The guards in the bank will be armed I think. We will need more than handguns to take care of them.'

'We are aware of that and at this moment two of our number are dealing with the Sicilians, they will supply us with automatic weapons, Kalashnikovs as well as handguns. You will have little difficulty if you hit them hard to begin with. There will be only one guard with a handgun and if he is stupid enough to resist, then shoot him. Should the police turn up then the automatic weapons will be a necessity.'

'You want to blow the strong room, boss, can we first try and hit when the vault is open? What about your man on the inside, Mario, could he let us in?' asked Luigi. 'There is no guarantee we will set the charge exactly, we might not blow the vault or we might bring the whole building down.'

'I have arranged for the manager to be away from the bank and our man will replace him for a day or two. He will help you gain entry to the vault and then you can set the explosives. If it means bringing the building down then so be it, but make sure you get the money out.'

A nervous murmur passed around the table, Luigi nodded thoughtfully as he considered the options.

'I will attend to it right away; it's a job for plastic explosives and I know just where to lay my hands on some.'

'Good, then if there are no more questions it just leaves me to give the order. Mario you have the funds ready to purchase all we need?' Franco's father nodded his head. 'Yes, I have cash waiting. If each man who needs money for his part in the plan comes to see me I can supply it.'

'You hear that gentlemen, if you need money then see Mario and do not be tempted to ask for more than you need.' He looked round the room to confirm his words were sinking in. Each of them was dishonest and each one might be tempted to line his own pockets, a perennial problem for Il Capo.

Standing, Il Capo closed the meeting and waited for each man to pass, kissing him on both cheeks, affirming their obedience and Franco as the most recent member of the *Famiglia*, was last.

'Franco you have an important job to do. Make sure you find a good hiding place for the guns and make sure no one, I mean no one, sees them and when we are ready, you will bring them to us and you must also plan the escape. I am relying on you.'

'I will make sure boss all is as you ask, you can trust me boss.'

'I trust no one Franco so be careful not to let us down. I am optimistic for you in the future. When we rob the *Banca d'Italia* we will have funds to make inroads into the drug trade, buy the best quality to sell to the rich and famous of this city and I want you to be the courier. Once this job is concluded we will talk again.'

'Thank you boss, I will not let you down.'

Il Capo's eyes bored into Franco's for a brief moment, the older man reinforcing his control before turning to speak with another of his lieutenants.

Franco and his father left the house together and walking towards the parked cars Mario spoke to his son.

'Franco, now you know of my involvement with the clan and I can tell you that you are well thought of by Il Capo. You have responsibilities now.'

He was stony-faced as he spoke, aware of his son's rise through the ranks and knew from experience that he was beginning to tread a dangerous path. Not only would the police be looking out for him but also petty jealousies within the local mafia would surface and then there were the Sicilians . . . If they decided to move into Venice, Franco could well be in the firing line.

'I am ready, I will show my worth, I will make sure my part in this operation is a success. And you father, I had no idea.'

'I know, Franco, but now you do know and you must not tell anyone, not your mother, your sister or even Claudio. Our code of silence protects us. You must be careful, there are eyes everywhere.'

If Roberto allowed himself a vice, it was tobacco. He enjoyed a hand rolled cigarette and although they might not be good for his health, they were good cover. He was a scruffy down-and-out the locals took for granted, invisible in full view, the way he liked it, and they did not begrudge him his cigarettes.

'Have you a light?' he asked a passing stranger.

'Yes, here you are,' said the man, producing a lighter. 'Why don't you get a job then you could afford your own lighter?'

Roberto shrugged his shoulders, said nothing but his eyes were alert. The man's smart suit was a uniform and the tell-tale bulge in his clothing confirmed it, a gun, he was mafia.

'Maybe I could but who wants to employ a tramp?'

'You could wash dishes. I know a few restaurants round here who need dishwashers. Try the pizzeria over there, tell them Vicente sent you and they will give you a job. Go on and don't be asking me for a light again scum.'

Roberto avoided the man's eyes, shrugged his shoulders and looked across the small square.

'Okay, but maybe you should introduce me; I mean they will not know me.'

The mafioso began walking towards the restaurant. 'Come on,' he sneered.

Roberto grunted and followed: a benevolent mafioso, that was a new one, he thought.

The job washing pots lasted just a few hours every afternoon and Roberto hated it but not as much as he hated the mafia. He persevered and on the third day, two men wearing expensive suits walked into the kitchen. The dishwasher noticed them enter, men in suits who would not normally pass through the kitchen, not unless they did not want anyone to recognise them. The dishwasher did though and one of them he knew was Franco Foscari.

'Hey you go find the boss,' Franco ordered the chef.

The man immediately stopped what he was doing and left the kitchen, returning within minutes with the restaurant owner.

'Luigi I have come for the tax and I want to introduce you to Pietro here. He is taking over from me as of today; he will collect the tax in future so no funny business or I will be back.'

The restaurant owner nodded. 'You are going on holiday?'

'No I'm staying at home, joining the church,' said Franco.

'The church!'

'Never mind, just give me the money.'

Roberto listened, kept his eyes on the dishes as his hands went through the motion of cleaning them. Could this be the lead he was looking for? Franco said he was entering the church, an unlikely calling for a thug like him yet there was something in his tone. He had brushed his words off as a joke, but the fact he did not want to dwell on the subject was significant. Perhaps it was a slip of the tongue but instinct told Roberto it was more than that.

'The money had better all be here,' said Franco, taking an envelope from the restaurateur.

It was, because no one in his right mind would dare short change Franco Foscari. Having a leg or an arm broken was too high a price to pay; it was all there plus Franco's commission. Stuffing the money into his jacket pocket he walked passed Roberto on his way from the restaurant kitchen and Roberto turned his face away. He could not afford to be recognised, his anonymity had protected him so far and one day it might save his life. As Franco passed he turned his head back, watched him leave and wondered if he should follow. He was sure something big was brewing and that Franco was involved.

Without a word, he let the plates he was holding sink below the surface of the washing-up water, removed his grubby white apron and after a quick glance round disappeared through the kitchen door. Keeping to the shadows, he followed Franco and his friend through the narrow streets trying not to lose sight of them. They were talking animatedly, unaware he was following and then, as they reached a main thoroughfare, they parted company and Roberto had to decide which of them to keep in sight.

He concluded that Franco was the main target and stayed behind him until he reached a small landing at the canalside. Then there was a problem – Franco hailed a water taxi and Roberto realised he could soon be whisked away at speed. He decided his best move was to try to get close, overhear Franco's instructions to the driver and hope to pick up his trail later in the day. So, quickening his pace, he joined a group of tourists standing close to the small jetty and gradually made his way through them till he was only metres away from the mafioso.

'*Ciao* Franco,' called the driver, 'where do you want to go?'

'To the station, I want to catch the next train to Mestre if I can.'

Mestre – he was for the mainland. Roberto, needing to keep on his tail, looked around for a way to reach the station, and caught sight of a vaporetto fast approaching. Dodging tourists, he crossed a bridge and ran along the canalside towards the next waterbus stop, reaching it just as Franco's taxi skimmed by. Digging into his pocket, Roberto pulled out the pass he always carried, stepped aboard, and for the next ten minutes looked anxiously for a sign of Franco. He consoled himself that at least he knew Franco was heading for Mestre and would go there in the hope of picking up his trail. However, unknown to Roberto, Franco had missed his train, forcing him to wait for the next and sitting alone with his thoughts was unaware of the tramp entering the station precinct.

The Church of the Virgin Mary is a modest affair, rebuilt with loving hands from the bombed out ruins of its predecessor and from the beginning the Bishops had entrusted its care to Father Giuseppe. He loved his church, loved his flock, a conscientious priest who had carried out his duties for so many years that he was beginning to look as if he too were part of the reconstruction. At the age of seventy-five, his determination to continue to look after his congregation was admirable; he had grown up in the area and had made it his mission to provide succour and support to those in need. Nevertheless, Father Giuseppe had a weakness, his kindness and trust in humanity. He could never see the harm in anyone – not even the mafia, and now it was Franco's turn to deceive him.

'Father Giuseppe.'

The old priest turned from the altar, shielding his eyes from sunlight streaming in through the stained glass window.

'Hello, who is that?'

'Franco, Franco Foscari, Father.'

'Franco Foscari, how long is it since I last saw you my son?'

'Oh quite a while Father, I have been working in Venice.'

'Venice, and now you have returned?'

'For the time being, I was an altar boy here when I was younger and I felt a need to visit the church.'

'I remember now, you could have made a good altar boy if it wasn't for your troublesome friends. No matter, you are here and I will thank God for that. Do you want to pray, do you want to confess your sins and start afresh?'

Franco smiled inwardly, Father Giuseppe was just as he remembered and he knew his task would be easy. As far as confessing his sins were concerned, he did not have enough time. Nevertheless, he did have time to hustle the old man.

'Yes I would like to pray for a while Father and then I would like to speak with you.'

'Good boy, I will leave you alone in the church for a while and afterwards you may come to see me.'

Gathering his frock Father Giuseppe walked a little unsteadily towards the church door, Franco alone to pray. Franco had little intention of praying, instead, as the priest closed the door he looked round the church for a safe hiding place. If Luigi Bellincioni had taught him anything, it was that churches made for good hiding places.

A hundred metres away, shielded by some bushes, Roberto watched the old priest pass and wondered why Franco would visit a church.

Chapter 8
Venice - Day 1

Less than a week after Franco had made his first visit to the Church of the Virgin Mary, Rory was looking out of the aircraft window during the descent towards Venice's Marco Polo airport. It was his second visit to the city, the third time he and Nadia had spent time together since Las Vegas and he was looking forward to the next few days. They had connected during their day alone, taking in the sights of Sin City, Nadia had told him all about the casinos and their history and he remembered wondering how she could be so knowledgeable about the place.

'I studied history and politics at university; I am interested in what makes a place happen.'

'Tick.'

'Tick?'

'Same thing, like a clock, tick tock, a mechanism I suppose.'

'That's a nice way of putting it Rory,' and then she had told him that he was not like the boys back home with their macho attitudes. 'You listen to me, they don't listen. They only want to tell me what to do.'

'You don't like that?'

'No I don't, would you?'

He remembered thinking that perhaps he had overstepped the mark at that point, and had told her he was just kidding. What was it he had said to placate her? 'I can see that you do not suffer fools easily. I like a girl with spirit.' That seemed to work and he recalled the feeling of relief knowing that she was not annoyed with him. After that, they had simply walked and talked, learning a little of each other's lives, their loves and hates, until eventually they had come across a café dedicated to the Harley-Davidson motorbike.

'Let's have a drink here; I like the look of this place,' he had said and it was there he told her of his solitary adventures on his motorbike, about the lochs and valleys of the Highlands, of the deserted roads and the occasional sightings of wild deer.

'It sounds lovely, not like the city where I live, traffic noise all day long.'

'You live in Venice; I would have thought that was a wonderful place to be.'

'The island maybe but I live in Mestre on the mainland. We have a big house there.'

He described the town where he lived, where he had grown up and his early life in the fishing community. Then he had told her again about the loss of the *Lurach-Aon,* this time in detail, and she had sympathised, reaching across the table to touch his arm.

'What about Venice, tell me about Venice because I know very little other than there is a lot of water?'

'Everything moves on the water, all the things you take for granted have to be moved by water, food, building materials, everything. Even the police and the ambulances services have to use boats.'

'I miss boats, small boats, not like the supply ship. In a small boat on a nice day there is nothing finer than shooting nets or hauling a few pots.'

'Pots?

'Lobster pots. We have the best lobsters in the world where I come from.'

'I must come and see one day.'

She had looked at him with her large brown eyes, clear, searching, and Rory had felt his heart melt, felt that he must not let this girl go.

'Yes you must, and I want to see Venice.'

'We will write no, we will write and you will come to Venice.'

It was as if a dam had broken. In those few, intimate seconds, it was like an electric shock setting off emotions he had not experienced before and he could see that she felt the same.

Ah memories, and now she was taking him home to meet her parents. He had not met them or seen the family house during his first visit to Venice. She had booked them into a pleasant little canalside hotel, away from prying eyes. 'For the next few days I want you to myself,' she had said. That was when they really began to get to know each other, when they were sure that they were in love and, a month later, she had flown to Edinburgh for a repeat performance. He smiled at that memory, her shock at the Scottish weather.

'Is this summer Rory? It's not as warm as Italy.'

'Aye, this is a Scottish summer and you're lucky we are having such a nice day. I worried that you might leave once you had experienced some typical Scottish weather.'

'Never mind the weather; it will be warm in bed.'

They had laughed; they were becoming used to each other, their lovemaking developing into something wonderful.

'Where are you going to take me, will I see the men in skirts, will I try whisky?'

'Hold on, the skirts are kilts and if you behave yourself I will buy you some of my family tartan.'

'What is that?'

'I'll show you later, first let's get to the hotel and settle in and then I'll take you out to dinner and feed you some haggis.'

'Haggis?'

Smiling at the memory, he felt the bump of the wheels on the tarmac as the aircraft touched down and a wave of excitement began to engulf him. Soon he was passing through passport control, and looking for Nadia. He could not miss her, waiting for him in the arrivals hall silhouetted against the glass entrance doors and waving her arm.

'Rory I miss you,' she said, embracing him and planting a kiss on his lips.

'I missed you too Nadia. It's good to be back, good to see you again. How's your family?'

'They are fine and they say they like to see you.'

'And your brothers, I guess I will get to meet them soon.'

'Don't ask. They are bad boys.'

'Oh . . . what's happened?'

'I tell you later, come I have tickets for the waterbus.'

Rory liked travelling by waterbus, the big clumsy craft with noisy engines called vaporettos. He liked them because they reminded him of the *Lurach-Aon* and as the vaporetto began to make its way across the lagoon, he took hold of Nadia's hand. Warm and soft he held it firmly and looked out across the water towards the spires and towers of Venice, wondering what the next few days might bring. Their relationship had developed into something serious and this time she had insisted he stay at the family home and the prospect had left him a little nervous.

'This is our stop,' said Nadia as the vaporetto bounced alongside a jetty.

Passengers began to stand ready to disembark. At first Rory did not move, his eyes fixed on the driver wrestling with the gears. The man was controlling the cumbersome beast, keeping it tight against the jetty, as the conductor secured the mooring line. Finally, Nadia convinced him to get up and as he passed the driving position he looked at the controls. He noticed how they differed from a fishing boat, but knew instinctively that he could handle such a craft.

Nadia and Rory disembarked at San Marco and made their way through the piazza, past white marble façades glowing in the late afternoon sun and Nadia, well versed in the intricacies of the narrow shaded streets, led the way.

'Where are we going, I thought you lived on the mainland?'

'To see Mamma, she has a shop here. Come, this way, it's not far,' said Nadia, turning to walk along a narrow canalside footpath.

Rory followed her over a small stone bridge where they negotiated the confusing interlocking streets towards the Grand Canal. Emerging at the canal side, Rory paused to watch passing water traffic. Venice was enthralling for him, its sights and sounds, the water taxis, delivery boats and vaporettos jostling for position along the waterways. Then there were the icons of the city, the gondolas propelled by the gondoliers in traditional attire.

Boats were Rory's first love and he marvelled at the sight. He heard a noise and looked up at the old buildings with their weather-worn shutters and peeling paintwork. A woman was retrieving her washing from a line strung across the narrow canal and calling to someone on the opposite side. Then his nose twitched as the smell of stagnant water reached his nostrils.

'Yes it can be a problem in summer,' said Nadia, catching his mood. 'Come we are nearly there.'

She crossed another stone bridge leading Rory towards a narrow shopping precinct, and half way along the street she stopped.

'Mamma, Mamma, *ciao*,' she called through the open door of a small jewellery shop.

'Nadia, is that you?'

'Yes Mamma, I have Rory with me,' she said, slipping back into English.

The curtains at the rear of the shop parted and Signora Foscari made an entrance fit for La Scala.

'Signor Rory, *ciao*, welcome to *Venezia*.'

'Thank you Mrs Foscari, nice to meet you,' said Rory holding out his hand.

Nadia's mother ignored the hand, came close and planted a light kiss on each of his cheeks. Standing back, she held his gaze for a second or two, a challenging look, and Rory knew that he would have his work cut out dealing with her.

'Mamma, we will come home with you, it is so much easier.'

'Good, maybe I get to know your friend a little better, learn what the English are really like eh,' she said with a twinkle in her eye.

The journey to the Foscari home was interesting; first, the vaporetto to the railway station and then the ride across the causeway to the mainland where Nadia's mother had parked her car. The last part of the journey to the family home took very little time and as the car turned into the drive, Rory looked the house over. It was an impressive, two-storey structure in the classic Italian style set in well-maintained gardens. Rory realised then that Nadia came from a wealthy family.

'I have a you room ready. Nadia, show him to his room,' said Signora Foscari as they entered the front door.

'Come Rory, I will show you to your room. Are we eating in or out tonight Mamma?'

'*Si* we eat at Luigi's at nine. I do not want to be cooking so we eat out. Papà will meet us there.'

Nadia's father was waiting at the restaurant, waving his arm as they entered. A thickset man wearing a smart business suit and Rory guessed he must be a professional, a lawyer or an accountant perhaps. And as they approached his table Nadia's mother took charge.

'Mario, order me a Cinzano and ice I've had a busy day,' then to Nadia and Rory, 'sit there.'

She seemed very different to Rory's mother, she was demanding, decisive, whereas his own mother had a gentler, thoughtful nature. Nadia's father raised his hand to summon the waiter, turned to his daughter and spoke to her in Italian.

'We will speak English in front of Rory, Papà, if you don't mind. He has no Italian. We will both have a glass of dry white wine.'

Her father nodded and when he had ordered their drinks, came to stand beside Nadia.

'This must be Rory, you a must introduce us Nadia.'

'Papà this is my friend Rory who I met in America.'

'Pleased to meet you,' said Rory offering his hand.

Nadia's father smiled and shook his hand, a necessarily brief introduction for Signora Foscari was one of the few people he could not ignore and she seemed to have plenty to say. Something was bothering her and it seemed Signor Foscari was the one to pacify her.

'I'm sorry Rory; please forgive my parents they are having an argument about my mother's shop. He promised to have someone come to fix the plumbing but no one has been and Mamma is scolding him.'

'Don't be telling everyone about my problem Nadia,' said her mother, breaking off her tirade.

'Sorry Mamma, but you are ignoring our guest.'

Francesca Foscari said nothing, her eyes stern, filling the air with tension until Nadia's father spoke.

'How was your flight, Nadia told me that you were to change at Barcelona?'

'Yes, it was the cheapest option. The flight was fine; it was the four hours I had to wait in Barcelona that was an inconvenience.'

'Well you are here now and you are with my daughter. She tells me every day that you are a good man.'

'Papà,' scolded Nadia. 'Papà you embarrass me. Are the boys joining us?' she added.

'No, they are away,' he said.

'Where are they this time, do you know Nadia?'

'No Mamma, they don't tell me much.'

The older woman's eyes clouded for a second or two and then she picked up the menu. '*Tagliatelle al frutti di mare* for me, the waiter says they have good fish today and he recommends it. What will you have Rory?'

'I think I will have the same. I am not very familiar with Italian food I'm afraid,' he said, hardly glancing at his menu.

'What is your job, how do you make a living?' quizzed Nadia's father.

'I work in the offshore oil industry, on a supply vessel.'

'And your family, what do they do?'

'Fishermen, we were fishermen until we lost the boat.'

Rory explained the loss, the accident, and then told them a little about the Western Isles, Lewis and about his family.

'That must have been a blow to your father, losing his livelihood.'

'It was to begin with but in the end he accepted it and looked to make a living onshore. He got a job on the fish farm and he gets by well enough.'

Again, Nadia's father nodded and was about to ask a further question when the food began to arrive and his wife took over the conversation.

'You like?' she asked Rory as he took his first mouthful

'Oh yes Mrs Foscari.

'You can call me Francesca, no need to be so formal. Nadia's father is Mario, no Mario?' she said to her husband.

His mouth full of food Signor Foscari could do little but nod agreement and sitting next to him his daughter smiled broadly. She had been apprehensive about her parents' first meeting with Rory but they seemed to have accepted him and that pleased her.

'You like Venice?' Francesca asked.

'Yes, what I've seen of it. Nadia showed me round last time but it was a bit of a whirlwind tour. Perhaps I will get to see more this time.'

'You must go to the islands, you will take him to the islands Nadia?'

'Yes Mamma and we will go to the Lido for one day, spend time on the beach. It is what the English like.'

Rory smiled at her, 'I keep telling you I'm not English.'

'Scottish, he is Scottish and doesn't like to be called English. A bit like us not wanting to be called Sardinian I suppose.'

Mario and Francesca nodded and then Francesca turned to her husband, speaking in Italian. '*Mi preoccupo per Franco.*'

'*Non adesso Francesca, parleremo di lui quando arriviamo a casa.*'

Rory did not understand the brief exchange, but the tone appeared to convey a conflict about Nadia's brother. The moment passed and the conversation turned to more mundane topics and when the time came to leave the restaurant Rory managed to ask Nadia, 'What was all that about?'

'I tell you one day, don't worry; it's not your problem.'

Venice - Day 2

It was past eight o'clock when Rory finally opened his eyes, stretched his arms over his head and looked at his watch. He was surprised he had slept so long. He looked at the white painted walls, the green shutters of his room; Nadia's home had taken him by surprise. Impressive in its size and architecture it was a more lavish residence than he had imagined. The ground floor consisted of two living rooms, a large dining room and a well-appointed kitchen. Each of the rooms contained elegant furniture and paintings on the walls, very different from his home on the Island of Lewis and Harris.

Guessing Nadia would already be up he climbed from the bed, dressed and made his way downstairs to find her in the dining room.

'*Ciao*,' she said as he entered, 'sit here and I will bring some breakfast for you. What would you like, bread and preserve I make myself or cereal?'

'I think bread and jam is just fine and can I have a cup of tea?'

'*Si*, of course. I know you like your tea you British.'

Just then, the sound of footsteps reached their ears and a good-looking, slightly-built man in his mid-twenties appeared.

'Ah Claudio, this is my eldest brother Rory, say hello Claudio.'

'*Ciao*, how are you?'

'I'm fine thank you.'

'You come to see my sister I think.'

'Er . . . yes,' said Rory holding out his hand.

'No problem, and you meet me now. Nadia bring me some coffee.'

Nadia frowned and pursed her lips, but she said nothing; instead, she placed the plate of freshly baked bread she was carrying in front of Rory and returned to the kitchen. Rory watched her go, mildly shocked at Claudio's manner but then he did not really know them, maybe that was how it was in Italy. He decided to engage Claudio in conversation.

'I hear you work on the water taxis Claudio.'

'Yes, I start work in one hour. It is our busy time with all the tourists, the city is getting full of them,' he said with some disdain.

Rory was surprised that he seemed so different to Nadia. She was talkative, so full of fun, sensible and friendly, yet he seemed moody and bad mannered and he began to wonder if he liked him. Then Claudio's attitude suddenly changed.

'Where you want to go Nadia, I take you in the taxi if you like.'

Nadia's eyes lit up. Claudio was being nice and it looked as if he did have his uses when it came to getting around Venice.

176

'Rory how would you like a ride in my brother's taxi?'

'Sounds good to me.'

Within the hour, they had crossed the causeway linking the mainland to the islands and walking through the station concourse, emerged into the sunshine. They descended a wide flight of steps onto the piazza where Claudio waved and called out to several passers-by.

'Your brother seems to know a lot of people.'

'Just about everyone, the boatmen must pass each other ten times a day on the water.'

Rory laughed; she was probably right, a good way to know everyone working on the boats. Claudio waved to yet another acquaintance and then he led them over a stone bridge towards several moored water taxis.

'This is a my boat,' he said proudly, removing a cover.

Rory could see why he was so proud. It was a beautiful boat with wooden planking so highly polished that it seemed made out of glass.

'You like?'

'I do, she's lovely,' said Rory, taking a look inside the cabin. 'It must have cost a bomb.'

'She no cost much, I have friends. Come and let me take you down the Grand Canal in style.'

For twenty minutes Rory sat beside Nadia on the white leather upholstery as canal traffic passed by on either side, an experience he would not easily forget. He revelled in being afloat, marvelled at the fine

Venetian buildings lining the canal until eventually the boat came to a stop alongside a hotel mooring where Claudio would collect his first fare of the day. It was where Rory and Nadia would have to step ashore and leave him to his work.

'You are quiet, is something wrong?' asked Nadia as they walked slowly along the canalside.

'Err . . . no, I was just wondering about your parents' disagreement last night. It seemed serious.'

'Is a problem with Franco, Papà worries he will get into serious trouble. He is young and how you say, flash, yes flash with the best clothes and his girlfriends. He has many girlfriends and he shows off, going to clubs and the Lido, spends more money than he earns I am sure.'

'What about Claudio, is he the same? He became pleasant enough once he had eaten his breakfast.'

'He is older, the eldest, and has a bit more sense I think. Not your problem and I do not want to talk about it anymore.'

'Hey I'm sorry, this is all new to me and I have no intention getting involved.'

'Good, then we don't talk about it again.'

Rory did not want to antagonise Nadia further and kept his peace, still he could not help feeling that there was something amiss.

The remainder of the day passed without incident and Rory began to enjoy simply sauntering through crowded streets in the Italian sunshine. They had no plans for his first day, just a visit to the Piazza San Marco like everyone else. Nadia showed him the sights; they lost themselves in the crowds, wandering wherever their fancy took them. Their relationship had blossomed and just being together was enough so they walked, talked, drank coffee, ate a pizza and in the early evening returned to Nadia's home.

'*Ciao*, I am preparing some pasta for dinner. It will be half an hour so go and pour yourselves a drink and bring me a Cinzano,' said Francesca as they walked into her kitchen.

'Where's Papà, is he home?'

'*Si*, he is in the garden. Go and see him, it will be good for him to know Rory a little more.'

'Do you want a beer Rory, I know you like a beer in the evening?'

'That would be nice, aye a beer please.'

Nadia poured her mother's drink and took a bottle out of the small fridge to give to Rory.

'Are you having a drink?'

'No, I will just have water for now,' she said, reaching up to kiss him. 'Go into the garden and find Papà and I will join you.'

A kilometre away Father Giuseppe was also in his garden. Kneeling, with his cassock gathered into a bundle between his legs as before crouching to meticulously scratch at the earth and remove weeds growing in the tiny plot.

'Dear lord I thank you for this wonderful garden you have provided for me and my congregation's enjoyment. You have made the flowers grow so beautifully and I thank you Lord, but could you see it in your heart perhaps to create not quite so many weeds? I am growing old and my knees are feeling the pain. Lord I am not complaining and I look forward to my journey into heaven but for the time I have left please could you make things a little easier?'

Father Giuseppe chuckled to himself, it was not a serious prayer, his complaint of hardship was tongue in cheek, for true believers carried their cross whatever and he was a true believer. In quiet, solitary moments though, he would often to speak with God one to one, discuss with him the problems of the day and causing more than one parishioner to wonder about his sanity.

The light was beginning to fade and he decided he should stop; he needed to return to the church to pray and close the doors for the night. Getting to his feet, he allowed his cassock to unravel, and walking a little unsteadily towards the rectory, oblivious to Franco and the other mafia soldier.

'Look there, Father Giuseppe, don't let him see us until we have finished. The store is just round here and no one must know what we are doing,' hissed Franco.

Franco's job was to the hide guns and explosives for the robbery and he congratulated himself on his judgement that no one would suspect the church. Il Capo had authorised fifty million lire for weapons, police uniforms and it was essential to keep everything out of sight and in a place without connection to the Family.

'Aldo keep your eyes open in case he comes back.'

The man nodded, following close behind Franco as the two of them made their way cautiously towards a small hut.

'Look here, the factotum's outhouse, where he stores his tools and building materials. For us it is ideal, but the lock is no more than a bent nail. You will need to replace that with something more secure. We have had a quiet word with the regular handyman, convinced him that it is in his interest to fall ill for a couple of weeks. While he is away, you will take his place and first, you must put a proper lock on the door. You can do that?'

'Yes, is no problem. I will attend to it first thing in the morning.'

'Good, it only remains for you to introduce yourself to Father Giuseppe. Let him know that you are working here until the regular man recovers. He is in the rectory so go there now and find him while I have a look round and I will meet you back at the car.'

Venice - Day 3

A motoscafo is a larger craft than a vaporetto, more stable in open water, the preferred transport for crossing the lagoon but for Rory, frustrating. The cockpit was above the passenger deck and he was unable to watch the driver manoeuvre the boat. Still, as it reversed away from the pontoon he could not help but be impressed. She was an old boat, her superstructure covered in flaking paint and she was showing signs of rust but she was powerful and that was what he liked.

'Today you have to sit here; maybe you pay me more attention than on the vaporetto.'

'I'm sorry, but these things fascinate me.'

'I can see. I never know anyone who likes the vaporetti as you do.'

'It's the *Lurach-Aon*; these boats are a little bit like her. Until we lost her she was my life.'

'I know, I am sorry, but you are alive and that is all that matters.'

Rory turned towards Nadia and put his arm around her shoulder, pulling her close.

'Today we don't worry about boats, today we have a good time on the beach and you can swim in the Adriatic for the first time. It will be warmer than your North Sea.'

'Everywhere is warmer than the North Sea,' he said, and sensing the engines begin to slow he stood up, leaned on the rail and watched as the craft came alongside the pontoon.

For the next few hours, they lay on the beach, splashed in the sea and Rory relaxed as he had never relaxed before.

'This is great, what a way of life you Italians lead. Does anyone around here work?' said Rory as he returned from swimming in the sea and flopped on the sand next to Nadia.

'Of course they do but we don't work like you or the Americans, we Italians know how to embrace *la dolce vita*.'

'The sweet life, at least I know that and I suppose it is okay for a while, but I would be bored just lounging about every day.'

'It's more than lounging about; it's about fun and love.'

'I suppose I could handle that,' he said, rolling over to smother her with his body.

'Oh . . . you are sandy, get off.'

'Only if you give me a kiss,' he said, sticking his fingers into her armpit and making her squeal.

'Ah . . . all right all right,' she said in mild panic, pursing her lips for him to kiss and Rory made the most of the moment.

He was happy, very happy, all the cares he had carried with him to Venice seemed to have evaporated, but after another hour in the sun, he had to admit that he could take no more and began pulling on his shirt.

'You are getting dressed?'

'Och, the sun is hot and I think I'm starting to burn. It's not a problem for you and your olive skin but I'm not used to it.'

'Let's go back then. It will take a while so we should be going soon anyway. We will take the motoscafo back to San Marco and the vaporetto along the Grand Canal. You like that Rory. I can see that every time we get on one you sit at the front and you never take your eyes off the driver.'

'They remind me of our old fishing boat, well the sound and feel of them anyway,' he said, gathering up his towel and swimming trunks.

Nadia did the same and together, holding hands, they left the beach, strolling in silence.

'Will you be a fisherman again?' Nadia said eventually.

'I don't know, fishing isn't what it used to be but I think I would like to give it a try.'

'And I will be a fisherwoman.'

'Ha ha, I doubt it, women don't go fishing and I don't think you would take to gutting and skinning fish very easily.'

Nadia pouted, feigned disappointment, and to Rory she looked so beautiful in the Venetian sunshine with her olive skin, bright brown eyes and dark hair cascading from the back of the red baseball

184

cap, a souvenir from Las Vegas and he knew then that he could never let her go.

'I fancy an ice cream,' she said.

'Yes, me too.'

Nadia pulled him across the street towards a gelateria. '*Stracciatella* for me, I like the little bits of chocolate.'

'And me, make it two.'

Taking the cones from the outstretched hand of the ice cream seller, they seductively licked their ice creams, eyes flashing in unspoken communication when suddenly an impish grin spread across Rory's face.

'You may not make a fisherwoman but you could be a clown,' he said, taking a small amount of ice cream on his finger and depositing it on the end of her nose.

If he supposed he was being clever he was sadly mistaken for Nadia reacted unexpectedly, pushing her half-eaten ice cream cone fully onto his nose before bursting into laughter.

'Now who is the clown, no you are Pinocchio and you are telling lies.'

For a few moments Rory's defences were down, his startled eyes wide open, his jaw sagging.

'I'm sorry, you are upset,' she said, taking the cone from his nose.

'No I'm not, in fact I'm impressed, I told you I like a woman with spirit.'

'Oh Rory I do love you,' she said, licking at the remains of her ice cream and passing her free arm round his.

'Nice of you to say so,' he said mockingly, wiping the remnants of the ice cream from his nose.

She grimaced, her eyes flashing in pretend hurt and then her face broke into a smile. She was happy, happy she had met the big Scotsman who made her laugh and made her feel safe. They had known each other for only a short time but she was beginning to believe that Rory was the man with whom she wanted to spend the rest of her life. However, there was a problem, if he felt the same about her then there were secrets she would have to share with him.

The terracotta tiled roof and spacious gardens of Nadia's house had made an impression upon Rory the moment he had set eyes upon it. He liked the neatly cropped hedges, the small individual flowerbeds and the mock Roman fountain in the centre of it all.

'You like the garden?' said Nadia, noticing how he looked at it.

'Yes it's lovely.'

'You are a romantic I think.'

'More the fact that we canna grow plants like this, just wee things in amongst the heather.'

'What a shame, never mind I will fetch you a beer,' she said, leading the way inside. Rory followed, unable not to glance back at the garden and it struck him again that the Foscaris must have money. They walked into the house and past the kitchen where Francesca was busy cooking.

'Just in time, your father will be home in a minute and your brother is here,' she said.

'Franco?'

'*Si* Franco.'

Nadia's eyes flashed and she looked at Rory.

'We should shower, it was hot today and I am salty from swimming in the sea. I will knock on your bedroom door when I am ready. We come back in half an hour Mamma.'

'No later, dinner is nearly ready.'

They left Nadia's mother stirring a large pan of pasta and after they had gone upstairs Franco appeared at the kitchen door.

'I heard voices, is Nadia back?'

'Yes, and she has her English boyfriend with her.'

'English boyfriend? I did not know she had an *English* boyfriend. How long has this been going on?'

'He is a nice boy; he is staying with us for a few days.'

'What, why does nobody tell me this?'

'Because Franco you are hardly ever here these days.'

'I come and go as I want Mamma, you know that.'

'Well you know now and don't go teasing her, she likes him.'

He frowned and returned to the living room but before he could settle again, his mother called out.

'Make yourself useful Franco, set the table and open a bottle of wine. We have a guest for dinner and I want to show him proper Italian hospitality.'

Franco grunted, more used to giving orders these days than taking them. When it came to his mother though, he had no defence.

'You have the way of an artist Franco, the table looks beautiful,' said Francesca looking over his handiwork. 'I will finish the cooking and we will eat.'

She returned to her kitchen and for a while Franco returned to his television until he heard footsteps on the stairs. He was not happy, Nadia with a foreigner was not right, she was a good-looking girl and she should belong to a mafia boss, someone who could guarantee his promotion.

'Franco, this is Rory, come and say hello.'

Nadia always tried to speak English in front of Rory, to make him feel at ease, and Franco spoke some English too but was not about to prove it.

Rory held out his hand, 'Pleased to meet you Franco.'

Franco grunted and said something in Italian to his sister causing her face to redden and she snapped back at him. What it was all about Rory had no idea but he guessed he was part of it. Then Franco's mood seemed to change and he held out his hand.

'Hello,' he said, but his eyes were steady and unwelcoming.

The atmosphere was tense, Nadia was upset and Rory had little understanding of why that might be. Why was Franco so moody and uncooperative? Then he heard the front door open.

'We are in here Papà,' said Nadia, seeking parental support.

'Nadia,' said her father entering the room, and seeing Franco spoke briefly to him in Italian. Franco pouted, replied fleetingly and left the room. 'Rory you have had a good day in Venice?'

'Yes, Nadia took me to the beach and showed me the Lido.'

'Good, good, and you Nadia, you have helped your mother.'

'We have only just returned from the islands, Mamma said she can manage. I think dinner is just about ready.'

'Claudio, is he here? Your mother said he was coming home early to have dinner with us and your friend Rory.'

'No Papà, Claudio isn't here yet.'

'Hmm . . . I will go and refresh myself before dinner and hope your brother turns up.'

Claudio finally arrived when they were half way through dinner, breathless and apologetic. He kissed his mother on the cheeks and then he spoke in Italian to his father.

'It sounds nothing, we will talk about it later, in the meantime sit and enjoy this wonderful dinner your mother has prepared,' he said in English.

Claudio nodded and Rory noticed the look he gave his brother. The two men had spoken little English and he had not followed the conversation, but it was obvious from Nadia's face that she had and something was wrong.

'Here, more pasta Rory, you are a big man and need a lot of food. You like my pasta?'

'Oh very much Francesca,' said Rory, holding his plate towards her for a second helping. 'Most of the Italian food I eat comes from a tin or a takeaway. This is very good I have to say.'

Francesca beamed as she spooned more of the pasta onto Rory's plate and he took great pleasure in sprinkling the grated cheese over the food in the Italian way. He liked Italy and, apart from Franco, he liked Italians.

'Nadia help me with the dishes while the men sit in the garden, and then you and Rory can take an evening stroll,' said Francesca.

'*Si* Mamma.'

'Come Rory, let me fill your glass and we will sit a while and watch the sun go down. The sunsets at this time of year are very nice. You can tell us about your home and what it is like,' said Mario.

'It's certainly a lot colder than here, and wet. It rains all the time,' said Rory holding out his glass.

'You like Italy?' asked Claudio coming to join them.

'Yes, what I've seen of it. I have only been here a few days but your way of life seems very relaxed.'

'Where is Franco, I want to talk to him?' said Mario, looking round for his younger son.

'He went to his room for something, he will be along soon,' said Claudio.

Mario nodded and led the way into the garden, Rory joined him but few words passed between them, something was obviously on Mario's mind and Rory began to feel that perhaps they did not want him around. He felt awkward, wondered what to do until Nadia put in an appearance and rescued him. She had tied her hair in a ponytail and she was carrying a bright red jumper.

'Come Rory, we will go for a walk so your food can settle.'

He needed little persuading and feeling relieved to escape the tense atmosphere followed her into the garden and away from the house.

'Is everything all right with your family Nadia, things seemed stressed and Franco doesn't like me, does he?'

'Ah Franco, he is a wayward boy, always has been. Be careful with him Rory he has some bad friends.'

'What do you mean?'

Nadia fell silent, she knew a little of Franco's dealings with the mafia, even suspecting her father was involved.

'You have gone very quiet.'

'Yes, I am thinking. There are things you should know and things you should not know.'

'Such as?'

'This is serious Rory; Franco is a violent man and I know he is always in trouble.'

'Trouble, with the police?'

'Sometimes the police, though mostly his own kind. He has come home covered in blood and bruises more than once. You are only here for a few days; keep away from Franco and all will be well I think.'

'What about Claudio?'

'Rory I cannot tell you anymore, I simply want to keep you safe and the easiest way for that is for you to keep away from Franco. We are having a good time together and I do not want him to spoil things.

Let's just enjoy the rest of your stay and next time I come to your island and meet your mother.'

'That would be nice. She asks about you, she would like to meet you and I want to show you off.'

'Silly boy, show me off. We are getting serious I think?'

'I think so too.'

Mario was concerned at Claudio's news that the police were making life difficult for the water taxis with demands to see driver's licences and permits. The clan had control of the water taxi business – made millions of lire each week and an investigation was the last thing they wanted.

'What is the trouble with the water taxis Claudio, are the police involved or is it just the municipality?'

'Both, and there were lots of them.'

Mario sat back in his seat, thoughtful, concerned. His job as the local mafia's banker was to keep an eye on the organisation's finances, launder it to reinvest in regular businesses. If the police from Padua were involved then it could mean real trouble because no more than a handful of them were on the organisation's payroll. The city of Venice police were different; almost every local commander and city official was receiving money or favours from them. If the problem was with the local police force he felt sure he could brush it aside but why the sudden interest? Could it be they had information about the pending robbery?

'You can still operate?'

'Yes, we have several days to produce our paperwork or be closed down. I am not worried.'

'And you Franco, will it affect you, this investigation.'

'I don't know. If it is only about the water taxis then no. I have nothing to do with them.'

'Fill my glass Claudio.'

Claudio took his father's glass and walked towards the house his brother alone with their father.

'Franco I have money available for guns and bribes but if this probe into the taxi licences is a cover for a wider investigation, we must be extra careful. I have heard nothing from the local police so it worries me that maybe the anti-mafia police are involved and they are less susceptible to bribes or threats.'

Roberto was tired; he had been on the go since six that morning and it was almost midnight yet he had decided to take one last look at the Foscari home. From the shadows, he studied the house, could see two figures in the garden but they were too far away for him to catch any of the conversation. Then the sound of feet on the pavement alerted him.
A couple were walking slowly towards him and he had to fade deeper into the shadows. They drew level, talking quietly, and as they entered the garden he heard the woman say Papà. So, were they part of the Foscari clan, the woman a daughter, a relative? Who was the man, he did not look Italian? He considered creeping closer, but these were dangerous men and he was tired. Working alone made him vulnerable and he could not risk discovery. Then he had an idea,

he would go to the church, find a pew on which to lie down and catch up on some much-needed rest. In the morning, he would have a good look round; see if he could get any closer to finding out what Franco and his friends were up to.

Walking quickly he reached the church, pushed open the heavy wooden door and made his way towards the Alter and lay down on a hard wooden bench. It was a fitful but much needed respite and hours later, as the sunlight began to stream through the stained glass windows. His eyelids twitched and adjusting his position, he began to wake, looking up at the ceiling and feeling the numbness in his back. His body was not as supple as it had once been; he was getting too old for this sort of work, the numbness caused by the hard wooden pew a stark reminder. Then he heard noise and opened his eyes wide. A door was opening; he heard the sound of a voice and was instantly awake, peering over the back of the pew. Breathing a sigh of relief, he saw that it was Father Giuseppe who had entered the church and was uttering a few words of prayer.

Swinging his legs off the pew, Roberto slipped to his knees and by the time Father Giuseppe drew level he was mumbling a prayer of his own. The priest noticed the scruffy, unkempt man and, taken aback for a moment, stood looking at him. Another poor soul down on his luck, he thought.

'Good morning my son, I see you have come to worship God. That is a good sign for although you may be troubled you still have faith and that is to be commended.'

'Thank you Father, yes I still have my faith; I still look for divine guidance whenever I am in need.'

'And you are in need?'

'Yes, I lost my job, there is little work and I cannot earn enough to keep body and soul together. I have no money Father and I have no choice but to live on the streets, but I manage.'

'You poor man, you are welcome here at any time. Have you eaten? You must come with me and I will give you bread, feed you as Jesus fed those in need.'

'Thank you Father I would appreciate that. I have not eaten for more than twenty-four hours.'

'Come with me my son and I will feed you.'

Roberto did as the priest told him, following the old man to his living quarters, sitting on a bench whilst Father Giuseppe went to find him something to eat. For a few minutes, he was alone in the churchyard and he wondered then just what Franco's connection with this church was.

'Here you are young man, some bread and Parma ham, the best, and a coffee,' said the priest returning with his hands full.

'Thank you Father, you have been most kind.'

'It is my work; I am here to help anyone in need no matter what. And now my son, I must go about my duties, I have another visitor coming to see me this morning, a young man who I thought we had lost but he has returned to the church, a nice young man called Franco.'

Franco! The mere mention of the name was enough to jolt Roberto and he knew then that he was onto something.

195

'Franco, is he a local man?'

'But of course, he grew up here but he has not been back to the church for many years. He wants to become involved again; I am pleased and will welcome him with open arms.'

'Oh, how will he help the church Father?'

'He says he can help with the restoration of the vestry, the walls are crumbling and in need of repair, he will recruit volunteers to help.'

Roberto was intrigued, Franco was no builder and he doubted any of his friends were either so what was he really doing?

Venice - Day 4

Nadia hardly slept for worrying. Rory was a good man, hardworking and she did not want him becoming involved with Franco. In Italy the mafia was a way of life for some, you accepted it and got on with things but Rory was different – he would not understand.

Rubbing her eyes, she rose from her bed, showered and after dressing went downstairs.

Rory was already in the dining room and greeted her with '*Ciao*' as she appeared and for all her worries, his tentative attempt at Italian brought a smile to her face.

'You are up early, where is everyone?'

'Your mother is in the kitchen, I don't know where your father or your brothers are.'

'*Ciao* Nadia,' said Francesca entering the room carrying a large coffee pot. 'You want some breakfast?'

'Yes Mamma, just some bread and honey.'

'What have you two got planned for you today?'

'We are going to ride down the Grand Canal on the vaporetto; Rory just loves riding on the vaporettos.'

'Vaporettos, they are a strange thing to like.'

'He says it reminds him of his fishing boat.'

Francesca laughed, who else would give the vaporetti a second thought. 'Well, have a good time; I have to leave for work soon. When Franco and Claudio get up give them some breakfast and keep them from bothering your father. Something is on his mind and when he is in that kind of mood, it is best to leave him alone. He is in the garden.'

'Oh Mamma, we would like to come with you to the station,' said Nadia in a tone Rory had never before heard.

Francesca pouted. 'Then they will just have to fend for themselves.'

Nadia seemed angry, and after her mother left the room, he asked her, 'What is the matter Nadia?'

'Nothing, I tell you later maybe. Get your things and we will go but first I will speak with my father.'

Nadia finished her coffee and went into the garden to look for Mario, Rory to gather up the dirty cups and plates. As he filled the sink with water, he caught sight of Nadia and her father, too far away for him to overhear, but he could see that she was upset. Mario placed a hand on each of her shoulders and spoke to her as if to assuage her of something.

'What was that all about?' he asked as she returned to the house.

'Nothing, I am just making sure you are not involved in anything you shouldn't be.'

'Why should I become involved?'

'Never mind, my brothers are still in bed so let's go and have a wonderful day together.'

Her mood changed, she seemed happy and carefree once more and after Francesca had kissed Mario goodbye the three of them left for Venice.

Franco was just rising as they departed. He had remained chatting with his father until well into the night when Mario had informed him of a worrying development. Franco's father knew certain police and local officials who could provide inside information. After hearing of the investigation into the taxi licences he had discovered that the anti-mafia police were somehow involved and it worried him and Franco remembered his words.

'Franco, the police and the anti-mafia brigade are looking at us more closely than ever before. National politics are mostly to blame and here in Venice the local police do not want the tourist industry disrupted by our activities. They should understand that we are the glue that holds Venice together. Without our involvement, there would be chaos, even so, if they are coming after us I am warning you to be careful. You remember a similar investigation two years ago. It decimated the leadership and put most of them in prison. You did not know it then, but I was one of the lucky ones, always in the shadows so the investigation did not reveal my involvement. It looks as if we might have a similar situation so we need to be extra careful. The bank robbery will help buy drugs from the Serbian mafia and pay bribes to ensure that the local police leave us alone.'

Their net was spreading wider and it was inevitable that the anti-mafia police would at some time show an interest in them. Perhaps someone had informed on them, Franco did not know but what he did know was that he should be extra vigilant and with that thought in mind he went downstairs, surprised to see his brother.

'Claudio, you are late this morning.'

'Today is a quiet day, the cruise ships have gone and the tourists are running out of money. Tomorrow will be busy. And you, what are you doing these days, I here you are no longer a tax collector?'

'No, a promotion and soon, my brother, I will be a rich man.'

'You have been saying that since you were a fourteen-year-old flower seller.'

Franco's eyes flashed.

'You will see. I will be more than a taxi driver like you.'

Claudio's grin receded, he had always teased his younger brother but when Franco's expression hardened as it did now, he retreated, well aware of Franco's reputation for violence.

'I wish you luck my brother. When you get your Ferrari I want to be the first to ride with you.'

Franco visibly relaxed, his eyes softened at the mention of the marque. Always he'd had a dream to own a Ferrari, show off to the girls – 'it is an Italian man's destiny', he would say.

'It is time I left for work; there will be plenty of people still wanting a taxi, still time to make some money,' said Claudio and when the door closed behind him Franco sat alone with his thoughts. The plan for the robbery was coming together; it was time to visit the Church of the Virgin Mary and check on the contents of the shed.

Father Giuseppe was sitting at the front of the church reading his prayer book when he arrived. Keeping out of the old priest's sight he carefully went round to the side of the building and towards the factotum's hut. Aldo had fitted a new padlock to replace the bent nail and trying the door, he felt pleased the hiding place was secure. For several minutes, he looked over the shed, thought about filling it with the tools for the job and wondered who might possibly see them when he saw Father Giuseppe approaching, and this time there was no escape.

'Franco you have prayed already?'

'It is a beautiful day Father and I could not resist coming to the church to pray and to admire your flowers. The colours, their fragrances are just wonderful and particularly enjoyable at the moment.'

'Thank you my son. I had another visitor yesterday who told me the same, a man down on his luck but a devout Catholic who had come very early to pray. I took him to the rectory to give him sustenance and he admired the flowers just as you do.'

Franco's ears pricked up, a destitute man, here, early in the morning. 'What did this man look like?'

Father Giuseppe described Roberto as well as he could, from the stubble on his chin to his clothes. Franco remembered someone of that description and began to wonder if it was it the same man he had noticed at the station and near the canal. He

201

remembered the warning his father had given him and he made a mental note to keep a lookout for this stranger because if the man were following him, if he was spying on him, prying into his affairs, he would need to eliminate him.

'If he returns will you let me know Father, it may be that with my connections he can be taken care of?'

'Of course my son, any help you can give the downtrodden will be looked upon with favour from above,' said the priest, looking skyward and entirely misinterpreting Franco's meaning.

'Thank you Father, now I will spend some time praying before I leave.'

Father Giuseppe smiled and nodded, turning his attention to the condition of his plants. It had been a dry month and he needed to water them.

Roberto was feeling the strain; after more than twenty hours on the go, he needed to rest. He had a base in Mestre, a small rented flat not far from the railway station that he used when the work was less demanding or he needed to recover as he did now. When he was working on the islands he would catch a few hours' sleep at one of the homeless shelters run by the City Angels, but tonight he would sleep in the flat.

Climbing the concrete staircase, to his flat he felt for the key hidden in a crack in the wall. His mind was troubled, if the local mafia were dealing with the Cosa Nostra then drugs, guns or both were surely involved. They were planning something, Franco Foscari was a big part of it he was sure, and if they could only catch him in some act of criminality . . . If they could, they might learn of the mafia's intentions and send Franco and his associates to prison. He wanted them all locked up, for his country to be rid of the cancer that was destroying it.

The captain had mentioned that he looked in need of a rest. 'Take a day off, stay in bed, watch some television,' he had said but Roberto could not relax. He was tired, he was in need of a few hours' rest, but he was not taking time off, this was his chance to strike back on behalf of his brother and all the other victims of the evil organisation.

Letting himself in his first task was to fill the coffee machine then he then went into the small bathroom and cleaned himself up. Three days without a wash had taken its toll but after several minutes under the shower, he emerged feeling refreshed and for a time sat with his coffee analysing the events of the past few days. He closed his eyes, tried to remember everything that had happened and wondered about Franco's next move.

He took a morbid pleasure in observing the comings and goings of the criminal class, reporting what he saw on the streets and canals of Venice, but working alone was exhausting him weary, lonely. The job demanded anonymity and his ability to move around the city with impunity had proved invaluable in the hunt for mafia thugs like Franco Foscari.

Finishing his coffee, he lay down on the bed to catch a few hours' sleep and for a while, he was oblivious to the world until a car door, slamming shut in the street below disturbed him. Rubbing the sleep from his eyes, he switched on the bedside light and looked at his cheap watch. It was one-thirty in the morning, he had slept for five hours, enough to leave him feeling rested and he contemplated venturing outside. What he might achieve at such an early hour he was not sure.

For a while, he pondered the question, finally deciding that he would leave the apartment, look at both the Foscari household and the church to see what he could turn up. Rising from his bed, he dressed in his well-worn clothing, looked in the mirror and smeared a tiny amount of black shoe polish over his face. He still had his disguise; the grubby persona staring back at him would not easily draw attention.

The Foscari household was almost two kilometres distant. It meant Roberto making his way through the dimly lit streets of his poor neighbourhood and across the deserted motorway to the more affluent area on the outskirts. Approaching the house, he noticed a solitary light burning but other than that, the place was in darkness. For several minutes he stood in the shadows looking the place over, finally parting the hedge and pushing his way through to creep closer. Moving stealthily he peered into windows searching for anything that might help him determine what was going on. The lack of light was a hindrance; he could see very little inside the house and decided that maybe it would be more profitable to look round the grounds. The double garage looked interesting and making his way furtively towards it he suddenly stopped. The sound of an approaching car had alerted him and crouching in the shadows he waited for it to pass.

Instead of passing by the car stopped at the gate and a figure of a man got out. In the gloom Roberto could not easily make out the person, perhaps it was Franco. He strained his eyes for a better look as the man opened the gate but shadows masked his features. The car drove into the grounds towards the garage before coming to a halt and the figure walked towards it, his feet crunching the gravel.

Creeping closer, Roberto watched as the man opened the driver's door and a woman emerged. They embraced, he heard her giggle and say something before the man bent her backwards and kissed her on the neck, then arm in arm they walked to the house. A light came on as they entered and he could see them more clearly, could see that the man was not Franco. He was taller, more muscular, with light-coloured hair that was not in the dark slicked-back style of a mafioso.

For several minutes the couple remained out of sight inside the house, before finally the woman re-emerged leading the man by his hand. Each carried a wine glass and passed only a few metres from where Roberto was hiding to sit on a garden seat. She spoke first, in English, a language Roberto understood marginally and from what he could hear it seemed she was Franco's sister and the man her boyfriend.

'You need to improve your dancing if you want to keep me Rory.'

'I know I have two left feet but if you think I'm going to prance about like some of your Italian men you are very much mistaken.'

'I tease you, you are not so bad. Kiss me again.'

The man reached over, held her head with his free hand and kissed her firmly on the lips. So, they were lovers, Franco's sister and this mysterious Englishman. What was he doing here, was there a British criminal connection and were the British working with the local mafia? He had no idea and before he could find out anymore they returned to the house, Roberto alone and feeling there was little else he could achieve by staying.

Carefully he retraced his steps and after a final glance around set off for the church. He found the big solid door unlocked and stood for a moment, listening, all was quiet, and so he pushed it open. He was alone and had the chance to look wherever he wanted and began by peering under pews and behind shelving but could find nothing particularly unusual. Maybe his suspicions were misplaced and yet he knew that Franco's actions were out of character. It was unusual for a man like him to visit a church on a regular basis, so there must be something in this church or the grounds that was capturing his attention and Roberto wanted to know what it was.

It was still very early, he felt there was little else he could do and so for the next few hours he lay on a pew and closed his eyes. He did not sleep, his mind was too active for that, and once the hands on his watch announced that it was six o'clock he decided the time right to visit the rectory and see if Father

Giuseppe had risen from his bed. Perhaps he could convince the priest to give him another breakfast and maybe he could manage a closer look at the rectory itself.

He slipped out of the church, turned the corner towards the rectory and noticed for the first time the small shed tucked away in a corner. At first sight it looked unremarkable except that it had a brand new padlock and to Roberto's inquisitive eyes that made it worth investigating. Walking quickly towards the shed he examined the lock, saw that it was of good quality, secure and difficult to open without the key. He had some knowledge of defeating such a device but he would need the specialist key of a locksmith and that he did not have. Frustrated, he looked around for something that might help him and as his gaze passed over the ground a metallic object half hidden in the grass drew his attention. Stooping down he saw a round of live ammunition, larger than that for a handgun, and his heart missed a beat. This was a significant discovery: it looked very much as if the mafia were storing automatic weapons here in this little shed.

Venice - Day 5

It was past ten o'clock when Rory finally awoke and his first thoughts were that time was running out, only three more days before he would fly back to Scotland. Nadia had said that today they would simply wander the streets and canals, maybe take a ride in a gondola, and visit Murano to see the famous glassworks, and he looked forward to that.

'So you have finally risen have you?' said Nadia as he walked into the kitchen.

'Sorry, I must have overslept but we did get in rather late last night.'

'What do you want for breakfast? I put the coffee on as soon as I heard you on the stairs.'

'Whatever you're having.'

Nadia pushed her plate towards him.

'I didn't mean literally.'

'Eat, I will cut some more bread but first I get your coffee and when you finish we will take a taxi to the station, I will ring for one.' She liked looking after Rory; it was becoming a natural part of their relationship. 'I have enjoyed these few days together

Rory, you have met my family and I think they like you, Mamma does.'

'What about your brothers? Claudio has been friendly enough but Franco has been positively hostile.'

'He is an angry man, he wants money and he does not care who he hurts to get it. He mixes with some bad people and I don't like it, he will finish up in big trouble one day I think.'

'Let's not worry about Franco; I'm sure he can take care of himself, maybe . . .'

Rory did not get to finish his sentence, interrupted as he was by the toot toot of the taxi's horn.

'Come, we have just enough time to catch the next train,' Nadia said, picking up her handbag, and before long they were journeying across the causeway.

Rory gazed from the train window and across the lagoon towards the airport reflecting on the past few days. He liked the city, the waterways, the hustle and bustle of the crowds, but above all he had enjoyed his time with Nadia. He was a happy man and when the train ended its journey at the Santa Lucia railway station, he led her with pride onto the piazza. Below them canal boats manoeuvred back and forth, all around stallholders filled pathways and open spaces imploring them to buy postcards and masquerade masks. Rory was finding it hard to refuse but Nadia took charge, telling him the prices were outrageous, she knew where to buy the same souvenirs at half the price. After negotiating the street market, the couple crossed a bridge and made their way towards the Grand Canal.

'You want to go on the water don't you?'

'I wouldn't mind.'

'We will save the gondola until later but first I will take you to Murano to see the glassmakers. The vaporetto stop is not far away.'

Rory's eyes lit up at the prospect. Of all his experiences of the past few days, riding those powerful boats were the ones that stood out.

'There look, the stop. Come on we need to buy our tickets before it arrives and I think it is that one coming,' Nadia said, pointing towards a yellow waterbus ploughing through the water.

They quickened their pace and just in time joined the short queue of people stepping aboard. Rory looked on with envy as the boat's engine roared, admiring the skill of the driver holding the craft close to the landing stage.

'I knew you would sit here,' said Nadia laughing at Rory who had found a place close to the driver. 'You will have plenty of time to enjoy the ride, Murano is a way off.'

'I will treat you to some glass for taking me there.'

'No, it's too expensive. My father has connections with the glassmakers, he brings home some of the things they make. I will give *you* some when we get back to the house.'

Mario Foscari's connection with the glassworks of Murano was not as Nadia imagined. As accountant for the local mafia it was part of his job to inspect the glassmakers' books. Il Capo did not trust anyone except a few of his closest associates but he trusted Mario. They had known each other since they were boys and Mario would let him know whether the businesses of Murano were paying the right amount of protection money or not.

Purely by chance, at the same time as Nadia and Rory were making their way to the island, Mario was in the office of Luigi Ranieri poring over his ledger.

'You keep your books well Luigi. I see you have had a good month with your sales up on last year.'

'Yes but I have to pay my glassblowers more. They are a dying breed; the young men are looking for work elsewhere these days, where they can earn more.'

'We are fair Luigi you know that and we will take into account your extra overheads but from what I see there will have to be an increase of one million lira a month.'

'What! One million, you will put me out of business.'

Mario looked at Luigi and could see that he was genuinely alarmed.

'Okay Luigi, five hundred thousand a month extra starting today and, if your sales drop off, we will look again. We don't want to kill our golden goose do we?'

'No, thank you Mario,' said a worried-looking Luigi, breaking into a sweat.

Caught between losing his business and having a leg broken he was not having a pleasant time of it.

'Franco will be coming to the island soon, I will tell him of our new arrangement.'

'Franco?'

'Yes, he has changed jobs and for a while he is the tax collector on Murano.'

Luigi knew of Franco, was aware of the mafioso's aggressiveness because their paths had crossed before. He had held back on a payment when working for his uncle several years previously and had the scar to prove it. He did not like Franco, feared him and wondered where he could lay his hands on the extra five hundred thousand lira.

After making several stops along the way, the vaporetto carrying Nadia and Rory finally arrived at the island of Murano.

'Enough of pretending to drive the waterbus, let's go and have a look around. There is much to see, the glassblowers put on a show so you can see how they do it.'

Nadia took hold of Rory's hand and pulled him away from the vaporetto. She had grown up in Venice, ridden the vaporetti hundreds of times, and she was a girl, mechanical things were of no interest to her. Reluctantly Rory followed her from the boat, joining a crowd of tourists wandering aimlessly along the waterfront.

'There is a show in this factory in ten minutes. I take you inside to watch the glassblowers,' said Nadia, eyeing an expensive piece of glass.

A hundred metres away a small motor boat with three men on board was edging effortlessly into a private mooring. A man jumped ashore, securing the boat to the narrow jetty, and another appeared from the small cabin. The third was Franco Foscari, filling in his time collecting taxes until they were ready to rob the bank and then he would have to produce the guns. He had safely hidden them away, the guns together with the police uniforms and dynamite in the church grounds ready for the order to go. Meanwhile Il Capo was utilising his skills amongst the glassblowers of Murano.

'Papà,' he said, surprised to see Mario appear from one of the factory shops. 'What are you doing here?'

'The same as you Franco. I have a list here of the rents to be paid and you, as the rent collector, will need it. I have finished auditing everyone's books and for some I have increased their payments. Here, take it and see what you can do while I hitch a ride back to Venice.' He handed Franco the sheet of paper and stepping aboard the motor boat and pointing at the driver said, 'He will be back for you in two hours.'

The glassblowers' demonstration was interesting enough for Rory and as it concluded he and Nadia left to walk along the waterfront when Nadia suggested they stop at a café.

'We can order a coffee and sit in the sunshine, watch the world go by.'

'You Italians have an easy life.'

'It's the weather I think, who wants to work when the weather is like this?'

'You have a point I must admit. I don't think I have ever, in my life, drunk so much coffee or just sat around doing nothing.'

213

'You are here to see me and see how I live; it's much easier here than Australia or in the casinos of Las Vegas. There I was expected to work all the time, very few coffee breaks then.'

'Yes you did work hard. It's a good job you did or I would never have found you.'

Their eyes met, the conversation halted abruptly and memories of that first meeting invaded their minds. Happiness spread across their faces and for a time they held hands, just enjoying each other's company.

'We should go soon if we are to have that gondola ride.'

Rory nodded and attracted the attention of the waitress to settle the bill.

'What will you do when I am gone Nadia, without a job you will be bored?' he said, as they strolled slowly towards the vaporetto stop.

'I could ask Papà for some money to go round the world again; I think that would fill in my time.'

'I think it would but I don't like the idea of chasing round the world just to see you again.'

'Ha, once was enough. I need to go back to school I think.'

'To do what?'

'Cooking.'

'Cooking, working in a kitchen all hot and stuffy, are you sure? Maybe you will eat too much and get fat. Yuk, I don't like the sound of that.'

'You don't like me fat?'

'No way, Jose, I like you just the way you are.'

Nadia giggled, her big brown eyes sparkling in fun. 'I want to open my own restaurant; I want to be a chef.'

'*Really*,' said Rory in surprise. 'Here in Venice?'

'Maybe, I do not know but if I go to school and learn to be a chef then maybe.'

'Well at least you will not be wasting your time and if you can cook anything like your mother does customers will be queueing at the door.'

She smiled and her eyes glazed over as ambition took root.

'I can see that you mean it,' said Rory, hardly noticing the vaporetto pulling up against the landing stage.

Finally, he turned to watch the boat begin its gyrations. The conductor jumped ashore with a line in his hand, steadied himself and began wrapping the stout rope about a capstan as one by one the passengers began to step ashore. Next, it was the turn of the returning travellers to board; Rory was last on and to his displeasure saw someone had already taken his favourite seat. He decided to stand in the aisle, looked back at the conductor holding his rope, and then, quite suddenly, the vaporetto lurched sideways and threw the man off balance. The violent action snatched the line from his grip him stranded and instinctively Rory knew that something was seriously wrong.

He turned to see the driver slumped forward, realised that he must have suffered some sort of seizure and had lost control of the vaporetto. The memory of the *Lurach-Aon* sinking was never far from his mind, and just as he had done then he reacted automatically. Stepping forward he reached the driver just as the vaporetto began to spin out of control away from the jetty and into the channel at an ever-increasing speed. Rory could see a disaster in the making and quickly pulled open the half door of the driving position, and using all his strength hauled the unconscious man out into the aisle.

Several women began to scream which threw everyone else into a state of panic. Rory did not hear them, instead, single-minded and determined, he slid into the driving seat and took control of the bucking beast. He glanced out of the window; saw the vaporetto was on a collision course with other boats in the channel, and knew it was vital he alter course as quickly as possible. Their only chance of avoiding catastrophe was for him to slam the gears into reverse and attempt to steer away. He had an idea of how the controls worked and with his mind racing, pushed a lever and throwing the gears into reverse. The engine growled in pain and fighting with the wheel, he managed to bring the boat back under control.

Onshore the conductor was busy raising the alarm. People stopped to watch and amongst them were Franco and his henchman.

'I think there will be a big accident Maurizio. That vaporetto is going to hit the motor boat.'

Maurizio said nothing, his attention, like that of Franco, focused on the impending collision. However, there was no collision; Rory's boat handling skills were good enough to avert disaster.

He twisted and turned the big vaporetto as if it were a mere dinghy and steered it from danger. He had quickly grasped the significance of the controls and this, together with his outstanding seamanship, had made sure they avoided disaster.

It was a close run thing as the vaporetto missed the other boats by a whisker but eventually he brought it under control and steered towards clear water to turn and return to the landing stage. It was a marvel to watch – the crowd onshore cheered, the relieved passengers on the vaporetto joined in and on the landing stage, the conductor stood open-mouthed. Soon the boat returned to its rightful place and relieved, he reached for the mooring line to secure it. Inside a German passenger helped Rory lift up the unconscious driver and together they carried him onto the wooden pontoon decking. Releasing him Rory stood up and Nadia could not help but throw her arms around his neck and kiss him fully on the lips.

'Rory you are a hero, I love you even more.'

Rory said nothing, standing still, letting his emotions subside.

'That was close; I hope he is okay. He must have had a heart attack or something.'

'A doctor is coming I think.'

Several metres away Franco looked on, anger written across his face as his sister embraced Rory. He did not approve of her courting a foreigner or kissing in public and unable to contain himself he pushed through the crowd to face the couple.

'Nadia what are you doing, come away, leave that Englishman.'

Rory looked across at Franco and with adrenalin still coursing through his veins, squared up to him.

'I am Scottish you Italian Sassenach. And leave your sister alone.'

For once, he was not prepared to take insults from Franco who was now red-faced and appeared ready to boil over. Then the man at his side said something in Franco's ear and, for once, he seemed unsure of himself. Growling an insult, he turned and disappeared through the crowd of onlookers Rory nonplussed.

'I've never seen him like that, he is dangerous if you cross him I know that,' said Nadia. 'Rory you are a hero and I love you and there are things I said I needed to tell you some day. Well I think now is the time.'

'What do you mean?'

Before she could reply, a member of the local police arrived to push back the crowd and allow room for the island's only ambulance. Rory and Nadia watched for a few minutes and then the police officer came up to them, gave a lazy salute and spoke in Italian. Nadia answered and he turned to Rory, speaking in halting English.

'You are a the one to save everyone?'

'Yes I suppose so.'

'You a must come to my office to tell.'

'Aye, if that's what you want. Looks like you will be the interpreter Nadia.'

The police officer pulled a sheet of paper from his drawer and began to write. Sitting side by side across the desk from him in the small office, Rory and Nadia looked on. After putting several lines of script down, the police officer began to ask questions that Nadia translated, giving Rory's reply in Italian. After several minutes and yet more writing, the officer put down his pen and sat back in his chair.

'So a you drive the vaporetto without a licence. This is against the law and I will a need to charge you for this.'

Rory was flabbergasted. 'What d'you mean, that boat was out of control and someone could have been seriously injured, maybe even killed. And what about the driver, he was in no fit state and needed to go to hospital. What does a licence matter under these circumstances?'

The police officer did not understand fully Rory's tirade and did not ask Nadia for a translation, instead he rose to his feet.

'I put you under arrest for driving the boat without licence. You can go to court, stay in the cell until your case comes up or you can pay a fine now.'

'A fine, how much?'

Without hesitation, the police officer said it would be twenty thousand lire immediately or Rory could take his chances in court where he might receive a prison sentence. Rory fell for it, twenty thousand lire now and he could walk away. It sounded an awful lot of money but with an exchange rate of almost two thousand to the pound, it was no more than one hundred pounds sterling, still a lot of money. He put his hand into his pocket but before he could withdraw any money, Nadia placed her hand on his arm.

'I think we will maybe leave now.'

The police officer sneered. 'No, you pay twenty thousand lire, I sign the paperwork and then you go.'

'Let me make something clear to you, Il Capo will not look kindly on a policeman who takes advantage of a tourist who has just saved a vaporetto and several people's lives.'

The police officer's eyes narrowed and his tone changed. 'You know Il Capo?'

'Yes and so does my father and my brothers, we are very close to Il Capo.'

The police officer swallowed, took hold of the charge sheet and screwed it up before dropping it into his waste bin.

'You have made a great service to us. You are free to go and make sure Il Capo knows we look after his people. Goodbye.'

Nadia did not waste any time. She tapped Rory less than gently on the arm and told him to follow her.

'Come on, we do not want to stop any longer than necessary, he might change his mind and we will never get out of here.'

Rory took little persuading and shaken as he was by such a blatant ploy to cheat money from him, followed Nadia to the street. He had become suddenly aware of the corruption that lay under the surface of Venetian life and it repulsed him.

'You have some explaining to do Nadia. You frightened that policeman.'

'*Si*, and you would be frightened too if you had offended Il Capo.'

'Who is Il Capo?'

'Not now, I tell you later but first we must get off the island. Look a vaporetto is coming.'

Joining the small queue at the vaporetto stop, they boarded and were soon heading out into the lagoon away from trouble and this time Rory was not much interested in sitting near the driver. At the rear of the boat Nadia leaned into Rory and began to whisper in his ear.

'Il Capo is the boss, the head of the mafia, and he is dangerous. I know a little about these people because of Franco, he is involved with them. I do not know how exactly and you must never breathe a word of what I am telling you. To anyone, *anyone*!' she emphasised. 'Promise on your mother's life?'

'That's a bit strong isn't it?'

'Rory I am telling you that these people are dangerous and they will stop at nothing if you cross them. They will kill you believe me.'

Her tone told him she was not joking and when tears appeared in her eyes, he understood.

'Franco?'

'Yes, Franco, he is very mixed up with them, Claudio not so much I think. He is just a water taxi driver, the taxis are controlled by the mafia but I think no more than that.'

'What about your parents?'

'My mother hates them but she can say nothing. If she does she knows she will bring trouble on us, maybe they kidnap me.'

'You, why?'

'Because I am easy to take and they know my parents would do anything to keep me safe.'

Nadia's statement was unexpected, disturbing and it shocked Rory to the core. Naturally, he was concerned for her but he was at a loss in knowing what to do. Then it began to dawn upon him that there was more to the Foscaris than met the eye. Franco was easy to read, a young thug, while the older Claudio seemed more amenable, without the mean streak his brother possessed, and yet it was Mario, Nadia's father, who worried him the most. He had seen a few gangster films and remembered that the quiet, respectable-looking ones were the worst. Nadia said that he was involved with the mafia and if he was, then with what kind of a family was he getting himself involved.

Taking a sideways glance, he tried to read Nadia's expression, wanting to know more but the look on her face convinced him to hold back. She believed she had told him too much already and she was probably right because her revelations had stunned him. Events had moved fast, his mind was in a whirl and for the rest of the journey to San Marco he remained silent.

'You haven't said much, are you all right?'

'Yes I'm fine but some of the things you have told me and the episode in the police station have made me think.'

'You don't want me anymore?' she said, her eyes wide, questioning.

'Don't be silly, of course I do but I can see our relationship is more complicated than I thought.'

'Franco?'

'Yes and your father. He must know what Franco is like yet he seems to condone his actions. How is he connected to the mafia?'

'No more talk please. Do not ask anymore, it is dangerous for you to know. I just want us to be together, happy, away from my family. I want a proper life and you are the one to give it to me, my Viking.'

'Viking, ha, where did you get that from?'

'You are tall and your hair is golden like the Vikings and you are brave. You saved those people . . . and me.'

She looked straight at Rory, a tear forming in her eye and Rory began to melt, Viking or not.

'Shall we forget the gondola ride; let's just go home. After today's excitement I don't really feel up to doing much.'

'*Si*, you are right. We will take the vaporetto to the station, that's if you still want to ride on one, my vaporetto driver.'

'Oh, I'm a vaporetto driver now am I?'

Again, they looked at each other and after a few seconds burst out laughing, releasing the tension and hand in hand they walked along the wide pavement leading to the piazza.

Roberto played his hunches now and then and earlier that same morning had decided to keep an eye on Franco. Taking the early train into Venice, he bought a newspaper, waited in the station concourse guessing Franco would turn up sometime and sure enough, Franco finally appeared. Dumping the newspaper in the nearest bin, Roberto began to tail him yet Franco's movements seemed to have little purpose. Eventually he reached the Rialto Bridge where Franco spoke briefly with two men who seemed to have been waiting for him and after several minutes, descended the steps followed by the men. They walked a short distance along the canal side and then they climbed aboard a waiting water taxi.

Clenching his fist in frustration, Roberto realised they had unwittingly outmanoeuvred him; their swift departure him stranded. He could not risk drawing attention by hiring a taxi, not in his condition, unshaven and scruffy. It would be out of character for a tramp to hire an expensive water taxi so instead he found a vantage point, watched the fast disappearing motor boat and attempted to work out just where it might be going. It was difficult to be sure but it seemed to be heading towards one of the smaller islands. He favoured Murano, well known for its glassmaking and he knew that the mafia controlled production there.

Still following his hunch, he ran to the nearest vaporetto stop for Murano and felt a wave of relief when he reached the island as Franco and another man emerged from a glass factory. Watching their progress, he followed, saw them enter a second glassworks and weighing up his options, decided to find a safe place and wait. Eventually they reappeared and then the sound of people shouting drew his attention towards the canal. A vaporetto was swinging crazily about on the water, narrowly missing boats and he craned his neck for a better view. The vaporetto seemed to manoeuvre dangerously amongst other boats before turning in the middle of the canal and returning to the jetty. Applause erupted, shouting filled the air and then he saw the passengers emerge from the boat, some crying and all looked shaken. Then he saw Franco by the water's edge. He had taken several steps forward and had begun to shout at a young couple, a young couple Roberto felt he should recognise. The woman seemed to freeze, the man retorted in English and Franco walked angrily away. What was all that about he wondered and the couple, where had he seen them before?

He took a closer look, could they perhaps be the pair he had seen arrive at the Foscari household two nights before, the British connection, was that it? He did wonder if there was an association and, intrigued, decided to follow them, but as the fuss surrounding the incident began to defuse, a police officer appeared and began to speak with them. Finally, he saw them leave the scene and he felt he had a problem, should he stay with the couple or follow Franco?

Things were getting complicated but again he had a hunch, deciding to loiter outside the office until the couple reappeared. When they did so, the man was angry and red-faced, the girl subdued and worried. They made their way back along the street towards the jetty and he followed, boarding the next waterbus with them. He found a seat from where he could try to catch their conversation unobserved but that turned out to be all but impossible. They were speaking in whispers, but he did pick up the words Il Capo, the boss, there was a mafia connection.

For the journey across the lagoon, Roberto was careful to make sure the couple did not see his face. At the end of the trip, he followed them from the vaporetto stop to the railway station, where they boarded the train for Mestre. After the short journey, the couple left the station and the girl hailed a taxi Roberto in a fix. On foot, he could not easily follow and asking one local taxi to follow another would draw attention. He watched in anguish as their taxi pulled away, frantically looking round for some means of following. Several bicycles chained to a stand were tempting but forcing a lock would be difficult and might draw attention to him. Then a passing police car caught his eye and without a second thought, he ran out into the road and flagged it down.

'I need a lift,' he said, pulling out his warrant card.

'Get in. Where is it you want to go?' asked the driver, relishing some excitement on what had been a dull and routine shift. 'Do you want the siren?'

'No, keep it quiet, just follow that taxi turning to the right,' he said, climbing into the rear seat.

The driver accelerated smoothly, reached the turn and followed the couple's taxi. Roberto had already guessed the probable destination, it had to be to the house of Franco Foscari, they had to be the man and woman he had seen arrive in the darkness.

'Drop me off here. Thanks for the lift.'

The police car pulled smoothly away Roberto alone in the road. He had followed Franco several times and was acquainted with the area, had a good idea where the Foscari house lay, and cutting across open ground, made his way towards it just in time to see the taxi . Of the couple, there was no sign so finding a place where he could loiter unobserved, he considered what he had learned. The woman was Franco's sister, he was sure, but the man was still something of a mystery. His features were not those of a southern European, he was heavily built and with flaxen hair and by his actions, the girl's lover. Then there was the overriding question as to whether he was a part of the suspected operation and if so what was his function? Darkness was beginning to close in and he felt there was little else he could achieve so he decided to leave and make his way to the church.

After his find in the grass, he desperately wanted to look inside the hut. Turning into the small courtyard he suddenly froze as a car's headlights swept towards him. Dodging into some bushes, he waited patiently, watched the car pull up and two individuals get out who began to walk in his direction. Fearful of discovery, he retreated into the shadows, hugging the stonework and then he heard the faint sound of a key turning in a lock. The men were obviously unaware of his presence and creeping closer he reached a bush no more than five or six metres away. They were in the process of entering the outbuilding engrossed in what they were doing. A flash of torchlight lit up the shed's interior and Roberto could see them leaning over something. His heart began to beat a little faster Here was his chance to see what they were concealing from the outside world and, forcing himself to calm down, he crept ever closer. Within just two or three metres of the open door he could see them holding something up, a dark blue uniform, a Carabinieri uniform, and they appeared to be trying it for size.

'You can be captain and I will be lieutenant, Maurizio, when we shut down the bank for Franco and the others.'

'These are good uniforms; I would not be able to tell they are fakes. The guns, we are to check the guns Alfredo, come on, let's open the boxes.'

The one called Maurizio produced a small bunch of keys from his pocket and wandered further into the hut to two boxes lying side by side while his accomplice shone the torch. Maurizio leaned over the first of them and Roberto could hear the sound of another key turning in a lock.

'What a beautiful thing,' he said, lifting an object wrapped in grey, oily cloth. 'I love the Kalashnikov,' he said, removing the cloth and casting his eyes over the weapon.

'Never mind playing, let's check the other box and then leave. If anyone finds us here there could be trouble.'

'Trouble, no,' said Maurizio pretending to spray the wall with bullets. 'With these there will be no trouble, not for us eh . . .!'

The hairs on the back of Roberto's neck stood on end. He had seen and heard everything; the full extent of what they were planning was beginning to dawn and it made him feel sick. Kalashnikovs were the chosen weapon of the Calabrian mafia, the Sicilian Cosa Nostra and now they were here in northern Italy. If the local mafia was about to use these guns in Venice with its many tourists, then anything might happen.

The sound of the lids closing on the gun boxes announced the men's departure. He heard Maurizio say, 'We will hit the bank so hard they will not know what has hit them,' and Roberto knew then the full extent of their plans. Fearing discovery, he retreated into the shadows, his mind in turmoil, and from a distance, he watched the figures emerge from the hut and secure the door with the padlock. Although he was disturbed by what he had just witnessed, Roberto had to admire their impudence. Storing the guns right under the nose of the kindly priest was a masterstroke, but equally it sent out a frightening signal and more than that, it appeared that the mafia were preparing to move the weapons.

Roberto's work in the shadows left him cautious, watchful, and his visits to Police headquarters in

Padua were no different. He had witnessed something profound, felt the need to report in person, and entering via a small side door, he took the stairs to the third floor and slightly out of breath, paused for a moment in the deserted corridor. Suddenly a door opened taking him by surprise striking him motionless. Then a man in police uniform appeared, saw him and was equally taken aback.

'Who are you, what are you doing here?' he demanded.

Roberto knew most of the police officers working in the department but the one confronting him was a stranger, tall and exuding authority. It was unnerving. It was dangerous for Roberto to let strangers know his identity and for a moment he held back, until he saw the police officer's hand move towards the holster about his waist.

Again the officer said, 'Who are you, what are you doing here?'

Roberto moved his hands away from his body, a submissive gesture, one willing the police officer to refrain from removing the gun from its holster.

'If you will not answer my question out here then you had better come into the office and tell me who you are. Antonio, come out here quickly,' he called over his shoulder. A second officer appeared. 'We have an intruder and I would like to know what he is doing on the third floor. In there, whoever you are.'

Roberto walked slowly through the open office door, heard it close behind him and knew that he had little choice but to co-operate.

'Sit down,' said the officer walking round the desk. 'I will ask you for the last time, who are you and what are you doing here?'

'You are not from this district are you, your accent is Milanese and your uniform, your shoulder flash, tell me you are a colonel of the *Guardia di Finanza*.'

The man's face was impassive. If he was surprised he certainly did not show it, instead he simply glanced up at his colleague.

'You are observant for a man of shabby and lowly appearance but I am also observant. Your hands are not those of a vagrant, you have entered this building unobserved and you know where you are going. I think it is about time you told us who you are. Let me tell you a prison cell awaits you if you refuse to co-operate.'

'I have come to see Colonel Barbonetti, the director of the DIA. I am a policeman as you are,' said Roberto, finally producing his warrant card.

'Hmm . . . you are with Preventative Investigations; it seems you are one of us. The colonel is unavailable at the moment so I suggest you speak with me, my name is Colonel Giovanni Luca and as you so rightly observe I am from the Milano office of the *Guardia di Finanza*.'

Roberto looked the colonel straight in the eye, saw a steely determination, a trait of the service, and knew he was dealing with a man of integrity.

'My name is Roberto Falcone, I work undercover hence my rather disordered appearance. My job is to look for signs of criminal activity on the islands of

Venice and further afield if needed. I report only to the colonel so I really cannot tell you anymore.'

'I think you can Roberto. The colonel is, shall we say, indisposed for a while, until the investigation into his activities are completed.'

Roberto froze; he understood instantly the implications of the colonel's words. The *Guardia di Finanza* was responsible for investigating many things, from financial crime to drug smuggling and the links between them, which usually meant the mafia. Colonel Barbonetti's department was supposed to investigate the mafia so why had they removed him from his post. Was he on their payroll?

'What has he done, is it a link to the mafia?'

'I cannot tell you but you are obviously an intelligent man Roberto. Shall we say that for the time being the department is under the control of the *Guardia di Finanza*? From now on, you will be dealing with me. Now that leads back to my question, why are you here?'

Roberto remained silent, analysing the situation. Colonel Barbonetti was in charge of the department, knew everything about Roberto and if he *was* in the pay of the local thugs then were they aware of his existence?

'I see you are thinking deeply Roberto but let me assure you we are all on the same side. We investigate corruption and we weed it out. You are in the same business so tell me what is it you have come to report?'

Venice - Day 6

Thursday, Rory's time with Nadia was nearing its end and standing under the shower he thought back over the previous twenty-four hours. He had come to realise that there was more to Nadia's family than he had appreciated and that worried him. She had explained a little of the family's mafia links, explained how the various families had spread their tentacles throughout Italy, and that the best way to cope was not to talk about it.

'You don't live here; you don't see what we do. They move in the shadows, they are violent and I do not want you to get involved. Franco is my brother and as a brother I love him but I don't like what he has become.'

'What about your parents, what do they say?'

'Papà says nothing but Mamma hates them, the mafia. She has spoken to Franco more than once but he just shrugs her off. We can do nothing to stop him, he will go to prison or one day someone will kill him.'

She had begun to sob and he had put his arm around her, determined not to let it spoil their relationship, but felt unable to do more in a world he did not understand.

'We should not speak of this thing again Rory,' she had said wiping her eyes, 'tomorrow we will simply wander round Venice and lunch somewhere special.'

Sighing, he realised that he should try to forget about Franco and his friends, instead enjoy his last days with Nadia. With that thought in mind he finished showering.

'Where is everyone?' he asked, walking into the kitchen.

'Working, only I do not have a job.'

'You live a sheltered life my love.'

'I will not for much longer, I received a letter from the college this morning, my application to begin the catering course has been accepted and I start in September.'

'That's good news, Nadia the chef,' he joked.

'Yes, one day. I am happy to be following my dream. Who knows where it will lead me.'

'You incurable romantic, you're only going to be a chef and I know it can be hard work. The Chinese chef on the ship, he . . .' He did not get to finish for Nadia suddenly burst out crying. 'Hey, what's the matter?'

'You, you are soon and I will not see you again.'

'What do you mean – not see me again?'

'You know my family are mafia and you will not want me after what I told you.'

Rory looked at her, lost for words, shocked by her unexpected outburst.

'I . . . er . . . I don't want to leave you, what gave you that idea?'

'Oh, I'm sorry, it's just that I've seen what can happen and Franco does not want us to be together.'

She took a step towards him and put her arms around his neck and he pulled her close.

'Franco, what's it got to do with him? What about your father, what does he say?'

'Papà looks after me, I am safe with Papà but if anything should happen to him Franco will make me marry one of his friends.'

'What! He can't do that.'

'He can if he becomes head of the family.'

'What about Claudio?'

'He is not like Franco, Franco will push him aside.'

'What about your mother?'

'She is a woman like me. Women have not much influence in Italian society, we do as the men say.'

'Like hell you will. I've a good mind to flatten your sodding brother. He needs a good hiding.'

'No Rory, he will kill you, if not him one of his friends will.'

Her statement made him think. He was in a foreign land, he could not speak the language and if they ganged up on him he knew he would not stand a chance.

'What are we going to do?'

'I don't know. You are the day after tomorrow and you will be safe back in Scotland. For that I am happy.'

'What about you?'

'If you go I am safe also – for now.'

'What do you mean, for now?'

'Nothing.'

'Nothing like hell. The simple solution is that you run away with me and we get married.'

'Oh Rory, if everything was so simple,' she said, gripping him tighter. 'Forget it for now, let's have a good day together and maybe we can think of something. Perhaps I can live in Germany or somewhere when I qualify and then we can be together away from my family.'

She relaxed her grip and stood back, her bright brown eyes looking to him for guidance.

'That's the solution isn't it, away from your family?'

'No more, I am upset,' she said, tears welling up in her eyes.

Mario was not a violent man, his sole function was to count the beans, add up the profits from the swindles and rackets. He worked mainly from a small office not far from his home, a place where Il Capo could easily find him.

'Mario we begin to move today, I am ordering our soldiers to get ready to hit the bank at the end of this week. I have it on good authority that the *Banca d'Italia* will move a larger amount of cash than normal. It seems that last week the security firm had a problem and had to forgo the transfer of some cash for one week so tomorrow they will move two weeks' money and that means maybe two million dollars, more than enough to entice the Serbians to deal with us. I have sent my best lieutenants to organise the attack on the bank and I want you to make funds immediately available to pay the foot soldiers. They will need to disappear as soon as we have robbed the bank and we cannot risk using the American dollars.'

'I will start immediately boss; I will have the money by mid-day. Where do you want me to take it?'

'I don't want you anywhere near the operation. No one knows of you or your work and that is how I like it. Franco will come for the money and he will take it to my lieutenants.'

'Franco?'

'Yes, Franco, he will do what is necessary. In addition, I have given him the job of the getaway, he will bring you the money we steal, and then you will hide it where no one except us can find it, *capiche*?'

'I understand. It will take several days to move the money to a safe place, one of the British tax havens I think, through our contacts in Panama, but I cannot do anything until Monday.'

It will be soon enough, but first we have to lead the Carabinieri on a merry dance, bribe and confuse them and for that we will need extra money, ten million lire I think.'

'It will be done.'

Franco was intimidating the shopkeeper, holding him by his throat against his shop door when Maurizio hailed him from a water taxi.

'You are lucky scumbag, I have to go but I will be back to make sure you are not cheating us,' Franco snarled, shoving the man backwards into his shop. 'Maurizio, what do you want?'

'A meeting, Il Capo wants you to attend a meeting.'

'Where?'

'The house.'

Franco nodded and leaped across the half metre of open water onto the boat. If Il Capo had summoned him, it must be important.

Roberto had seen guns and uniforms hidden in the church, overheard conversations, but none of it told him exactly what the mafia Family were planning. All he knew was that a bank was involved and things would become violent and he knew he must speak with Colonel Luca. At their meeting the colonel put him at his ease, opening his silver cigarette case and offering one to him.

'Thank you colonel, it makes a nice change to my homemade cigarettes.'

'I expect it does, these are very good quality,' said the colonel, striking up his lighter and holding it out for Roberto and for a moment there was silence as the men took long drags on their cigarettes.

'It's the local mafia, they are worrying me. Last night I saw them with two Kalashnikovs and uniforms of the Carabinieri. I expect they will have handguns as well and that is quite an arsenal. From what I overheard I know they are planning to rob a bank but I cannot figure out which one. All I know is that it is imminent and innocent people could be hurt.'

'Kalashnikovs, damn, that changes things. If we were dealing with a few handguns we could probably cope easily enough but automatic weapons are something else altogether. Do you think they will hit the island or stay on the mainland?'

'Venice, the island, because they are after tourist money, money they can easily hide or use to buy drugs, probably from the Serbians or the Montenegrins I think.'

'How do you know that?'

'I heard the word dollars I'm sure.'

'Dollars, hmm, just a minute.' The colonel went to an adjoining door and opened it. 'Antonio come in here a minute will you. You know Captain Capizzi I believe.'

The two men acknowledged each other, 'We have met.'

'Antonio is my very capable assistant and I want him to hear what you have to say.'

Roberto took a long drag from the cigarette and repeated his fears, told Captain Capizzi everything he knew, finishing with his belief that the mafia gang were after foreign currency, lots of foreign currency, and were about to rob a bank with violence.

'What do you think Antonio?'

'I think we have a very bad situation colonel. A bank, obviously, nowhere else is really worth robbing if you are going to use such fire power and you say foreign currency.'

Captain Capizzi was a very bright young man and, more than that, he had an almost photographic memory.

'Since being posted to Padua I have made it my business to find out where the most likely targets for

239

the mafia might be, the size of an establishment, the type of valuables including cash, and just how easy it would be to rob. I have by no means conducted an exhaustive survey, however, several candidates spring to mind. The savings banks, but they are mainly away from the islands of Venice, and there is the casino which is always awash with foreign currency.'

'Anywhere else you can think of?'

'There are one or two large jewellery dealers, gold, precious stones. They could be targets but getting rid of the proceeds would not be so easy.'

'The casino sounds favourite I think.'

'It does, but it is by no means certain they will hit there.'

'And there is the *Banca d'Italia*; they handle lots of foreign currency.'

'So we have several possibilities. I cannot take any risks, not with automatic weapons. Captain, get on to the Army and ask them to put a special operations unit on standby. Roberto you must go into the city and look for any likely place they might hit, look for known criminals and report immediately what you see. I will arrange for an undercover unit to keep an eye on you just in case you are recognised for you will be exposed.'

Roberto felt his stomach churn, all his hard work seemed to be crystallising in this one moment. The colonel was taking him seriously, unlike his predecessor who always seemed to have a reason not to pursue his leads. It was obvious now: Colonel Barbonetti was in the pay of the mafia.

'Thank you colonel, if you send an undercover squad then I will be on the Rialto Bridge at ten o'clock. We will need a coded phrase to identify each other, they should say *I hear there will be a thunderstorm soon* and I will reply *Maybe later this evening.*'

'An apt phrase Roberto let us hope that the storm passes without incident. Good luck.' The colonel stood and gave Roberto a salute before turning to his subordinate. 'Let's get moving captain, we don't know how much time we have and worse we don't know where they are going to strike.'

There was a car waiting for Franco and Maurizio when the motor boat reached the port area to whisk them across the causeway. Franco was intrigued, was the operation to rob the bank underway? Clenching and unclenching his fists, he ran through all the possibilities until twenty minutes later the car crunched to a halt on the gravelled drive.

'Just you Franco,' said the man in the dark suit guarding the front door.

Franco looked at Maurizio who simply shrugged his shoulders. He was not of the inner circle, not invited to what appeared to be an important meeting. He, Franco, was on the inside and going places at last.

'Franco welcome,' Il Capo said, kissing him on both cheeks in greeting and a show of authority. 'Men of honour,' he said to those sat around the table, 'the time has arrived to put our plan into action . . .'

For a while, Roberto walked the streets and canalsides of the Rialto district the well-appointed businesses were prime targets and almost every time he visited, he came across some thug or other. Crossing a bridge, he descended to a precinct where only a few days before he had seen Franco and wondered why today it seemed devoid of the criminal element.

'Where are they all?' he muttered to himself, walking past a restaurant, a constant target of the mafia, and was surprised to see a notice proclaiming 'Under New Management'. It was a successful business so had the mafia taken it over to launder their ill-gotten gains? If they had then he would have a closer look when the present situation was over but this morning he had an appointment he did not want to miss.

Sauntering past a vaporetto stop, he pushed his way through tourists waiting to board and making his way to the Rialto Bridge, he climbed the steps.

'Buy a flower mister?'

Turning round he saw a boy of twelve or fourteen holding out a rose for sale. Another budding mafioso, he thought, and waved the boy away before moving towards the midpoint of the bridge. He found a space and rested his elbows on the stonework, looked down at the canal, the passing water traffic and moments later heard a voice behind him.

'I hear there will be a thunder storm soon.'

Roberto looked up at the sky, 'maybe later this evening.'

'You think so?' said the man leaning on the parapet.

He looked at Roberto, taking in his features before moving on with his female companion and Roberto began to feel a little more secure. He had made contact with his backup but time was passing and he had not yet come across any mafiosos he recognised. Perhaps he was looking in the wrong area, maybe he should try further along the canal towards the heart of San Marco. It seemed the right thing to do under the circumstances and then, as he was about to leave the bridge, a passing motor boat caught his eye. It was familiar, the same motor boat he had seen Franco climb aboard not so long ago. Racing to the opposite side of the bridge, Roberto pushed through a group of complaining tourists for a better look.

It *was* the same one, he was sure, and hurtling down the steps, he darted along the bank of the main canal after the boat. He crossed several bridges in his pursuit before coming to a dead end, the only way forward was to negotiate a warren of narrow side streets. Cutting across a secluded square he crossed a bridge over a small canal and, gasping for breath, stood for a while to regain his composure. He had a good view of the main canal and looked anxiously for the motor boat but there was no sign. Retracing his steps, he thought he might at least catch a glimpse of Franco's motor boat somewhere on the canal, but there was so much traffic and from a distance so many of the boats looked the same.

It seemed he had lost his quarry and so, with his hands in his pockets and a dejected look on his face, he wandered aimlessly until he came across the *Banca d'Italia*, a nondescript building backing onto a small canal. Standing for a minute or two, he reflected on his wild goose chase, worrying that he was getting nowhere when he saw the motor boat again nudging slowly into the canal in front of him. Hardly moving, it slowly came to a halt at the side of the *Banca d'Italia*.

He could not see inside the boat from where he stood but if he could have, he would have witnessed Franco and Maurizio looking along the waterway, noting each building, every feature, and gauging the canal width. Once Franco had seen enough he ordered the driver to move and slowly the boat reversed back into the Grand Canal to leave Roberto to wonder what was going on.

Folding his arms across his chest, he cocked his head sideways, narrowed his eyes and then he smiled as a realisation dawned.

'What are you doing here?' said a gruff voice behind him.

Turning round he came face to face with two men he recognised as minor mafiosos, the clan's foot soldiers, and they were staring straight at him. There was no escape, he felt trapped, faced them and prepared himself for violence.

'I know you, you are always mooching about, who are you tramp?'

'Uh . . . what do you mean, I'm just looking for something to eat.'

'Eat this,' said one stepping forward and hitting him in the soft part of his belly.

Roberto doubled up in pain, gasped for breath and braced himself.

'You are spying tramp, you are spying for the police aren't you?'

Roberto groaned, unable to speak properly, the man hit him again sending him sprawling to the ground, and instinctively he curled into a ball.

'Kill him; we'll dump him in the canal. One less tramp on the streets will be a blessing.'

Roberto groaned again, his head began to clear, his eyes focussing on his assailants and he then heard the metallic click of a flick knife opening. The sound sent a shiver down his spine, his life began to flash before his eyes, and flinching in expectation he called out to God.

Then the world exploded, the mafioso's head suddenly snapped backwards, a hand covering the mouth, the sound of a scuffle, no words spoken, silence, save for dull thuds and when his vision fully returned Roberto became aware of a hand reaching down to him. To his astonishment, it was the hand of a woman, the companion of the man on the bridge.

'Th . . . thanks,' he managed to say.

Next, he heard the crackle of a shortwave radio and within a few minutes several men appeared to haul away the two recovering mafiosos.

'Lucky we didn't lose you. You were moving at quite a pace and it would have been easy for us to take a wrong turn,' said the woman in a much deeper voice than Roberto might have expected.

'Very lucky,' said Roberto, holding his stomach.

'Are you all right, do you need medical attention?'

Roberto was in some pain but medical attention was the last thing on his mind. He was sure now that he had found the target of the mafia's impending raid, he just did not know when.

Franco was feeling somewhat agitated. While he was more than capable of extracting money with violence from defenceless business owners, he was not a gifted organiser. Far from it, intelligent to a point he had his limits and time was running out. He had twenty-four hours before they hit the bank, time in which he needed to pull his part of the plan together. Each component of his brief was in itself manageable but having to consider them all at once was putting a strain on him. Organising the gang's getaway was a point in case; he had most of the plan in place except that he had still not found a reliable driver.

'Maurizio, this driver, who is he?'

'Arturo Fabrizzo, a friend of mine.'

'Can he be trusted?'

'I think so, he is not one of us but he will do it for the money.'

'He will see faces, it is a risk. How good a friend is he?'

Maurizio looked Franco in the eye, understanding. 'He is just an acquaintance, not really a true friend.'

He had just signed Arturo Fabrizzo's death warrant.

'Good, promise him double what he expects and bring him to the depot at four o'clock.'

This was Franco's chance to show Il Capo what he could do but the pressure was beginning to tell, robbing a bank the size of the *Banca d'Italia* would not be easy. He was aware of how necessary it was to the future of the organisation, and to him personally. With enough foreign currency, they could enter the lucrative drugs trade in a big way, flood the rich northern Italian towns with drugs and make themselves rich men.

Il Capo had explained that the drug route from Afghanistan passed through Serbia before crossing the Adriatic. Venice was the ideal destination, open to the sea, easy to smuggle the contraband into northern Italian cities and to feed the habit of the middle classes. First, they had to empty the bank's vault – and the responsibility for making a clean getaway rested on his shoulders.

The beating Roberto received left him bruised, his ribs hurting, but he was thankful to be alive and discovering the likely target of the mafia had left him elated. Immediately he had set off for the police headquarters in Padua to see Colonel Luca and reveal his suspicions.

'I am convinced they are about to rob the Venice branch of the *Banca d'Italia* colonel. Not only did they try to kill me for being in the area, but I saw Franco Foscari there. He is the common thread running right through this mafia plot I am sure. Each time I manage to get close to finding out what they are up to, he is there.'

'Your two minders saw him. A good job they were there I think, and he has been back to the church.'

'The church?'

'Yes, I have taken the precaution of putting the church under surveillance. Resources are limited but the lady who got you out of trouble is spending quite a bit of time praying for salvation.'

'Lady?'

'Yes, he's good at it isn't he? If I didn't know better I might even fancy her myself.'

'Well I don't know about that but he was damn good with those two thugs.'

'They are in hospital under guard and will survive but there may have been others, we don't know. We do not want anyone suspecting the hand of the authorities in that little incident and I am concerned that you might have blown your cover. Which brings me to the point: I am pulling you off the case.'

'What! After all I've done.'

'Don't take it to heart Roberto; it's for your own safety. You are a very good undercover cop but I believe that you could have compromised your position. If any of the gang suspects you are working for us, it could wreck the whole operation. What if someone with enough common sense can see that really you are a police officer and not a tramp then what do you think would happen, eh? That could blow this whole thing and I am not prepared to risk it. From now on you will not be involved, and, until we reach a conclusion, you will not go into Venice.'

Roberto's jaw dropped – off the case – he was shocked to the core.

'Am I being reassigned?'

'No, I want you to go home and stay there until I deem it right for you to come back.'

'How long for?'

'Until I say so, weeks, perhaps months, you will remain on full pay but I cannot afford for you to be seen by any of the mafiosos. They will torture you and when you have told them everything, you really will finish up in the lagoon, and next time we will not be around to save you. I don't want that on my conscience.'

Roberto remembered feeling numb and upset but it hadn't stopped him from firing a parting shot at the commander.

'In that case I will do as you say colonel but I hope to God you do not let these bastards slip through your fingers as easily as your predecessor.'

'Don't worry my friend, I won't.'

Was that enough, words? Would a simple statement put the men of honour behind bars? He doubted it, Colonel Luca's predecessor had used only words and nothing he ever did brought the gangsters to justice. He was annoyed that the colonel had ordered him not to return to Venice and perhaps he was right, but he was determined he could no more let go of the case than end his support for the Azzurri.

Still fuming at the colonel's disregard for all he had done, Roberto entered his neighbourhood, and walked along the uneven footpath towards the apartment blocks with his hands stuffed into his trouser pockets and his mind on the *Banca d'Italia*. Engrossed with his own problems, he did not notice a small Fiat go past. In the passenger seat, Franco sat deep in thought and hardly noticed the scruffy man mooching along, until fifty metres further along the road when he suddenly exclaimed.

'*Che*, that man, I know him. Turn round Maurizio I want to take a closer look at that vagrant. I see him in Venice, why is he here in Mestre?'

Alarm bells were ringing. There was something familiar about the unkempt individual; he had seen him before in San Marco and he fritted father Giuseppe's description of the man who had visited the church. His face set into a scowl, the faint odour of police involvement permeating his nostrils. Maurizio responded immediately, the car's tyres screeching on the tarmac as he changed direction, and that sound was the first indication of impending danger for Roberto.

Perhaps he was on edge after the beating, or was it simply an inbuilt survival instinct that caused Roberto to react? Almost without thinking, he took a sharp glance back along the street, saw the little Fiat making a one hundred and eighty degree turn and with his heart rate picking up, began to run as fast as he could. He swerved off the path, leapt over some bushes and ran between two apartment blocks to re-emerge breathless in the next street.

'Where is he, he was here only a minute ago? Try over there, circle those buildings and find him quickly. If he is running then I am sure that he is the police. Find him and I will make sure he doesn't spy on us ever again,' screamed Franco, his temper rising.

Coupled with the pressure of the job he was in no mood to be gentle. If the tramp was an undercover police officer then the whole enterprise could be in jeopardy and he might not get his hands on a Ferrari.

'There is no one here Franco, just those two women pushing prams.'

'Pull up, I will ask them.'

'Have you seen a tramp come here in the past minute?' he said, leaning out of the car window.

The women looked at him and then at each other. 'No, no one has been here, just us, isn't that right Marie?'

'Yes, just us for maybe ten minutes.'

Franco was not one for thanking people and today was no exception. 'Try over there.'

Maurizio continued to drive the little car round and round but they saw no one save some boys playing football.

'Are you sure you saw whoever it is we are looking for?'

'I was, I still am, but we will not see him again so soon I think. I will put the word out to the soldiers; tell them to keep their eyes open for the tramp.'

A few meters away Roberto pressed his body hard against a wall. Almost in view of the Fiat, he could hear Franco's voice questioning the women and feared that if the mafiosos looked his way he would be undone. They did not; instead, they drove away, him breathing a sigh of relief and able to make his way home unhindered.

He entered the building feeling decidedly shaky and ran up the stairs to burst through the door of his flat, slamming it shut behind him. He flicked the latch, leaned against the wall and tried to regain his composure. For maybe ten minutes he did not move, his mind trying to catch up. He had not seen the faces of the men in the Fiat nor recognised the voice of the one asking questions but he would bet a year's salary it was Franco Foscari. Eventually his eyes stopped staring, he looked up at the ceiling and drew in a long, measured breath and, feeling more secure, went into the small bathroom. Turning on the shower, he left it running while he went into the kitchen and filled the coffee pot. Over the years, he had learned that a hot shower and a strong Italian coffee made for a good catalyst to facilitate deep thinking.

As he stepped from the shower, the smell of the fresh coffee reached his nostrils. He stepped over his ragged clothes spread across the floor and looking down at them knew he would not need them again. The alternative was not a great deal better – a white shirt, a pair of dark blue slacks and a lightweight jacket, the legacy of an earlier time. He had no other clothes so they would have to do.

Sitting in his armchair, a towel across his midriff he sipped his coffee and contemplated his predicament. He was in trouble, naked and unarmed, yet he was confident he had given the mafiosos the slip and could use this oasis of calm to make a plan, redefine himself. First, he would shave, rid himself of the stubble he had lived with for so long and, finishing the coffee, he returned to the bathroom.

As the white shaving foam covering the lower half of his face gradually contracted, he turned Colonel Luca's words over in his mind. He was off the case, a case he had followed for weeks. He felt angry – he was close to solving the mystery of the weapons hidden in the church, sure he knew the target, and now he felt impotent. What could he do, should he just give up?

Wiping away the last of the shaving foam he peered at himself in the mirror: the tramp was finished and a new personality was taking shape. The face looking back at him belonged to Roberto Mancini, private citizen, a man who did not need to take orders from Colonel Luca.

Dressing in the shirt and slacks, he took a further, determined look in the mirror and wondered what else he could do to change his appearance. He could alter his hairstyle, cut some off to appear respectable enough until he could find a barber. Then there was the problem of a new hideaway because there was always a chance they might come looking for him. He could go back to the colonel for help, but he was sure that would not work, no, he needed someone not directly connected with the police, someone he could trust and there was only one person he could think of.

Valentina saw him first. As normal on a night like this, the hotel was practically deserted as either the guests at the exclusive hotel had gone to bed or they were still out on the town. She noticed a figure appear in the hotel foyer, his cheap-looking clothes out of context in such an opulent setting and becoming suspicious she approached the doorway. She noticed that he was a man in his early thirties, handsome and he reminded her of her dead husband, and then it struck her.

'Roberto, what are you doing here?'

'Oh Valentina, thank God I have found you. I need your help. Is there somewhere we can talk?'

'Yes, follow me,' she said, puzzled, and led him to a door near the reception desk.

'This is a surprise; I have not seen you since Tomaso's funeral. What have you been doing for the past two years and why have I not heard from you?'

'This is a surprise for me too Valentina, I can explain. How have you been?'

'Fine, thank you. Now what are you doing here, how did you find me?'

'I heard that you had started working here after the force, but I did not know for sure you were still here, it was a gamble. Listen, I am in trouble and I need help. You will not know it but since Milan, I have been working undercover for the anti-mafia police in Padua. I was mad at those bastards who call themselves men of honour. That's the last thing they are and I've made it my job to hunt them down.'

His eyes flashed and the passion of his feelings was all too apparent to Valentina. She had suffered her own pain; ever since Tomaso's murder she had felt a hollowness and Roberto was the one person with whom she could share that pain. She looked him over and felt a lump come to her throat, memories dormant for so long re-emerging, memories of her late husband, gunned down by the mafia.

They had said it was a routine investigation but it was far from that – the Sicilian mafia were waiting

254

for him. Someone had tipped them off, told them when Tomaso and his partner would arrive to arrest a prominent suspect. The two police officers did not stand a chance, shot at close range and left for dead. Someone in the department had informed the mafia thugs she was sure and Roberto too suspected a colleague. Both were none the wiser as to whom it might be and from that moment on the thought of working alongside corrupt police officers. It was the final straw for both Valentina and Roberto, both felt that they could no longer work for the Milanese police force and both resigned on the same day.

'You've lost weight,' she said finally. 'I hardly recognised you when I saw you but the eyes don't change Roberto.'

'No, I suppose they don't, and you, you are looking well. I'm glad.'

'So, what brings you here in such mysterious circumstances?'

Roberto felt tired; it had been a stressful day, and pulling up a chair, he sat down.

'Where to begin,' he said wearily. 'I suppose I am on the run.'

'From the mafia?'

'And the police.'

'What! This does sound serious. You had better tell me everything that is going on and what it is you want of me. If I can help I will, but I make no promises.'

'Thank you, I know that. I told you I have been working undercover, I heard of a vacancy working out of Padua and I applied. My job is to gather intelligence on the mafia, track their movements and find out anything of value that I can. I often feel the work I do is not fully appreciated but I keep on doing it.'

'What do you mean?'

'Very few of them are ever arrested and even fewer go to jail. I have my suspicions.'

'We know all about that,' said Valentina with a sigh of resignation.

'I called in to report a few days ago and found that the head of the department was under arrest and a colonel of the *Guardia di Finanza* was in charge. I think he is a good man, he listens to me, and earlier today I went to see him to tell him of my suspicions. I believe that the local clan are planning a big operation, a bank robbery.'

'Why would you run from the police if he is a good man?'

'Because he has pulled me off the case, just when we are really getting somewhere. I have dedicated my life to catching these criminals and now, when we are so close to smashing their organisation, he has told me to go home and stay out of it.'

'You think he is corrupt?'

'Not really, those *Guardia di Finanza* boys are generally incorruptible but I cannot be sure. I suppose technically I am not yet on the run from the police but I will be by tomorrow because I think I know which bank the mafia are about to rob and I want to be around to stop them.'

'The mafia, you said you are on the run from them.'

'Franco Foscari, a little shit who thinks he is the godfather. He is in this thing up to his neck. This afternoon, I think it was him, he came after me in Mestre, he suspects I am working with the police and he is right. My worry is that they will abort this operation and cheat us of the chance to put them all behind bars.'

'How can I help, what is it you want from me?'

'I need a place to hide, to rest and I need some decent clothes. As a vagrant, I was practically invisible to those arrogant bastards but now Foscari suspects me they will be looking for a tramp. You haven't seen me in my working clothes, my stubble, my smell, have you? I need to change my appearance and I have decided to become Roberto Mancini again, to carry on as myself.'

'That is dangerous; perhaps the colonel is protecting you.'

'Maybe he is, but even so, I don't want to be taken off the case. So as a private citizen I am going to keep an eye on things, help where I can.'

'There is a room on the top floor you can use for a few days but only a few days. Tell me your size and I will find you something to wear, something fashionable maybe.'

She smiled a smile that masked a deep-seated worry for Roberto's safety but she knew him well enough, respected his commitment, and she would do what she could.

The *Banca d'Italia* was busy, the queue at the tellers' window long enough for Roberto to wander about without drawing attention. It was the first time he had entered the establishment, as a vagrant he would not have been welcome, today though he was not a vagrant but a respectable-looking citizen. Valentina had found some clothes left behind by guests and for Roberto it was a transformation. Dressed in an expensive shirt, trousers and an Armani jacket, he looked every bit the successful Italian business executive. He took note of the customers, mostly Americans exchanging their US dollars through the metal grille separating them from the tellers. He wondered how Franco and his friends might gain entry to the vault – even the glass entrance doors were robust, reinforced with thin wire and above them shutters to secure the bank for the night. They could rob the bank at any time during the day but it would be full of customers, surely an inconvenience, even a night-time raid had its own difficulties. He wandered over to a shelf by a window and made to peruse some of the literature on show and from what he had learned so far, it seemed the best time to hit the bank would be at closing time. That would be when it was almost devoid of customers and contained the maximum amount of cash.

He could not be completely sure, of course, and he did not know which day. Nor did he know anything about the bank's system of moving money or where the vault might be, but he would try to find out and, feeling in his pocket, pulled out a small bundle of notes. The money was from Valentina, to tide him over, not much, but he reasoned that it would be enough to open an account.

Joining the queue, he waited in turn, looking past the cashiers, trying to understand the bank's layout until it was his turn.

'Can I help you?' asked the girl behind the screen.

'I would like to open a business account.'

'You are local?'

'Not completely, I have business interests in Venice but I am from Milan.'

'Just a moment,' she said, getting to her feet, knocking on an office door and entering to speak with someone inside. 'Wait over there.'

Roberto half smiled his thanks and moved from the counter to a window overlooking the canal. He was curious as to how the gang might force their entry and tried to identify a possible escape route once they had snatched the money. The canal running alongside the building did not have a footpath so it seemed unlikely they would come from that direction and then a voice disturbed his thoughts.

'You wish to open an account?'

He turned from the window to face a handsome dark-haired woman in her mid-twenties.

'Er . . . yes, that is my intention.'

'You are Italian, you live here in Italy?'

'Yes.'

'That makes things easier, if you were a foreigner we would need more paperwork, passport, maybe a letter of introduction. Come into my office and we can speak privately.'

Roberto followed the woman into the small office, his body language oozing the quiet confidence of a successful entrepreneur. She was attractive and he could not help mildly flirting with his eyes. The woman responded with the air of someone used to such attention, giving him a shy smile, and then it was all business.

'What kind of account do you want to open, a current account, a savings account?'

'A current account.' He leaned forward, lowered his voice just enough to add an air of mystery. 'I deal in commodities, frequently move large amounts of merchandise and I need to be able to pay in various currencies. Is that possible?'

'Of course, we are the foremost bank in Venice dealing in foreign currency.'

'Good, will I need a foreign currency account?'

'That depends, we can easily open a dollar account, that is our main foreign currency dealing but we can cover any currency. Are dollars what you want?'

'Yes, I buy and sell in dollars.'

'Then it's probably best to open a dollar account, it will save you money in the long run. What kind of amounts are you thinking of?'

'I can move a million dollars a month on occasion.' He paused, noted her reaction. 'Most deals are around a quarter of that but I sometimes need to complete several deals over a short time period and then I will need such a facility.'

'Oh, that is a little more complicated, a million, I think perhaps you need to talk to the manager.'

'I have another question that you might be able to answer. Sometimes, in fact many times, my dealings are in cash. Could I draw say two hundred thousand dollars in cash if I need to?'

'Again, I'm afraid I cannot really answer that, you will need to speak with the manager. Amounts so large would only be available at the end of the day I think. Friday would be the best before the security firm comes, but that would mean you carrying a large sum over the weekend.'

'That isn't a problem; I will be on my yacht at weekends, miles away from here.'

'Shall I make you an appointment?'

'Yes, that would be a good idea but I'm afraid that at the moment I am rather busy.'

'Is next week convenient?'

'I think so, probably Tuesday.'

'I will check the diary. Wait here,' she said, getting up to leave the room.

After she had gone Roberto closed his eyes and imagined himself as a mafioso, imagined how he might rob this bank. They would already have the information the girl had just furnished him with and it dawned on him that closing time on a Friday would be the ideal time and that would be tomorrow.

Returning with a large diary, the girl placed it on the desk and turned over several pages.

'He is free next Tuesday, all afternoon, will that do?'

'Yes, that seems perfect. Do you have a card in case I need to contact him beforehand?'

She did not but she did have a pen and a note pad and scribbling the manager's name and telephone number passed it across the desk to Roberto.

'Who shall I tell him will be coming to this appointment?'

'Just myself, Vincenzo Zanetti.'

The woman wrote the name in the diary and Roberto took his leave after flashing one more admiring look, a glance he imagined a rich and successful businessman might give a beautiful woman, and satisfied with the outcome, left the bank. He had learned a little of the business method, that the largest amount of dollars held by the bank would be on a Friday and he reasoned that the following day would be a favourite time to carry out the robbery. It seemed that he would not have long to wait.

In Padua Colonel Luca had not been idle. He believed Roberto when he said the local mafia clan were going to rob a bank with violence and had immediately set to work on a plan.

'Antonio, what have you got for me?' he said, walking into Captain Capizzi's office.

'We have a man watching the church and we believe they may have already moved the guns.'

'Where to?'

'We don't know. I could order a raid on the workman's hut and if we find the guns then all well and good but if they are missing a raid might alert the gang.'

'Do we know the target – do you think the undercover officer is right about the *Banca d'Italia*?'

'We have a few candidates and I am having them all watched including the *Banca d'Italia*. If any of the local boys turn up we will know the target.'

'But it's no good if they turn up to rob the place. We need to be ready for them; simply having a ringside seat is not good enough. I do not like the idea of a gang of thugs running loose with Kalashnikovs. I want them locked up and I must admit I have wondered about pulling them in, but what can we charge them with, possessing weapons? A couple of the lesser members will take the rap and the rest will remain free to cause mayhem. It has become a difficult situation for us. If we let them carry on, we risk serious injury or even death to innocent bystanders...'

His words tailed off and Captain Capizzi nodded, understanding their predicament very well.

'The undercover man, why did you take him off the case, he could be useful?'

'He could quite possibly be useful but those two thugs recognised him and others could too, besides, although he has done good work I fear he has burned himself out. It is difficult working as he does, alone with little or no backup. What mafioso would think twice about killing a tramp? I pulled him to avoid compromising the investigation and for his own well-being. I don't want his death on my conscience.'

'Where does that leave us colonel, what do you want me to do?'

'I have asked the Carabinieri for a squad of armed specialists and more of our own men are coming from Milan. My reading of the situation is that we have too many targets to worry about, the roads and canals on the islands are not exactly easy to negotiate in an emergency and on top of all that, we have innocent tourists to worry about. Have any bank managers gone missing?'

'Bank managers, missing?'

'It used to be a favourite ploy of the Sicilian mafia, kidnap or threaten a bank manager into working for them. I know of a couple of cases where the mafia kidnapped a bank manager and threatened his family, the terrified victim would then let them into the bank.'

'I'll ring round. I have a list of numbers.'

'I will see you again at four.'

Saluting his superior officer, Captain Capizzi returned to his office and for the next two hours worked through his list of numbers. He spoke with bank managers or their assistants and it transpired that no manager had disappeared unexpectedly though the young woman who answered the telephone at the *Banca d'Italia* told him that the manager was away, quite legitimately, for several days. She said a temporary manager had taken his place. Under normal circumstances, Antonio Capizzi might have thought no more of it but his analytical mind would not let go. Perhaps the replacement manager was under the control of the local mafia. At the top of a clean sheet of paper in his notebook, he wrote *Banca d'Italia* and after chewing the end of his pen for a few seconds, picked up his telephone to ring the number in Milan.

The meeting at the house of Il Capo was underway and, for Franco, going well. He reported that he had just moved the weapons stash to the garage and that his plan for their escape after the robbery was at an advanced stage. Il Capo seemed pleased, inviting another of his lieutenants to speak about his arrangements for the robbery. The man, experienced, a tough-looking gangster began to speak.

'We have made sure the bank manager will be absent, the assistant manager is in our pocket and he will make sure the vault is open when we enter the bank. Our men will close off the immediate area outside and once that is done enter the bank itself, threaten the staff and make them open the internal door.'

'And when you have gained entry, what will you do?'

'Four of us will force our way into the back office area and the vault. The Kalashnikovs should be enough to deter any resistance. I will set the charges and then, bang, we will make our escape with the money.'

'Franco you are handling the escape, you say you have everything under control?'

'Yes, I have the transport arranged. Once we are clear we will transfer the money and kill the driver. I have a question. What about the bank staff, what if any of them should see our faces, what if they recognise us in future?'

'No need to worry about them, I think they will be wise enough to look at the wall and not at us. Gentlemen I think we are ready, we will put the plan into action tomorrow afternoon just before the bank closes. I wish you luck and prosperity. I will be here if you need me, I have a visitor coming from across the water and as soon as I know we have the money I can begin to set up the drug route from Serbia and then, my friends, we will all be rich men.'

Three ambitious, violent men sitting opposite him smiled, thin crocodile smiles, as the prospect of the riches the drug money would bring them sank in. As the junior member of the top table Franco's ambition was no less, he too wanted money and to taste power just as much as they did.

'Get the American currency, lots of it and you can all have a Ferrari, the top of the range,' said Il Capo, bringing the meeting to an end, and each lieutenant passing him showed respect by kissing him on the cheek and he blessed them with the secret code of the mafia brotherhood.

The dark-suited men left the house and dispersed to their cars parked on the gravel while Franco walked to his scooter. From a Fiat parked a hundred metres away a man watched them through a pair of binoculars.

'There they are,' he said and sitting next to him in the passenger seat a second man lifted his camera and focused on the small group. The sound of the rapidly clicking camera shutter filled the small car for a few seconds and then there was silence until Franco appeared on his scooter. The camera focused on him.

'He's the one we have orders to follow. Captain Capizzi told me we should keep an eye on the young dark-haired one, the one with the swagger, and I think that is him.'

The two men were part of the *Guardia di Finanza* elite surveillance squad that had received the call in

Milan. Immediately they had set off for Venice with orders to stake out the house and, equipped with the Leica thirty-five millimetre camera with the super sharp Carl Zeiss lens, they had set to work.

Franco did not notice the Fiat as his scooter emerged onto the road, nor was he aware of it following him as he sped along the highway. The streets were clear and the Fiat had little trouble keeping him in view until Franco reached the railway station. Dismounting he chained his scooter to some railings and his stalkers had little alternative but to leave their car and follow on foot.

'Even a thief worries about thieves,' commented the driver dryly. 'It looks like we are about to take a train journey Carlo.'

'I am, but you must take this film to Captain Capizzi,' said Carlo, rapidly removing the film from his camera and replacing it with a fresh roll. 'At least in Venice I will be less conspicuous carrying a camera.'

'Be careful my friend, these men can be dangerous.'

Carlo looked at his partner with a sombre expression. 'I have been in this job long enough, don't worry about me. Now take this to the captain, I will report to Padua as soon as I can. Give me Captain Capizzi's number.'

The driver took the roll of exposed film, exchanging it for a piece of paper with the scribbled telephone number of Colonel Luca's office, and then the two men parted company. Ahead of them, Franco had already purchased his ticket and was climbing onto the train, forcing Carlo to hurry if he was not to lose him and two minutes later, ticket in hand, he too boarded the train for the short journey.

Franco alighted at Santa Lucia, walked quickly from the station precinct, descended the steps to the waterfront and hailed a water taxi.

'Take me to the shipyard Sant'Elena.'

Several metres away Carlo watched in horror as the water taxi sped off along the canal. He could not afford to lose Franco and spotting a taxi disgorging some tourists, ran towards it. After a quick negotiation, he persuaded the driver to take him. 'It's my first time in Venice and I do not have much time. If you will take me anywhere I fancy I will pay you well.'

The driver smiled, it was not the first time he had carried an oddball with more money than sense and the chance of a big payday was very welcome.

'For one hundred thousand lire I take you anywhere you want to go for two hours.'

'Good, go that way,' said Carlo, pointing in the direction of Franco's taxi.

Having occasionally worked in Venice, Carlo knew his way around well enough and could see that Franco was intent on travelling a long way; his taxi was keeping to the middle of the Grand Canal and showing no sign of slowing down. He noted the boat's curved transom and had little difficulty keeping it in sight until they passed under the Rialto Bridge. The tourists were out in force, gondolas were clogging the waterway, slowing the taxi, and further along the canal, near the Academia Bridge, traffic increased so much that Franco disappeared from view.

In mild panic Carlo searched the waters, worried that Franco might have gone ashore until, just as he was about to lose heart, the curved transom reappeared entering the wide reaches of the Giudecca canal.

Sitting back somewhat relieved, he took several shots of Franco's taxi and wondered where he was leading him. They were nearing the Piazza San Marco, maybe he was heading there or even the Arsenale further along. None the wiser he sank back into his seat and waited.

Fifty or so metres ahead of him, Franco was planning his next move. He had ordered three subordinates to meet him at the boatyard Sant'Elena where a recently serviced vaporetto was waiting to go back into service. He had conceived a plan to use it for the escape. If they could handle the robbery with skill and determination it seemed obvious to him that they could get away unobserved on a vaporetto. The Grand Canal was full of them and they all looked the same. Drumming his fingers on the armrest, he turned his plan over in his mind and the more he thought about it the more he considered himself a genius. For a further twenty minutes, he could think of nothing else until, finally, his water taxi turned into the Rio di Sant'Elena, a waterway separating the main island from the marina and not far away, on a landing stage, Franco saw his men waiting and waving his arm, attracted their attention.

Some way behind, Carlo's taxi followed and instinctively Carlo realised that this backwater was the final destination and that his own taxi might appear conspicuous.

'Stop anywhere here for now driver, I fancy a look around.'

The driver nodded and stopped at the canalside before looking at his watch.

'I will give you a bonus if you wait. I could get another taxi maybe?'

The driver pouted, spread his hands in a gesture of settlement and Carlo stepped ashore to see Franco some way off talking with some men. He did not relish bumping into them and climbing the low embankment he used the trees to break their line of sight. The men were undoubtedly mafia – dangerous – and he needed to find better cover before taking any more photographs.

Franco was waving his arms about, making some kind of point as Carlo took several shots. He was still a long way off and for a better view of the men's faces and needed to get at least a little closer. Keeping to the tree line, he reduced the distance further but before he could begin to take more pictures, the men moved away. They were walking towards the marina, a dead end, so unless they took a boat, he knew that he would find them again.

Entering the marina to look over his prize Franco felt more than a little excited. After speaking with contacts, paying bribes, he had discovered that there was always at least one recently overhauled vaporetto in the marina at Sant'Elena awaiting reassignment and it became obvious that he should use one for the getaway.

'Which one are we taking Silvano?'

'That one,' said Silvano, pointing to the first of two boats moored side by side.

'Is the driver ready, can we trust him?'

'Yes, he will come when we tell him and he will keep quiet. We will pay him well and for that he will say nothing.'

Franco nodded – the driver *would* remain quiet after their escape because he would be dead. Looking at the solid yellow boat, he could see that it was ideal for the purpose he intended and narrow enough to negotiate the canal once they had robbed the bank. All he had to do was transfer the money from the bank to the vaporetto. After that, they would enter the Grand Canal where the water traffic would render them invisible and then head for the rendezvous where others would be waiting to move the cash on. It was there that he would kill the driver and abandon the vaporetto.

'We are going to hit the bank just before closing time. That will give us just over an hour to move to the canal ready for the getaway. Maurizio, bring the driver here for two o'clock tomorrow. This will be the biggest job we will have undertaken and I do not want to mess things up. If we get it right we will be rich.'

The men grinned and slapped each other on the back in congratulatory gestures and from fifty metres away Carlo recorded it all with his camera.

Colonel Luca was sitting behind his desk, chain-smoking and studying the newly printed photographs provided by the surveillance team. Together with these images, Roberto's information and Captain Capizzi's intelligence he believed that the mafia hit would take place sometime during the next twenty four hours, but he was still not sure where. What was significant about Foscari's visit to the Sant'Elena marina? There were still too many unknowns but at least he had not been idle, arranging the distribution of the suspects' photographs to local commanders and ordering that they should report to him immediately if any of them were spotted. As an afterthought, he had also ordered the undercover couple who had rescued Roberto to stay near the *Banca d'Italia*. If Roberto's hunch was right, he did not want to look foolish by not covering that eventuality.

Only a few minutes earlier Captain Capizzi had named several locations which he believed were noteworthy of further examination and, before their meeting, he had emphasised that the name of the *Banca d'Italia* had crept into his investigation more than once.

'I would put the chances of it being this bank at more than fifty per cent. The fact that the manager is missing and the information Roberto Mancini provided all point to it as a strong possibility. There are two other institutions they could rob but this, in my opinion, is the favourite.'

The captain's words were still echoing around Colonel Luca's head as he stubbed out his cigarette amongst a growing pile in his ashtray. Clasping his hands together and with his elbows resting on his desk he thought long and hard. The fight against the mafia was becoming more successful but he had limited resources and if the department was to prevail, he would need to husband them very carefully.

Venice - Day 7

Sleeping in a comfortable bed in a posh hotel had worked wonders for Roberto and as he strode purposefully towards the waiting waterbus, his mind was clear and he knew what he should do. He was convinced they were about to rob the *Banca d'Italia* and from what he had learned, today would be the ideal time to carry out the robbery. He believed Franco Foscari was key, young, ambitious and brutal, the textbook attributes for a mafioso. The only problem was that as Colonel Luca had taken him off the case and he did not have access to any current information that might help him thwart Franco's ambitions. His only contact with the forces of law and order was through Valentina and that was unofficial. He had told her all he knew and she had promised to find out what she could from former colleagues, but could promise nothing.

'If they find out I am helping you I could be in trouble. I will ask a few questions but you know the police as well as I do, if they become suspicious of my questions they will come looking.'

'It's a chance I am prepared to take. I believe there will be a robbery at the *Banca d'Italia* quite soon and

274

I think there could be a lot of serious injuries if we don't stop them.'

'You can do little on your own.'

'I can try. Do me a favour Valentina – get me a gun in case I get myself cornered. I don't want to go down without a fight.'

'You are mad Roberto, mad but brave and wonderful like your brother. I will see what I can do.'

Her words helped, he did not feel so alone and the gun in his pocket gave him the confidence to confront the mafia dogs should he need to. His vague plan was to risk everything on one endeavour, to concentrate on the bank rather than go looking for Franco. If he was right, they would appear some time towards the end of the working day and then he would have an opportunity to take them on. His only real worry was that his tiny automatic pistol would have little chance against the Kalashnikovs. He must make sure that they did not get the chance to use them.

Time was passing quickly for Rory and Nadia too, it was their last full day together. They had decided that it should be a day spent relaxing, a day to look to the future, a day just wandering the Venetian canals.

'You must write to me every day for I will miss you. I want to know everything you are doing.'

'Whoa, steady on, I'm no letter writer, I will try but I can't promise. Anyway, if I'm working at sea I might not be able to post a letter for days. It's only when I can get ashore I can post stuff.'

'Then you must write long letters, six pages at least. Tell me everything.'

Rory laughed, looked at her with loving eyes and pulled her to him. 'I will do my best.'

'When can I come to meet your mother, soon?'

'Soon enough, I will get my next leave period in a month. You could come then, it will still be warm back home and you will not have started your cooking course.'

'I will fly to Edinburgh and you will drive me to where your family lives?'

'Aye Edinburgh, it's about the only airport with flights from Venice. What do you recommend for today madam? Where shall we go, what can I see that I have not seen before?'

'The Arsenale.'

'The what?'

'The Arsenale, it is where they used to build the ships when we were a great city state, from where the fleet would set sail to conquer foreign lands, that is until the Ottoman empire put a stop to it.'

'That's interesting, I didn't know that.'

'There is a lot you don't know about my city and today I educate you Englishman.'

'I'm not English, I'm Scot . . .' He was about to say Scottish when the mischief in her eyes made him laugh aloud.

'First we will take the vaporetto and travel the full length of the Grand Canal and you can treat me to a coffee in St Mark's Square.'

'You're on, which vaporetto do we take?'

'This one,' said Nadia, leading him towards a waterbus already filling with tourists

It was a crush, standing room only, and they had to hold onto leather traps hanging from the roof. All around the tourists chattered their alien tongues filling Rory's ears and strangely, he felt at home. They passed through the stone arches of the Rialto Bridge, Nadia pointed out landmarks, the palaces of Grimani di San Luca and Doña Della Madoneta. She seemed to know them all and soon she was pointing out the Guggenheim museum as they reached the end of the Grand Canal and began to head into the wide reaches of the Giudecca canal.

'Look Rory, the gondolas, we still have not ridden in a gondola.'

Smiling broadly, he watched as gondoliers negotiated the canal traffic in their sleek black craft, dodging fast motor boats and cumbersome vaporettos, the vibrancy of Venice thrilling him. Then there was Nadia, her arm through his, her body close and he knew he did not want this wonderful experience to end but, in a very short time it must.

The vaporetto passed a large domed church and Nadia told him it was the Basilica di Santa Maria. 'We call it the Salute, it is very famous, it was built as an offering to stop the plague, the Black Death the same as you had in England.'

'Did it work?'

'Something must have for the city survived.'

Rory nodded as the building slipped past and the vaporetto turned into the Giudecca canal. At the Piazza San Marco, they disembarked and wandered slowly through the square finding seats outside a bar.

A waiter in a long white apron appeared and Nadia to order Rory sat back to take in the scene.

'Why didn't we sit near those musicians? That is the Venice I had heard of before I came here, art, music,' said Rory.

'You haven't had *il conto* yet.'

'The bill, why is that important?'

'You pay double to sit near the musicians. It is very nice but we can hear them from where we are sitting.'

Nadia was right, Rory's eyebrows rose in mild shock when he saw the bill and she shook her finger at him.

'I told you it would be expensive, just think if it had been twice as much. I should look after our expenses I think. Come Scotsman and I will show you the Arsenale and then maybe we can go and have a look at Sant'Elena.'

'Sant'Elena, what's that?'

'The marina Sant'Elena.'

'More boats, good.'

'Si more boats, you are mad about boats so I show you where they keep the vaporettos.'

Rory liked the sound of it, liked the idea of a stroll round a harbour, he missed being on the water in his own boat, a small boat. It was almost three years to the day since the sinking of the Lurach-Aon, when he was so sure he was about to die in the open reaches of the Minch. He thought of his father and how he had managed to hang on until the helicopter was able to winch him to safety. They had been very lucky but the boat was gone and with it his future as a fisherman.

Why was he thinking like this? He looked at Nadia, her black hair, her olive skin, she was beautiful and he felt his heart soften. She seemed happy and he realised that if events had been different he would not have met her, not be here in Venice walking alongside the canal.'

'Penny for your thoughts.'

'*Che cosa*, what?'

'What are you thinking about, you looked lost in thought.'

Her brown eyes turned to look into his and a faint blush filled her cheeks. 'Nothing.'

'I don't believe that.'

'I was thinking about you – us.'

'Funny, so was I.'

She looked at him, her eyes somehow willing him to speak and almost as if a guiding hand had taken hold of him he said, 'Let's get married.'

'Oh Rory I thought you would never ask. You are tomorrow and I worried that we might never see each other again.'

The dam broke, his pent up feelings spilled out and he did the only thing he could. Taking both of her hands in his, he knelt on the pavement in front of her.

'Nadia Foscari, will you marry me?'

'Of course my Viking, of course I will. Now stand up and kiss me.'

Rory got to his feet, wrapped his arms around her, pulled her close and kissed her firmly on the lips. He was so happy and about to tell her so when a round of applause stopped him in his tracks. So engrossed were they in each other that they were oblivious to passers-by who had noticed him drop to one knee and realising what he was doing could not help but cheer. It was a warm sunny day in Italy, Italians appreciate a good love story, and here was one playing out before their eyes.

'*Grazie, grazie,*' Nadia called to the well-wishers, her face glowing with happiness. 'I love you Rory,' she said, wrapping both arms around one of his and pulling him close and for a time they walked, saying nothing, simply happy to be together.

'Is this where we are going?' said Rory eventually.

'Si, the Arsenale; look the entrance, the old buildings.'

Rory looked across the small square to a wide canal passing between two tall towers.

'It looks closed.'

'It is, the public are not allowed in but we can walk around the outside and you can see the old Venice, the real Venice.'

'You are proud of your city aren't you?'

'Of course, are you not proud of your city?'

'You can hardly call Stornoway a city, but yes I am proud of it. It's rather different to Venice but it is home.'

'I want to see your city.'

'You will.'

For an hour they walked around the perimeter of the medieval shipyard, scrutinising the old buildings, the cranes, equipment from a bygone age, and Nadia took great pleasure in informing Rory of the Arsenale's history.

'Many years ago we were the main city state in the Adriatic, Venetian ships traded right across the sea and that is why we have such wonderful architecture. We were rich and we could build the best ships. Do you know they could build a ship in only one day here in the Arsenale?'

'Really,' Rory was impressed. 'What happened?'

'The Ottomans, Napoleon and the sailing ships that could travel all round the world. They build galleys here which were fine for the Adriatic but they could not go much further.'

'It happens to us all; look at the British Empire – gone.'

'Never mind history, for us is only the future Rory.'

He put his arm around her waist and together they walked a little further towards the easternmost part of the main island until Rory caught sight of masts towering into the sky.

'The marina, it's over there is it?'

'Yes, but first we stop and share a pizza, I am hungry.'

'And I could do with a beer, it's getting warm.'

Franco was on edge; Il Capo had sent word that he should be at the *Banca d'Italia* for six, no later because the raid would start then. He had completed all the tasks given him except one. He had only to take the vaporetto and move it to the canal running

281

alongside the bank and wait, but he had still not seen the driver.

'Maurizio, you said he would be here for two o'clock. Where is he?'

'I don't know Franco, I told him to be here by now. Maybe he has got cold feet.'

That was the wrong thing to say, the driver was key to the final part of the plan, without him they could not move the vaporetto. Franco's eyes flashed menacingly.

'I will kill him. Go and find him and if you do not I will kill you.'

Maurizio's face turned several shades paler and without another word he hurried away.

'What are we going to do if he doesn't find the driver?' asked Luciano.

Together with Maurizio and Franco, he was part of the getaway gang and he knew as well as anyone that without the driver they were in trouble. If they did not pull off their part of the plan, it could mean a serious beating or even death, for Il Capo did not tolerate failure and this was the biggest job they had ever attempted.

'We find another one and quick.'

Franco lit a cigarette and began pacing back and forth, his temperature rising. Luciano knew to keep out of his way and for half an hour the two of them remained silent, far enough from each other to avoid any friction, and awaited Maurizio's reappearance.

'There he is,' said Luciano, spotting his fellow mafioso.

'Where is the driver?' growled Franco as Maurizio approached the boat alone.

'I don't know, he was not at home and his wife said she has not seen him since yesterday. She thinks the police were looking for him.'

'What, the police. Do they know?'

'I doubt it, Alfonso is often in trouble with the police. He is a thief and they know him.'

Franco was close to boiling point, so much depended upon him being able to make a clean getaway with the proceeds of the raid and now he could see it all slipping away. If he failed to pull off his side of the robbery the outcome did not bear thinking about. He felt angry, cornered.

'What are we going to do?'

'Do? We are going to find someone else who can drive this thing if Alfonso cannot. We need someone who drives these things for a living, a regular driver. Who do we know?'

'I don't know anyone else.'

Franco snapped, lashed out at Maurizio sending him reeling against the side of the vaporetto and was about to lay into him with his fists when he saw his sister. Was it her? What was she doing here? At first, he could not believe it was Nadia strolling aimlessly along the footpath with her boyfriend.

'Huh, the Scotsman with my sister and holding her hand. I want to kill him,' he muttered to himself, his eyes narrowing as his anger transferred from Maurizio to Rory and he felt for his knife.

The movement was a natural one for a mafia killer and Maurizio saw it, backing off in fear for his own life until Franco barked at him.

'You stay here, I have an idea.'

A few metres away, oblivious to the tensions on the vaporetto pontoon, Rory and Nadia were walking slowly, talking about the future, their future. After Rory's proposal it was apparent they would be together for the rest of their lives but first they had to figure out how to make it work.

'I still want to go back to college to learn to be a chef. Maybe you can get a job in Venice to be with me until I finish the course.'

'Doing what, I have no real skills and I am not going to be a waiter, no way.'

'Maybe you can work on the ships of the commercial port on the mainland. Ships come from all over the world, big ships.'

'They will be seagoing, away for months at a time, that's no good. Maybe there are tugs or a dredger, that would work but I don't have any tickets other than as a deck hand and I don't speak the language. Besides I earn good money in the North Sea, we'll need money.'

'Ah . . . I suppose so.'

'Maybe you could learn to be a chef in England or Scotland; you speak good English so it wouldn't be too hard for you.'

'Maybe, perhaps I can . . .'

She got no further.

'Nadia, Rory, this is a surprise. What are you doing here in the marina?'

'Rory likes boats and I thought as it is our last day together I would bring him down here to look at the yachts and the vaporettos,' said a puzzled Nadia.

'Of course the vaporettos, you are an expert I think,' said Franco in a salesman like voice. 'I am with Maurizio and Luciano looking after vaporettos for the day. The company is worried about vandalism and we are guarding them. They are over there; come and have a closer look my friend.'

Rory was already looking across the pontoons at the newly refurbished and repainted vaporettos.

'I wouldn't mind,' he said, looking at Nadia.

Nadia was not so sure; she knew her brother and did not trust him, but then if he were only keeping an eye on the boats it would do no harm.

'Come, follow me and you can have a good look round, at the engine, the equipment.'
Rory was astonished at Franco's friendly manner and his ability to speak at least some English. Taking control he led the way down some steps to the pontoon moorings and out of Rory's sight he gave Maurizio a knowing look.

'You first, climb onto the deck and if you go down towards the engine you can see everything.'

'Is this where they maintain the vaporettos?' asked Rory, climbing into the boat's interior.

'No the vaporettos go to the dockyard on Pellestrina Island for maintenance; here they just keep them ready for service.'

It was neither a clear nor explicit explanation but then Franco knew little or nothing about mechanical things and Rory was not really listening, more interested in looking. He poked around the engine compartment for ten minutes or more and when he finally looked up it was into the barrel of a handgun.

'What!'

'Be quiet my friend and no one will get hurt.'

'What do you mean, where's Nadia?'

'She is safe, she is with my friends and if you want to see her again then you had better do as I say.'

Rory felt cold, cold and angry, but at least he had the sense to remain calm and not antagonise the young thug. He looked at the floor, said nothing, his mind racing, wondering if he could overpower Franco and take his gun away but the thought of Franco's thuggish friends holding Nadia held him back.

'You are going to do a little job for me my friend, a job I know you can do because I have witnessed you driving one of these things. Are you listening?' said Franco with a snarl.

'Yes I'm listening.'

'Good, then we can start. You are going to drive this vaporetto to where I tell you, that is all, easy isn't it?'

Rory remained silent, not moving until Franco shoved the barrel of the gun into his back. 'Up there, into the driver's seat.'

'Where's Nadia first. If you harm her . . .' He didn't finish, there was nothing he could do, he felt helpless. 'What is it you want me to do?'

'Sit in the driver's seat and wait. I will be on deck for only a minute and if I find you have moved I will shoot you in the leg, just enough to make you do as I say. I won't kill you straight away if you disobey me but be assured I will if you try anything serious.'

Rory knew he meant it, felt sick in the pit of his stomach but he realised he must go along with Franco until he saw Nadia again and hope a chance of escape would present itself.

Roberto watched the bank frontage from across the canal, pacing slowly back and forth, keeping close to the bridge. Working alone was not an ideal situation, he had no backup, no information of any new developments, but he would do what he could. Settling into a routine, constantly on the lookout for anything unusual and trying to look as inconspicuous as possible, stopping every minute or two to peer into shop windows. At least he could be mistaken for a tourist or a bona fide businessman as he scanned the reflexions in the window. It was frustrating, nothing seemed to be happening and he was beginning to wonder if he had it wrong. What if they were not going to rob the *Banca d'Italia* – perhaps another bank or the casino was the target – did he have the wrong day?

Exhaling in frustration, he tried to calm his nerves and returned to scanning the immediate area. There was nothing out of the ordinary, just the usual tourists and the locals working in the bars and shops. Then two Carabinieri appeared, walking along the footpath at the opposite side of the canal and catching his eye. Strange he thought, he could not remember ever seeing Carabinieri officers in this part of Venice – local police yes but not Carabinieri.

Perhaps Colonel Luca had sent them and they were securing the bank.

That did seem to be the case as the two uniformed officers reached the *Banca d'Italia* and began waving their arms about, giving orders and clearing the street. Then two more men dressed in white overalls appeared carrying plumbers' tool bags. They walked past the Carabinieri, neither pair acknowledging the other and yet to Roberto they appeared to be working in unison. His eyes narrowed, he concentrated on each pair and suddenly an alarm bell rang in his head – was he witnessing the beginnings of the raid? He remembered the hidden police uniforms at the church. Of course, these were bogus Carabinieri and the tool bags the perfect place to hide the weapons. The revelation forced him into action.

Running towards the bridge, he dodged pedestrians all the time keeping an eye on the Carabinieri. Luckily their attention was elsewhere, they had their hands full keeping stray tourists away from the bank and that gave Roberto the chance to cross the bridge unobserved. He swiftly descended the steps on the opposite side, found safety in the shadows of an arch and pressing his body against the stonework, looked towards the bank. The two police impostors were now no more than metres away and the workmen were just entering the bank where the staff and the few customers would be unaware of developments outside.

Unseen by Roberto the first of the men in white overalls entered the bank and reached into his bag; letting it fall as he pulled out the Kalashnikov. His accomplice did likewise and he barked his orders to a stunned audience.

'You, stand away from the desk,' he shouted at the cashiers.

The terrified women stared through the grill and as the realisation dawned as to what was happening, did as the thug told them. Raising their hands they stood back against the wall while the second raider waved his weapon menacingly at the remaining customers. Visibly shaken, they too offered no resistance apart from one woman for whom the situation proved too much and she began to sob.

'Shut up your snivelling,' said the man waving his weapon threateningly at her and addressing his accomplice asked 'has the stand-in opened the vault yet?'

The second man moved towards a door, pushed it open and looked along the corridor. A metal grille door was open and inside the replacement manager was holding a piece of paper as he systematically keyed a code into a keypad attached to the solid looking vault door.

'He's working on the strong room door.'

'Tell him to hurry up we don't have all day.'

The second man grunted and made his way along the short corridor, returning almost as soon as he had left.

'He's got it open.'

'Keep this lot covered while I bring the others inside and we can lock the doors. We have to get the money out of the strong room quickly. The two Carabinieri can take over looking after the bank staff and these customers while we move the money and I can set the charges in the outer wall.'

From his hiding place Roberto witnessed the two Carabinieri enter the bank and watched as the door closed behind them. He guessed that the robbery was underway but he dare not risk taking them on, outgunned as he was and there was always the possibility of innocent people finding themselves in the firing line. He needed help and quickly but he had no means of contacting the police and none were to be seen. Feeling at a loss, he retraced his steps onto the bridge to look back across the canal for help and it was then he noticed the vaporetto. The yellow hulk was lying motionless alongside the bank wall, out of place in the narrow canal. A vaporetto would rarely strayed from the main canals and if they did he was sure they would never use this one.

Was the vaporetto to play a role in the mafia's plan? As if to answer his question a dull thud shook the ground and a section of the *Banca d'Italia*'s outer wall bulged before several blocks of masonry fell with a splash into the canal. A cloud of dust cloud accompanied the low-level explosion and as it began to clear, he could see the vaporetto moving slowly forward and he knew then that it *was* to play a part in the robbery. The hole they had blown in the bank's outer wall was not large enough for a man to squeeze through but it was large enough for money bags and as the explosion was so low key, no one in the vicinity seemed to have noticed it. He watched in fascination as the vaporetto's bulk moved slowly to conceal the site of the demolition and he could make out movement as the robbers transferred the proceeds of the robbery to it.

Inside the vaporetto, Franco too watched the falling stonework, pressing the barrel of his gun against the back of Rory's head and ordering him to drive forward.

'There, stop where the wall has collapsed. Maurizio, you and Luciano take the money when we get near.'

Franco's heart was beating so fast he felt that his chest might burst. He had done it, positioned the vaporetto in exactly the right place at the right time and now they were reaping their reward.

'Stop here,' he said, a faint quiver in his voice.

Rory had little choice but to obey and gently easing back on the throttle he brought the boat to a halt but not before he had caught sight of shadows moving inside the building. He sensed Franco behind him, heard him call out to his men, he had not looked round since first sitting in the driver's seat but now, as the tension rose he dared to look round. The two men with Franco were busy taking sack from those inside the bank and for a few moments, Franco's attention was on them. He looked back through the cabin, beyond the men, shocked to see the forlorn figure of Nadia, trussed in rope bindings and lying awkwardly on a seat. It shocked him to see her like this, he felt helpless, could do nothing but stare at her and wondered what could he do. There were three of them and they were armed, he had nothing but his bare hands and then Franco turned round.

'So you see Nadia. That is not good Scotsman, concentrate on the driving, we are right now.'

Once more Rory felt the coldness of the gun barrel on his neck. It seemed as if there was no way out, the mafia were probably going to kill him when they had no use for him and he believed they would probably kill Nadia too. What kind of a person would kill his own sister? A thought that percolated through his whole being, and as the anger within him, he took a deep breath. The situation had become a matter of life and death and he must do something, he could not let them win.

'Move!' screamed Franco.

Rory felt a coldness engulf him as he eased the throttle and as the engine growled, he turned the wheel and steered the vaporetto smoothly away from the fractured wall. He was mad and becoming madder by the second, a hatred for Franco building up inside him as the vaporetto began to pass under the bridge and into the Grand Canal.

'Turn left when you get us into the main canal, we have people waiting. I will tell you where to go next.'

Rory did as Franco told him, his mind racing, searching desperately for a solution. Without a weapon he was helpless and as he steered the boat under the bridge, from the corner of his eye, he noticed a movement. It happened so quickly that he could not make it out but he did feel a barely perceptible thump as something hit the roof above his head. Had someone thrown something off the bridge? He did not have time to think about it as Franco growled, 'Left, I said go left.'

'I am turning left, it takes time, damn you.'

Franco seemed to accept Rory's view and turned back at his accomplices to cast a greedy eye over the proceeds of the robbery.

'Maurizio come here and look after the driver. I don't want him trying anything that might cause us a problem.'

Rory heard the words he spoke but did not understand them yet he could not help feeling that something was changing. Franco was loosening his hold on the situation, perhaps he felt they had succeeded in their endeavour and that he need not worry anymore. Then, seconds later the blade of a stiletto knife appeared, interrupting his thoughts and he glanced sideways to see the grinning Maurizio who had just announced his arrival.

'No try anything a funny Englishman or I slit your throat.'

Rory involuntarily jerked his head back, his feelings of fear and apprehension increased tenfold. Maurizio's lips parted to reveal a cruel smile as the blade of the knife withdrew into the handle and a sharp intake of breath betrayed Rory's relief.

'Watch a the canal,' advised Maurizio, his bad teeth showing as his lips parted in a warped smile.

Rory gripped the wheel and swung the boat into the main canal slipping in amongst the congestion of rapidly moving water taxis, vaporettos and gondolas. It took all of his concentration to avoid them, he could not afford a collision for Franco might finally blow and then anything could happen and for a few seconds it took his mind of his predicament.

Swinging the steering wheel from side to side, he plotted his course through the mayhem that was the Grand Canal and then the thought struck him. He had considered that as he was unarmed he was at a distinct disadvantage, yet here in his hands was a weapon of sorts. He looked down at the steering wheel, out of the window at the boats gliding past and then he thought about Nadia lying helpless at the rear of the cabin and a plan began to take shape.

Behind Rory, at the back of the cabin Nadia lay uncomfortably on a seat where Maurizio and his fellow thug had unceremoniously tossed her. Then they had forgotten her, their minds on the robbery but from her position, she had borne witness to events. She had seen Franco and then Maurizio threaten Rory, heard the dull thud of the explosion and seen bags come aboard the vaporetto. She knew well enough how the mafia operated and it frightened her enough to attempt to break free of her bonds. Wiggling her fingers, constantly twisting her wrists, she finally succeeded in loosening the rope enough to free her hands. She had little chance of escape so she decided that it was prudent to keep her bonds in place for the time being. She would watch what they did, bide her time and hope that she might escape and that Rory would too.

At the midpoint of the boat, she could see her brother inspecting the bags of money. No doubt he was estimating their worth, confident they had managed to steal millions of dollars and were getting away with it. She was right and after scanning the sacks of money, he looked through the windows at the canal traffic. There were no police boats in sight, he felt that they were invisible amongst the canal traffic and all that remained was to transfer the money to the safe house. After that, he would get Maurizio to dispose of the driver, kill him and dump him in the canal, and then there was Nadia to consider. Even he could not kill his own sister but he had somehow to prevent her from talking. Perhaps she should marry a clan member, or maybe a year or two's exile in a remote convent up in the mountains would dull her memory.

In the spacious main cabin, Franco stepped back alongside the vaporetto driver, telling Maurizio to go and get ready to transfer the money while he instructed Rory where to go. He stood, feet apart, steadying himself with one hand as the vaporetto ploughed steadily along the Grand Canal through the throngs of water traffic, past eloquent buildings with their fading facades and towards the bend where they must turn off. Beside Franco Rory sat hunched in the driver's seat.

From the corner of his eye, Rory kept Franco in sight, aware that time was running out and yet he still had no idea of how to stop this madness. Maybe he could run the boat into one of the bridges or plough into the boats moored along the canalside but with the volatile Franco so close, it was a risk and did not look to be a particularly good option. After the initial excitement of the getaway, the participants had settled into a reflective mood and it did at least give him time to think about his own situation.

Above them Roberto lay, sprawled on the roof and desperately clinging to an air vent. His situation was precarious, the wakes of passing boats were buffeting the vaporetto and he was in danger of falling, his time was running out, he guessed that the journey would soon be over and he would need to act. He had soon realised the significance of the loitering vaporetto, its connection to the explosion. Without considering the consequences, he had leapt from the bridge onto the its roof and as he lay there he remembered his conversation with Colonel Luca. He hoped that his words had stirred the colonel into some sort of action and that help was near at hand.

Lifting his head as much as he dare he looked at passing boats, the thought of attracting someone's attention crossing his mind. The gangsters below him were armed and dangerous and he knew that he could not risk indiscriminate shooting. Suddenly he felt the tone of the vaporetto's engine change and it began to alter course. He lifted his head and saw they were entering a small canal off the Grand Canal, tall buildings towering above him on either side.

He guessed that they would soon be stopping because the canal would become too narrow for the bulk of a vaporetto and they would need to unload the money. Once they had unloaded, they would disappear through the warren of tiny interconnected streets. After that, finding them again would be an impossible task. The thugs would get clean away and all his work would be in vain, somehow he had to try to stop them. Shifting his position, he felt for his gun– some assurance at least – and he dared to lift his head again but to his dismay, a bridge with little enough clearance was looming towards them. Fear of decapitation forced him to press himself flat on the vaporetto roof, the hairs on the back of his neck rising as air trapped between the narrow space under the bridge and the back of his head rushed past.

The woman on the bridge reacted first; Roberto was unmissable spread-eagled on the roof of the vaporetto and digging into her handbag, she pulled out a shortwave radio.

'All stations, all stations, we've seen them. They are on the vaporetto, just turned into the Rio di Foscari,' he said, the irony of the canal's name lost on him.

After a crackled acknowledgement, he and his partner hurried along the canal keeping the vaporetto in view for as long as possible until the path ended against a blank wall. It forced them to take a different route through nearby streets and passages making it increasingly difficult to keep the vaporetto in sight. The location was always part of Franco's plan for he knew that anyone attempting to follow on foot would find it almost impossible. The endgame was fast approaching.

'Stop there by that landing stage,' he snarled, pointing to a wooden structure thirty or forty metres further along the canal.

Rory heard him, saw him signal for Maurizio to take his place and felt his mouth run dry. The thug came forward sneering, waving his knife slowly back and forth. At the rear of the cabin, Luciano too was aware that they were near the end of their journey and went to check on Nadia. She saw him coming and allowed the loosened bonds to slip from her wrists. That action freed her hands completely and as Luciano reached her, she made her move.

'What's that on the floor, look, it fell out of one of one of those bags?' she said, nodding her head in a general direction.

'Eh . . . what?' said Luciano, taken unawares.

His natural reaction was to turn and look for the object of Nadia's remark and as he did so, the girl rose up from her seat. Now with her hands free she swiftly removed one of her shoes, raising it high above her head to bring it down with as much force as she could muster onto the back of Luciano's head. The action took him completely by surprise, he did not know what had hit him, and he fell to the floor unconscious. Leaping over his prostrate body, Nadia rummaged through his clothing, eventually finding what she was looking for.

Taking the gun firmly in her hand, she kicked off her remaining shoe and feeling sick with fear she made her way towards the forward end of the vaporetto where Franco and Maurizio were watching the approach to the landing. If either of them should see or hear her they would not hesitate to use violence. So with her heart beating furiously, she moved cautiously forward.

In the driving seat, Rory's knuckles had turned white with tension as he gripped the wheel. His jaw was set with concentration as he steered the heavy craft between towering walls on either side of the narrowing canal. His eyes scanned ahead for obstacles and every few seconds he looked round, occasionally managing to glance in the rear view mirror. Then, to his horror, he saw Nadia making her way gingerly between the rows of seats and that she had a gun in her hand. He saw the figure of her mafia guard lying face down on the floor and if Franco or Maurizio saw her, she was in trouble. The adrenalin began to pump through his system. Somehow he must protect her and thinking quickly he opened up the throttle as far as it would go.

The engine growled like a wounded tiger, the vaporetto turned into a charging beast and Rory used all his strength to swing the steering wheel from side to side. It was enough to set up a wave motion in the narrow canal, throwing the craft violently towards the walls on both sides, his aggressive action taking everyone by surprise. As the motion became ever more violent the vaporetto began to hit the canal sides with force, throwing everyone off balance and that included Roberto.

The policeman was unaware of the events unfolding below him, only that the violent motion was causing him to lose his grip and eventually he could do nothing to prevent himself sliding across the roof towards disaster. His arms and legs flailed in panic as he grappled with anything that might arrest his progress, his foot catching a metal protrusion the only thing preventing him falling into the canal. The leg began to shake uncontrollably and swearing under his breath, he tried to change position, swinging his free leg to try to find some purchase but it was to no avail and he slid off the roof and onto the deck below.

Franco saw Roberto fall and swung his gun in his direction, lunging towards the doorway but the motion of the boat made it difficult for him to keep his footing. It was a brief respite, enough to give Roberto the chance to get to his feet and pull out his own gun to face Franco as he emerged onto the deck. Franco's gun was pointing straight at him and without hesitation, the young thug fired. His aim was wild yet good enough to catch Roberto's right arm, forcing the gun to spin from his grasp. Roberto yelped in surprise and unable to hold himself steady, he slumped to his knees.

Rory saw it all from the driver's seat; saw that Franco was not about to miss for a second time and his anger finally boiled over. Leaping from the cramped compartment, he raced onto the open deck and lunging straight at Franco, sent him crashing against the superstructure. Without doubt his action prevented the second fatal shot and then, swinging a muscular arm round the Italian's neck, he forced Franco's head backwards and grabbed at the gun. Franco fought back, twisting and turning to escape Rory's iron grip but the Scotsman was too strong and too angry for him, gradually forcing the Italian to his knees with an arm securely round his neck.

Alerted by the sound of the gun firing Maurizio looked up to see the vaporetto driver lunging at Franco. He staggered forward but finding it hard to keep his footing he was unable to offer immediate help. Eventually he managed to find a handhold and emerging onto the deck produced his flick knife. He was a killer intent on violence and he would have stabbed Rory in the back if it were not for a female voice screaming in his ears.

'Drop it or I will shoot you'.

Turning his head the thug came face to face with Nadia and the barrel of a gun. He sneered, she was nothing more than a slip of a girl, no match for him and passing the knife from hand to hand, he faced her, saw hesitancy in her eyes. He guessed she did not have the courage to shoot and he lunged towards her, but before he could make contact, there was an almighty crash as the wildly swinging vaporetto hit the pontoon. Such was the force that Maurizio lost his footing, his knife fell from his hand and when he finally looked up it was to see a fearful Nadia still pointing the gun at him.

The vaporetto had bounced along the wall and wedged itself against the pontoon, its engine was still running and the craft was bucking like a rodeo steer. Nadia gripped a seat back and the gun with equal force to keep her adversary at bay but eventually the violent motion caused her to slip and she fell backwards onto a seat. Try as she might she was unable to keep the gun pointing at Maurizio and that afforded him the chance of escape. He stepped forward, forced Nadia's arm and the gun away from him before gripping round her throat with a huge gnarled hand. It was enough to subdue her and in one swift movement, he snatched the gun from her grasp and spun her round, imprisoning her with his free arm.

From his vantage point in the police helicopter Captain Capizzi had watched events unfold ever since the vaporetto had made the turn into the side canal. Colonel Luca had believed that they could control events better from the helicopter and had contacted the police in Milan for the use of theirs. Aware of the difficulties in pursuing fugitives through the narrow canals and streets of Venice it seemed logical that an observation post high above the city would aid them.

The captain looked down to see a woman emerge from the cabin, and behind her, a man with a hand on her neck and in the other, he was holding a gun. Captain Capizzi judged that it was time to let the criminals below know that there was no escape, flicked the switch on the microphone and the loud speaker burst into life.

'Stay where you are. Put your hands above your heads.'

Rory looked up dumfounded and released his grip on Franco as they both raised their hands. For Maurizio though, surrender was not an option and dragging Nadia to the rail, he waved the gun for the benefit of those in the helicopter and planting against Nadia's temple, he waited for negotiations for his escape to begin.

In front of him, Franco was free of Rory's grip but with his weapon gone, he was helpless, the police were closing in and his resistance was fading.

'Franco, we can get away. Come, help me take this woman ashore and we can use her as a hostage.'

Franco looked on with horror at the plight of his sister, her face pale with fear and for once, the violence shocked him. His own sister, he had never meant for her to be hurt, he only ever wanted to get rid of the Scotsman and now, with nowhere to go, he felt trapped. He looked at Rory whose eyes seemed calm, cold, they were watching Maurizio and Nadia, and then he looked up at the helicopter and knew that for him, it was all over.

'Damnation, they have a girl hostage,' Captain Capizzi said to himself, his mind racing as he adapted to the new situation. He turned to the radio operator sitting beside him in the rear of the cramped cabin and told him to inform headquarters of developments.

Many miles away Colonel Luca lit yet another cigarette and inhaled deeply, a hostage situation was not good news, they had planned for the possibility but after the raid, he had presumed all on board the vaporetto would be gangsters. He picked up his telephone and called the Milan number again. He had asked for military assistance and now it seemed that he would need it.

'Colonel Moretti we have a bad situation here in Venice, we could well need your sharp shooters. Will you liaise with Captain Capizzi and order your men to take up positions to assist him.'

The voice on the other end of the telephone spoke rapidly before Colonel Luca thoughtfully replaced the receiver and no more than a minute later, the receiver on board the helicopter crackled into life. Captain Capizzi took the headphones from the wireless operator and spoke into the microphone. The captain was a good officer, thoughtful and calm under stress but he did not like what he was witnessing.

Below him, on the vaporetto, Rory's heart was pounding, he felt mildly sick but his concentration was absolute. Maurizio was talking with Franco, glancing occasionally in his direction and then up at the helicopter. Presumably, they were planning to use Nadia as a hostage. He was angry and if even the smallest chance of rescuing Nadia presented itself he would take it, then Nadia's voice cut in.

'Franco what are you doing, you are going to let this man hurt me, your sister. Do I mean nothing to you?'

Franco's brow creased, he was already of two minds and Nadia words had struck a nerve.

Rory saw an opening.

'You cannot kill Nadia, she is your sister, you have robbed a bank yes, but it is not murder. What is wrong with you man?'

Franco turned his head towards Rory and Rory could see he was troubled but then Maurizio said, 'Come Franco, we can get out of here with her as hostage. Grab a sack of money and let's go. Come on!' he shouted, his patience tested.

'Captain Capizzi could hear nothing of the conversation but he could see something was happening. The well-built blonde haired man seemed to be entering the vaporetto and seconds later the

304

churning water from the propeller subsided and the boat settled.

Rory had told Maurizio that they would all be better off with the engine stopped and after obtaining his agreement had turned off the ignition and looked frantically for a weapon. He had only seconds before Maurizio might start shooting but he could see nothing of any use. Then a movement caught his eye, Roberto had somehow managed to wedge himself between the wooden deck seat and the side of the vaporetto and nobody had noticed.

'You get back out here,' said Maurizio in broken English. 'Fetch some of the money Franco.'

Franco was subdued yet he did as Maurizio told him, returning from the boat's interior with a small sack and together they began to make their way off the vaporetto and onto the narrow pontoon. Maurizio pushed Nadia in front of him in preparation for their escape but as he lifted his foot to cross the threshold he was forced to lean back, countering a slight movement of the vaporetto and that was enough for Rory.

Springing forward he pushed past Franco and made straight for Maurizio. Nadia screamed in terror and then from nowhere Roberto emerged from his hiding place to grab hold of Maurizio's gun hand. He was weak from a loss of blood and no match for Maurizio who swept him aside. Then the killer turned his attention to Rory, levelling his gun at him but Rory was in full flight. Crashing into the thug, he knocked him sideways and sent the gun spinning from his grasp and then, with his fists moving like pistons, he forced Maurizio backwards.

'Franco, the gun, get hold of the gun!'

Franco seemed lost and did not move, Rory managed one last punch to knock Maurizio off his balance, his foot slipped, and his leg went into the water him trapped between the pontoon and the wall. With Maurizio temporarily disabled Rory turned his attention to Franco.

'All right Scotsman, I give up. It is not worth losing my sister. What would my mother say?'

Rory looked at him, saw a softening and realising that Franco would not present any more trouble. He glanced at Nadia, silent a vacant look upon her face.

'Nadia, are you all right?'

She looked up and their eyes met.

'You saved my life.'

'It's not over yet,' he said pointing to Maurizio lying half on the pontoon half in the canal his face contorted in pain. 'Looks as if he's broken something but even so he could still be dangerous. I think Franco might have just seen the light but even he might be a problem. Here,' he said picking up the guns and giving one to Nadia, 'keep that one covered.'

Nadia's eyes flashed at her brother, her anger showing through and he turned his head away, reward enough for Rory whose attention focused on the wounded Roberto.

'Are you okay mate?'

'Don't worry about me my friend; I think maybe I will live.'

Rory nodded and looked up at the helicopter, and then towards the entrance to the canal as he heard the shriek of approaching police sirens.

Epilogue

I first read of Rory's escapade in the national press, the *Daily Mail* picked up the story a day or two after the event and I had to read the article twice to believe it. Details were vague, though the report seemed to intimate that Rory was involved with the Italian mafia. I was flabbergasted, was it really our Rory?

'Have you seen this Marion? Remember Rory, my friend from home, well he is in big trouble.'

Marion took the paper and read the article. 'I thought you said he was a hardworking, honest sort of chap, more like a criminal I would say.'

I must confess it did look that way and for a time that was all I had to go on until one day there was a knock at the door.

'Rory, bloody hell, what are you doing here? I thought you were rotting in some Italian jail.'

He looked at me and grinned.

'What does it look like I'm doing here? I've come for a cup of tea.'

'Come in, come in – Marion look who's here?' I called to her in the kitchen.

My wife was preparing our evening meal and our little girl was in the living room watching television, but as soon as she heard me call out, she came running.

'Who is this Daddy?'

'He is my friend Rory; you have heard me talk about Rory haven't you?'

I was a little too quick in introducing Rory to Megan; she did not miss a trick.

'He robbed a bank; you said he was in prison.'

'Oops, I'm sorry Rory, out of the mouths of babes and all that.'

He seemed unfazed, leant over and touched her hair.

'She's a bright kid Malcolm, gets it from you does she?'

'Hardly, go and watch your television Megs and mummy will call you when your dinner is ready.'

She gave us a look that told us she did not really understand and scampered back into the living room. I said for Rory to follow me into the kitchen to see Marion. She looked up from preparing the meal and smiled a greeting.

'Your daughter seems to think that I have been in prison,' said Rory.

Feeling a little embarrassed I said, 'You must have got off with good behaviour then, it was only a couple of months ago wasn't it. I think you need to fill us in with a few details.'

'That's why I'm here, well one of the reasons.'

'What's the other?'

'All in good time,' he said with mischief in his eyes.

'Go on Rory, we are intrigued to know what happened to you,' added Marion.

'Aye, it's a long story all right. I could get ten years you know.'

I looked at Marion; her jaw dropped almost as far as mine. 'Oh Rory, they gave you ten years, what for?'

'Well maybe not ten years.'

'Less?'

A lot less, just a fine.'

'A fine, how much?'

'Price of a pint,' he said, grinning from ear to ear.

'You rotten thing, you are winding us up.'

'I am, and it was worth it just to see your face. No nothing will happen to me, I haven't been in prison but I will have to go back to Venice. They are giving me an award or something.'

'Wow, what for?'

'Let me start from the beginning. You remember when I came to see you in Edinburgh well shortly after that . . .'

It was quite a story he told, Las Vegas, Venice, the mafia and then he told how he had thwarted the bank robbery, the undercover policeman and how he had saved him from being shot. When he finished his story, I began to realise just how far he had come since the loss of the *Lurach-Aon*. Back then, it really did seem that without qualifications or skills he would find it difficult to earn a good living. I had a degree and finding a safe, steady job, was easy enough but he had could do no more than fish the waters around our home but here he was, having

310

lived an adventure. He had achieved what few others have done in life, things for which qualifications mean nothing. Above all else, he had proved himself a man. Then I remembered him mentioning that there was something else.

'You said there were two things, what was the other?'

'Malcolm, I can think of no one else who can speak in public as you do.'

'You're doing it again; go on, what do you want?'

'I want you to be best man at my wedding.'

'You are getting married! Congratulations,' I said.

It seemed simple enough until he added, 'but there is a catch.'

'A catch, what?'

'The wedding is taking place in Venice.'

'Oh . . .,' Marion swooned. 'Venice, are you getting married in Venice? You lucky thing, I hope that I am invited.'

'You're invited because Malcolm here will need someone to dress him properly.'

'Cheeky sod, hey, you're on I would love to be best man. In fact it will be the greatest honour I have ever had bestowed upon me.'

'Now who is taking the Mickey?'

'That's done then. Is it the Italian girl, the one we still haven't met?'

'Yes, Nadia, she is coming here next week. She wants to meet my mum.'

That was almost four years ago, golly how time flies. If you are not careful, life can pass you by so it was good to see him again and the following week we finally met Nadia. I have to say he is a lucky man, she is very attractive, a dark eyed beauty and her English is very good. Once she started talking, it was hard to stop her particularly when she got round to relating her part in the story. She had witnessed Rory's heroics first hand and I could see just how much respect she had for him. On the other hand, I also learned about her brother Franco, the villain in the story. She spoke quite openly about him and I was surprised to hear just how forgiving she was towards him.

Six weeks later, Marion and I together with Rory's parents and his sister travelled to Venice for the wedding. It was there that I learned a little of his in-laws. Rory introduced me to them all, Nadia's mother and father, her brother Claudio and of course Franco whom the authorities allowed out of prison for just one day to attend the wedding ceremony. Having kidnapped his own sister and tried to kill Rory I expected the relationship to be frosty to say the least. However, he did appear friendly enough, acting as if there was no problem although I could see coldness in his eyes. Rory kept away from him, leaving it to Nadia to introduce Marion and myself and we did not dwell in conversation with him. Her elder brother Claudio was more forthcoming, telling me about his water taxi and then there were her father and mother.

Her mother spoke passable English but her father spoke very little and Nadia had to translate. I found out that he was an accountant for a small local firm and seemed the stereotypical accountant, an insignificant sort of man. Francesca was quite different to the males in her family and it was obvious that she was Nadia's mother. She liked to talk and I must say she is the type of Italian matriarch I had always imagined. She dressed very well, putting the Scottish contingent to shame, she was expressive, flamboyant and after the trauma she must have endured because of Franco's arrest, she held the day together very well.

The wedding ceremony itself was an interesting affair, longer and more involved than back home. It took place in a church on the outskirts of Mestre and conducted by an old priest with a round, ruddy face. His voice was soft yet no one could fail to hear his words and after the blessings, we left to celebrate in a restaurant taken over for the day by the wedding guests. Francesca was in her element, her daughter was married to someone she approved of and she had family around her, aunts, uncles, cousins from near and far and she took pleasure in mixing with them all but I couldn't help but wonder if in part it was to keep everyone's mind off Franco and his recent misdemeanours.

As for Franco's father, he seemed to take a back seat once he had performed his wedding duties, although after the meal and the speeches, I caught sight of him and Franco separated from the other guests. They were in deep conversation and I guessed the old man was giving his son a good telling off before the prison officer came to collect him. I do not know if Franco has returned to the straight and narrow but I did hear that shortly after the wedding, the authorities placed him under house arrest and that to me, seemed almost as if they had set him free.

We did not have a lot of time for sightseeing after the wedding because we had to return home to the children. Oh yes, we have two little girls now, Molly turned up two years ago and is developing into a proper little madam. Even though our time there was short, the wedding in Venice was a wonderful experience. I must say how pleased I am that things have turned out so well for Rory, I have never seen him look so happy and before we left, I had time to say goodbye.

When I finish writing today's events in my diary, we are going out as a family to see Rory and Nadia. They came to live back in Stornoway around the time of Molly's birth and no one expected that a girl from Italy would cope so well with the Scottish weather. She has surprised us all seemingly thriving in the cold Atlantic air and as for Rory, well he has finally bought himself a twenty foot fishing boat. He goes out most days to tend to his lobster pots, catch a few bream and haddock and brings them home to sell to the tourists in the small restaurant they run.

'Are you ready Malcolm, you are forever writing in that note book of yours. The girls are waiting and if we don't go now we'll be late.'

Well I must go now I do not want hold things up.

'You look pretty girls, are you both ready?'

'Yes daddy, are we going to the Italian place mummy?'

'Yes darling, the one belonging to Uncle Rory and Auntie Nadia. She is a super chef and she does work so hard Malcolm. I don't know how she expects to cope once the baby arrives.'

Other books by this author

iGoli, City of Gold

In Southern Africa at the end of the nineteenth century, the discovery of gold created a stampede to claim those underground riches. Unscrupulous men mixed with the hard working miners and the thousands of black labourers. Greed and dishonesty permeated both sides of the racial divide leading to industrial strife and insurrection. Caught up in these events an immigrant Scotsman seizes an opportunity to enrich himself while on the other side of the racial divide a young black labourer struggles to provide for his family

Amsterdam Traffik

Since the breakup of the Soviet empire corruption and political favour has ruled Ukraine. The regime, controlled by the oligarchs mutes any opposition but a group of young women activists, called FEMEM, dares to protest. Baring more than their souls, they grab the media's attention at a demonstration, causing the President's displeasure. It is the beginning of a terrifying ordeal for one of their number, and through interwoven connections, MI6 becomes involved.

Pickpockets and Zulus

In Victorian London, conviction for even minor offences can lead to prison or transportation but for one teenage boy the choice was prison or the army. Recruited at the tender age of fourteen his adventures take him to South Africa campaigning the length and breadth of the country. In the Lands of the Zulu, another boy too becomes a warrior, following his King's bidding until the final battle.

The Last Zulu Warrior

After defeating the Zulus, the British subjugate the Kingdom, forming thirteen Kinglets administered by favourites. It is not long before old tribal rivalries surface and civil war ensues. Famine and hardship stalk the land and in his kraal, one brave warrior strives to save his people. He learns the ways of the European, their language, the use of firearms and working as a tracker joins a group of blockade-runners. Embroiled in conflict with the chief Induna he becomes an outcast and forced to leave the village, he meets an army deserter and a Boer farmer and together they make their way to the diamond mines of Kimberley.

Made in the USA
Columbia, SC
26 September 2017